THE BODACIOUS KID

**Center Point
Large Print**

**This Large Print Book carries the
Seal of Approval of N.A.V.H.**

THE BODACIOUS KID

Stan Lynde

CENTER POINT PUBLISHING
THORNDIKE, MAINE

To Lynda,
who shares my trail,
and to the memory of my Dad,
who loved a good yarn.

This Center Point Large Print edition is published
in the year 2007 by arrangement with Kleinworks.

Cover art courtesy of Cottonwood Publishing, Inc.

The text of this Large Print edition is unabridged. In other
aspects, this book may vary from the original edition. Printed in
Thailand. Set in 16-point Times New Roman type.

ISBN: 1-58547-907-1
ISBN 13: 978-1-58547-907-8

Library of Congress Cataloging-in-Publication Data

Lynde, Stan, 1931-
    The Bodacious Kid / Stan Lynde.--Center Point large print ed.
       p. cm.
    ISBN-13: 978-1-58547-907-8 (lib. bdg. : alk. paper)
      1. Frontier and pioneer life--Montana--Fiction. 2. Montana--Fiction.
    3. Large type books. I. Title.

PS3562.Y439B6 2007
813'.54--dc22

2006025601

ACKNOWLEDGMENTS and FORWARD

Nobody writes a book alone. At the very least an author relies on those who wrote before, writers who created and furthered the form, and whose works inspired and influenced him or her in the first place.

I owe much to many. To Larry Delaney, for his encouragement, savvy, and service as drill sergeant, mentor, and friend. To Jael Prezeau, whose editorial skills enhanced the book and made me seem a better writer than I am. Also to Laura, to Judie, to Tim, and of course to Lynda, for her unwavering belief in the project and in me.

Although the events in this book are set in 1882 Montana Territory, the names, characters, places, and incidents are entirely fictional. There was, for example, no Progress County in Montana Territory in 1882, although there were 11 other counties at the time, some as large as European nations.

The reader may note that in referring to the cowboy's leather leggings, I spell the word the way it should be pronounced—"shaps"—rather than "chaps." I'm in good company; cowboy author Will James spelled the word that way in *his* books. I do so not to impress but to educate, and as a public service. Those who mispronounce the word here in the West (with a hard *ch)* are branded greenhorns at best, and at worst may cause Westerners to shake their heads and grin broadly.

bo • 'da • cious *adj (1845)*

1 Southern & Midland: OUTRIGHT, UNMISTAKABLE.
2 Southern & Midland: REMARKABLE, NOTEWORTHY.

—Webster's Ninth New Collegiate Dictionary

PROLOGUE

When I rode out of Dry Creek, Montana Territory, that August fore-noon in '82, all in the world I wanted was to hire on with some cow outfit as a rider of their rough string. I was headed for the county seat of Shenanigan, where the big cowmen do their banking, and the weather that day was hot as the very hinges of Hell.

I had growed up around Dry Creek, and I liked the town. I can't tell you *why* I liked it, I suppose it was the people, but anyway I did. Dry Creek took its name from a muddy, sometime stream that flowed west out of the foothills of the Brimstone Mountains and drug itself on past the city limits for a mile or so before it petered out entirely. Leastways that's what it did most years, but that particular summer the creek had already been dry since the twenty-third of June. Barring a flash flood, it wouldn't flow again until spring.

There was nary a cloud in all that brassy sky, and the sun burned hot upon my back and shoulders as I drew rein atop a sandrock ridge. The big gelding I rode was neither sweated nor winded, while I was both. Seldom if ever had I forked a saddlehorse with a gait as punishing to the rider, but the animal had heart, and during our brief acquaintance I had found him to be steady, willing, and double-tough.

I had taken to the ridge in the hope of catching a cooling breeze, but found no movement to the air at all, cooling or otherwise. Down below, a whirlwind scampered out across the valley floor, growing bigger as it spun. In the distance a band of antelope shimmered white, black, and orange in the heat waves, and high overhead a red-tailed hawk drifted upward like burnt paper from a stovepipe. I envied him; I druther have been drifting on air myself than setting astride of the rough-gaited roan.

A half-hearted, random scatter of scrub cedar trees dug their claws into the sandy soil along the ridge, and even though the shade was scant I figured it was better than no shade at all. I stepped down off the roan, took my canteen and the cold hotcakes I'd brought from breakfast, and made for the nearest cedar. After I kicked some loose rock in under the tree to spook out any rattlers that might be dozing there, I hunkered down cross-legged in the dirt.

It didn't take long for me to wolf down the cakes. I was still enough of a kid in those days to be hungry most of the time; I doubt a man could have filled me up with a scoop shovel. The hawk was still gliding upward, and I took to watching him again. Somehow, seeing him brought to mind the many times I had set on a ridge and watched a circling hawk with my Pa, and I felt my throat grow tight as the gut-lonesome sadness fell upon me again.

I had stood there at the Dry Creek cemetery with my hat in my hands and grief in my heart while the preacher droned on about Pa and what a fine feller he had been. A hot, gusty wind rattled sand and grit against

8

Pa's coffin, and I tried to imagine him laying inside with his hands folded across his chest, or up yonder in Heaven a-playing harp, but I could not. The only way I could picture him was the way I'd seen him most, a-horseback, and setting his old Texas saddle—the same rig that was now cinched upon the withers of the roan.

Soon as I could manage it I pulled my mind away from the hurt of remembrance and got to my feet. I dusted off the seat of my breeches and wiped my eyes on my shirtsleeve. Then I set foot in the stirrup, sunk spur, and took the road again. Had I knowed at the time where *else* that road would lead me, I might well have rode the other way.

ONE

In Jail and Out Again

Pa had told me once there were six saloons in Shenanigan, but that Cherokee Bob's was the best of the bunch, so it was there that I headed when I rode into town. Pa said Cherokee Bob was a squaw man but an honest saloonkeeper, and that most of the local ranchmen liked him. They drank at his bar, made their deals there—both paper and handshake—and they oft-times came there to do their hiring. Pa said Bob had a way of knowing who was looking for men and who was looking for work, and I figured maybe he could put me onto a riding job, if there was such.

It was there, as I reined up at Cherokee Bob's, that I

first saw Androcles Wilkes. He was leaning against the hitchrack in front of Dollan's saddle shop with his thumbs hooked in his pistol belt and his big hat pulled low over his eyes, and he looked like he held title deed to the world. He was a big man, big of body, belly, and rump, but there seemed no softness to him for all of that, and I reckoned he was a man to take note of.

When I stepped down, my right foot hit the ground harder than I meant for it to and the jingle-bobs on my spur rang the rowel like a mission bell. Looking across the polished seat of my saddle I caught him sizing me up, but he didn't seem much impressed. He sort of grinned underneath his big walrus moustache, like at his own private joke, and I have to confess it riled me some.

Frowning at him, I loose-tied the roan. "What the hell are you lookin' at?" says I, trying my best to look fierce and scary. I guess it didn't work all that well, because his grin just got wider.

"If a cat can look at a king," says he, "I reckon a man can look at a jackass."

I was taken aback some, but I tried not to let on. My arm went loose and limber, and my hand sort of hovered above the big Dragoon Colt on my right hip. "You don't *know* me well enough to go callin' me names, mister," I said.

"And you don't know *me* well enough to try t' booger me with that old cannon, kid. You even *touch* that smoke-pole and I'll blow out your lamp."

He came walking toward me across that dusty street

through the horse apples and old playing cards, and it was then I saw the tin star inside his vest catch sunlight. He pulled his pistol as he came and centered it on my belt buckle while he lifted my Dragoon with his other hand. Now I only weigh about one-thirty soaking wet, and I tend to be slender of hip and belly, but as I watched that six-shooter study my middle with its cold eye I couldn't help wishing I was slimmer yet.

"Trouble is, that horse you rode in on is *stolen*," he said, "although I expect you'll claim you didn't know that."

"No, sir, I didn't," says I, the "sir" part being due mostly to his six-gun, "I bought that horse over in Dry Creek a week ago."

"Then I expect you can show me a bill of sale."

"Well, yes, I could, if we was in Dry Creek! I don't carry it *with* me!"

I have to admit I was running a bluff with a two-color flush right then. I *had* bought the roan, but the one-eyed Mexican who sold him to me didn't offer a bill of sale and the price was so good I didn't ask for one.

All of which means I had a fair idea the horse *was* stolen, although I sure didn't aim to confess that just now.

"I've been a peace officer since the hogs et Hildegarde," says he, looking me in the eye, "and I've got to where I can tell when a man is lyin' just by the tone of his voice. You don't *have* a bill of sale, do you, son?"

"All right, no, I don't!" I replied, "but I ain't n-no

11

dang horse-thief, n-neither! H-How did my t-tone of voice sound on *that* one?"

For a long moment he just stood there, looking at me. His eyes were cold, hard, and savvy, and the way he studied me put me in mind of a cat sizing up a dickie bird. My face felt hot and I'd just heard myself commence to stutter, which I only do when I get riled.

Of a sudden he grinned like he did before, as if some secret joke tickled him. He handed my gun back and holstered his own. "Sounded like a man tellin' the truth," he said, "but I still need to talk to you about that roan." He jerked a thumb toward Cherokee Bob's front door. "I'm Androcles Wilkes, Sheriff of Progress County. Can I buy you a beer?"

"Yes, sir, you surely can," I told him, "I'm Merlin Fanshaw, from over Dry Creek way, and I'm lookin' for a ridin' job." Then we shook hands and walked on into Bob's.

A man I took to be Cherokee Bob himself sat dozing on a high stool behind the bar when we came in, but he woke up fast when he heard the sheriff's dime hit the hardwood. "Two beers, if you please, Bob," said the sheriff. Bob drawed us a pair, and we carried them over to a felt-topped table by a window near the front and set down.

The saloon was cool and dark after the hot sun outside, and I drank half my beer before I came up for air. I looked around and saw we pretty much had the place to ourselves, except for a bored chippy playing solitaire and a blue-tick hound stretched out near the back door, dreaming of rabbits while he thumped out a rhythm with his hind leg.

I took another pull at my beer and studied Wilkes across the rim of the stein. He was watching me, too, and I felt there wasn't much his old eyes didn't take in. Beneath the brim of his Buckeye Stetson his thinning black hair and his soup-strainer were streaked with gray. He had wrinkles aplenty, some from sun and some from laughter, and his jowls sort of pooched out at the bottom like a bulldog's. An old scar cut down through his eyebrow and just missed the corner of his right eye, and even though he had to be pushing fifty his smile showed a set of strong, white teeth. I decided then and there that Androcles Wilkes was no swivel-chair lawman; he'd heard the owl and seen the elephant, and his sunburnt face was a battle map.

"All right, son," says he, "tell me more about you and that horse out yonder."

"Like I said, I bought him a week ago over at Dry Creek from a one-eyed Mexican. I don't know the feller's name, but I've seen him around Dry Creek now and again. He's a hard-lookin' old boy, with a pot belly and a black eyepatch, and he smells like the downwind side of a distillery"

"He generally does. That'd be Emiliano Vasquez, called *El Borrachon*. He rides with the Starkweather gang."

"Never heard of no Starkweather gang," I said.

"No reason you should have, although you did purchase that cold-jawed hay burner from one of its more

13

colorful members. The gang is a rustler outfit, mostly, although they sometimes rob a bank or a coach when they run low on operatin' capital. Heard they even hit an Army paymaster last month.

"The boss of the outfit is a hardcase named Original George Starkweather, and I shot him in the buttocks once in a skirmish over in Silver City. Was aimin' at his belly, but he moved."

"Thoughtless of him. How'd he get that name?"

"Story is his daddy admired General Washington, so named his first boy after him. Then he had three *more* boys and named *them* George, too. Must have *really* liked the name. There was Little George, Red George, Slow George, and of course his first-born, Original George. I don't know what happened to them other Georges, but Original George is a bunion on the big toe of decency. I would admire to put him and his trail trash out of business on a permanent basis."

I had finished my beer while he'd been talking, and reckoned it was my turn to buy a round. Cherokee Bob had settled back into his *siesta,* so I spoke up loud enough to be heard. "Hey, Bob," I said, "We need two more here when you get a minute."

"None for me, son," said Wilkes, "I never drink while I'm on duty"

"What was that you just had," I asked, "buttermilk?"

"I sometimes have *one* beer when I'm *partly* on duty," he explained, "Now let's get back to you and *El Borrachon.*"

"Well, I come from over at Dry Creek, like I said.

14

Grew up with my folks on a hard-rock farm in the badlands with dirt so poor it wouldn't grow weeds. Mother died when I wasn't but ten—of consumption and perpetual despair, the doctor said—and Pa and me scratched out a livin' breakin' broncs and sellin' 'em to the cowmen along the Big Porcupine. Then last month Pa was buckin' out a crazy black stud at the home place and the fool horse took him off a rimrock."

I don't know whether it was drinking that beer fast like I did or just remembering Pa, but all of a sudden my eyes misted up again and my voice got tight. "Killed him outright," I said. Bob had fetched me a second beer like I asked, and I cleared my throat and took a quick drink of it.

"Anyway," I went on, "it turned out Pa owed everything we had and a little more to the Cattleman's Bank of Dry Creek. Bankers took our farm, the horses, the old milk-cow, even the dang chickens, and sold the whole outfit at auction. I had to go to work at the livery stable just to pay back the undertaker for buryin' Pa.

"Pa had hocked his old Sharps rifle and this Dragoon Colt I'm packin', but the banker had a generosity fit and let me keep Pa's Texas saddle and his spurs. I had enough money left to get the guns out of hock, so I strapped on the Colt and sold the Sharps for twenty-five dollars cash.

"Well, I was settin' there in the shade of the livery barn dreamin' of bankers boilin' in oil and wonderin' what on earth I was goin' to do when this heavy-set Mexican walked up. His horse was a hot-blooded

Spanish barb that I'd took care of a time or two at the stable—you know, gave it extra oats and such. Anyway, the old boy seemed to like me. Asked if I'd like to buy a good horse, and I told him if money was dynamite I couldn't blow my nose.

"Well, he threw his head back and laughed like that was the funniest thing he'd ever heard. I stood there watchin' the sunlight dance off his gold tooth and waited 'til the hilarity passed. He looked at me kind of thoughtful and scratched his big belly. 'How much *dinero* you got, *chico?*' he asks. Holding back five dollars, I told him twenty and he walked me around behind the barn where his barb was loose-hitched to the corral. Tied next to it was the roan. He said, 'I like you, *chico*. I sell to you this very fine *caballo*.'"

Wilkes leaned back in his chair and stroked his moustache. "So," he said, "*El Borrachon* unloaded a stolen horse on a country boy and picked up a fast twenty bucks to help quench his terrible thirst." He hooked his thumbs in the pockets of his vest and grinned at me with his cat-that-et-the-dickie bird smile. I could almost see feathers on his lip.

Well, he just made me feel like a dang fool, and I reckon I showed it. "Yeah," I sulled, "I guess that's about the size of it."

Wilkes squinched up his eyes and studied the hanging lamp above the table like he was fixing to buy it. He looked back at me then, and I thought I saw sympathy in his eyes. He dropped his hands to his knees and leaned forward. "It does seem to me," he

16

said, "that you have a few problems, son.

"From what you tell me, you're maybe four bits away from vagrancy, and you've rode all the way from Dry Creek to look for work. Trouble is, you rode in here on a stolen horse, and it's my job to return the animal to its lawful owner. Which means you're not only broke, you're afoot. But that ain't the worst of it."

"I have a feelin' you're about to *tell* me the worst of it."

"It's my painful duty, son. You are in possession of another man's horse without a bill of sale. I'm afraid that qualifies you for a one-way trip to the territorial pen and a new career makin' gravel out of boulders with a twelve-pound sledge."

I jumped up and kicked my chair back so hard it woke up the dog. "I t-told you I d-didn't steal that horse—you said you b-believed me!"

"Set down, son, and keep your hands away from that hogleg. I have my Colt's Peacemaker trained on you under the table here, and believe me, you don't want to be shot where I'm pointin' it."

That calmed me down some. I eased back into my chair, keeping my hands high.

"I *do* believe you, son," Wilkes went on, "but there's nothin' I can do. The law don't care what I believe, it only cares about evidence. Now I feel real bad about it, but I'm gonna have to lock you up 'til the circuit judge comes around next week."

I told him I sure didn't want him to feel bad on my account, and thanked him for the beer as sarcastic as I knew how. For the second time that day he took my Dragoon Colt off me, and we walked out of the cool darkness of Cherokee Bob's onto Shenanigan's sun-baked street.

"It's all right, sheriff, there's no hard feelin's," I lied.

By the time we'd walked to the sheriff's office at the far end of Main Street, I had sweated through my shirt and was panting like a lizard on a rock. The front door was propped open and so were the windows, I suppose in hopes of catching a breath of cool air, only there wasn't any.

Stepping inside, I saw a big man who I took to be Wilkes's deputy sitting astride of a chair near the back door, eating watermelon and spitting the seeds outside. He wore a black hat but no shirt, and his shoulders and chest were hard-muscled, white, and shiny with sweat. He gave me a bored glance, shrugged, and went back to his melon. Wilkes pushed me on across the office to another door and opened it.

I stepped in through the doorway, and there beheld the inner reaches of the Progress County Jail. The walls were made of rough-cut granite, and there were four cells maybe twelve feet square, divided floor to ceiling by iron bars. Along one side ran the cell doors and more close-set bars, off a kind of hallway which held a chair and a small table. The whole layout seemed dark and dim after the brightness of the street outside, and it took a minute for my eyes to grow used to the gloom.

Directly, things began to come clear and I was able to

make out some detail. I saw that each cell contained a pair of beat-up iron beds, with a straw tick and a ragged gray blanket on each one. It looked like the bunks had been white once, but the paint had mostly all chipped away, showing bare metal underneath. High up the wall were two narrow, barred windows and below, at the back of each cell, stood a white enamel slop bucket.

Wilkes swung open the door to the first cell, and I heard the rusty hinges groan like a lovesick cat. Then he nudged me inside, and the heavy door slammed shut behind me with a clang like the crack of doom.

That was my first time in jail, and if you've never been locked up there's no way I can tell you what the sound of that closing door is like. If the words "trapped" and "helpless" each had their own sound, it would be something like a blend of the two, combined with the hollow thud of a shovel on a coffin. I hadn't felt so flat-out scared and lonesome since Pa died.

The sheriff had taken my belt, spurs, and pocket knife—so I couldn't hang myself or cut a hole in the granite wall, I suppose—and for what seemed a long time I just laid back on the bed and felt sorry for myself.

I thought it was a crying shame that a fine, upstanding, young man like me could be took advantage of by a one-eyed drunken bandit and forced to buy a stolen horse.

I pictured myself growing old and feeble-minded in the Territorial Prison. I almost commenced bawling like a baby, not so much because I saw myself an old geezer in the pen but because my life of crime had been so puny and piddling. I hadn't robbed any banks, coaches, nor army paymasters. I hadn't rustled stock nor killed scores of men in desperate gun battles. My only claim to fame as a bandit was that I'd bought a cheap roan horse I had a pretty good idea was stolen and stepped off the animal right in front of the Progress County Sheriff. All things considered, I figured I was too dumb to live, and the most pathetic example of an outlaw there ever was.

I don't know how long I laid there wallering in self-pity, but somewhere along the line I must have dozed off. When I came to myself again it was dark outside and someone had lit the lamps in the hallway. As I listened, I heard the sound of footsteps from inside the sheriff's office. Then the door opened, and this good-looking young girl swept into the room like a sweet song on the wind.

She was slender and pert, and she carried a napkin-covered tray in both her small hands as she entered the hallway. Under the yellow light of the oil lamps her hair was the color of sunlight shining through a honey jar, and she wore it soft and loose about her slim shoulders. Her dress looked to be of white cotton, high-necked and close fitting, and her skirt sort of billowed out as she closed the door and carried the tray to the table across from my cell.

"Supper time," she said, "beef stew and biscuits. Stand back from the cell door, if you please."

I did my best not to stare at her, staring at her all the while, and stumbled back and set down on the bed like

I'd been pole-axed. There was a kind of pass-through built into the door just big enough for the tray, and the girl set it there and stepped back with a quick, shy smile.

"You ain't at all what I expected," she said, "I thought you'd be older, you know, and *mean* looking."

She stood there with her hands on her hips, sizing me up with a set of big brown eyes that put me in mind of a newborn fawn. I picked up the supper tray and carried it back to my bunk.

"I reckon I must have looked mean enough to the sheriff," I said stiffly, "and the old devil didn't seem to worry much about my tender years, neither."

Her smile got bigger. "The old devil is my daddy," she said, "and when he told me we had a horse-thief to feed I expected he'd at least be older than *me*."

"I reckon I *am* older than you, little girl," I said, "I was prob'ly breakin' wild horses when you were havin' tea parties with your dollies." I sounded puffed up and stuffy, even to myself, but I felt like she was mocking me. I didn't enjoy being studied like a critter in a cage, even if I was one.

"That is hard to believe," she said, "how old *are you, sir?*"

"I'm almost twenty-one, if it's any of your business."

"You telling me you're *twenty?*"

"Well, not exactly. More like nineteen."

"When exactly did you *reach* that great age, sir?"

"All right, I'll be nineteen in June. I'm eighteen."

"I apologize, old timer," she smiled, and this time her

21

smile like to have lit up the whole jail, "you *are* older than me. *I* won't be nineteen until *July.*"

I felt my ears burn and knew my face was red. I didn't know what to say, so for a mercy I said nothing. I just took the napkin off the tray and went to eating the stew and biscuits she had brought.

She kind of leaned back against the hall table and cocked her head sideways, like a dog hearing a train whistle. "I'm Mary Alice Wilkes," she said, "What's your name?"

"Name's Fanshaw, miss, Merlin Fanshaw. I'm pleased to meet you, but I druther it was some other place."

"Yes," she said, her eyes big and serious, "I'm sorry to see you in jail, Merlin Fanshaw."

I thought about saying she wasn't half as sorry as I was, but didn't. Instead, I finished off the last of the stew and wolfed down the second biscuit. I thought the meal was as good as I'd ever had, and I wondered whether she'd cooked it.

"Daddy is sorry you have to be in jail, too," she said. "I'll bet."

"My daughter's right, son, I am," said the sheriff, who stood now in the open doorway that led to his office, "I've been tryin' to find some way I could let you out of there, and I believe I've maybe thought of one, if you're interested."

Well, of course I told him nothing would interest me more, and that I would surely like to hear about it, whatever it was.

Sheriff Wilkes walked slowly over to the table and stood next to the girl. "You see, son, I have the authority to furlough you, pending the arrival of the circuit judge next week."

"Furlough?"

"Turn you loose until your trial. I believe I might be inclined to do that if you'd be willin' to cooperate with *me*."

"Cooperate how?"

"My deputies and me have been huntin' for Original George and his boys ever since they robbed that army paymaster last month, but we haven't seen hide nor hair of 'em. On the other hand, it appears that you *have*.

"Now just suppose you was to go back over Dry Creek way and run into that one-eyed *pistolero* again. And then suppose you was able to find out from him where the gang is holed up. And then further suppose you was to pass that information on to me. I would then raise myself a posse and go apprehend those gents."

Wilkes looked thoughtful; for a long moment he was quiet. Then he said, "I believe the judge would be impressed by your willingness to cooperate in this matter. I would of course speak to him on your behalf, and I reckon he might even be inclined to dismiss the charges against you entirely."

The sheriff put his arm around Mary Alice and smiled at me. "How does that sound to you, son?"

"Anything that gets me out of here sounds good," I

told him, "but I'd be less than honest if I didn't tell you it seems to me there's a whole heap of supposin' in your plan."

The sheriff's smile faded. He shrugged and turned back toward the door to his office. "Well, there's no real hurry, son," he said, "take your time and think it over for a day or so. The circuit judge likely won't get here 'til late in the week, anyway. If he gets here at all."

I walked to the cell door and looked at Mary Alice. She was studying me with those big brown eyes again, her face serious and sad. She stood only a foot or so from me, just beyond the bars. I saw that her chin came up about to the level of my shoulder, and I caught the smell of lilac and saw the soft shine of her hair in the lamplight.

"That won't be necessary, sheriff," I said, "I'm your man."

Wilkes broke out in a broad smile. "Why, that's just fine, son," he said. He stepped into his office and came back with the cell key on its big ring. While he was gone I'd looked close at Mary Alice again and saw she was smiling, too. I don't know whether it was the prospect of getting out of jail or seeing her face light up the way it did, but right then I felt like I could take on the entire Starkweather gang all by myself.

TWO

Back to Dry Creek and Beyond

The battered swivel chair behind the big oak desk squawked in protest as Wilkes eased his considerable bulk down onto it. I sat across from him and watched as he took my belt, knife, spurs, and holstered pistol out of a drawer and pushed them across to me. The weather had cooled down some with the coming of evening, but there was still a dry, scorched smell from outside where the street had baked all day under the August sun. Through the open windows I could see flashes of heat lightning off to the south. A coal-oil lamp hung above the desk throwing deep shadows and soft yellow light over the office, and three big dusty moths had fluttered in and were looping and battering at the flame behind the chimney like they were loco, or drunk.

Mary Alice stood at the door to the street with the supper tray and empty dishes, looked back, and smiled her bright flash of a smile.

"I'll leave you gentlemen alone now," she said, "it was nice to meet you, Merlin."

It took me a second or two to realize she was talking to me, and before I could answer she was already gone. In the first place, nobody had ever called me a gentleman before, even by accident. Second, I don't recollect a pretty girl *ever* saying it had been nice to meet me.

25

Anyway, I was sitting there, half turned, with my jaw hanging open like the tailgate on a wagon and my eyes on the empty doorway, when Wilkes cleared his throat, impatient-like, and I realized he'd been talking to me.

"All right," he said, "here's how we'll play it. We'll spread the word that you got hold of the keys and broke jail, stealin' another horse in the process. I can't let you take the roan, of course, but I've got a tough little buckskin out back you can put your saddle on. He's a little rank, but he's tough as a ten-cent steak and there ain't no quit in him."

Wilkes stood up and the swivel chair gave a groan of relief. He took a double eagle from his vest pocket and handed it to me. "Here's twenty dollars travelin' money, kid," he said, "make it last."

I took the coin and turned it over in my fingers. It glowed warm in the yellow light, as if it had a life of its own. Above me, one of the moths had found its way inside the lamp chimney, and it suddenly flared bright and perished in a flash of fire. "Well," I thought, "so much for reaching your *goal.*"

I couldn't rightly put a finger on it, but there was something about Wilkes's proposition that left me feeling cat-eyed and goosey. What he'd said about the reward money made sense, I guess, but whenever he spoke about the Starkweather gang his voice took on a hard edge that caused me to think there was more to the deal than he'd told me, something secret, and well, *personal,* somehow.

"One more thing, Merlin," he said, "if I don't hear

from you in a week or so, you'll damn *sure* be hearing from *me.*"

The buckskin was tied high and short in a small corral behind the sheriff's office, and while Wilkes held a lantern I set my saddle on him and pulled the latigo snug. The gelding seemed steady enough, and he did look to be clear-footed and tough. His ears were laid back and his nostrils moved like the gills on a trout as he took my measure, but I had seen a horse or two before and I figured we'd get on all right.

In the corral behind the sheriff's office, I opened the gate and led the buckskin outside, then walked him up and down in the dark, untracking him. I was about to set foot in the stirrup and ride out when here come Mary Alice, her white dress soft and pale as woodsmoke in the gloom. She sort of glided up to me and smiled as she handed me a small, loose-wrapped bundle. "Some more of those biscuits you liked," she said, "it's a long ride to Dry Creek."

I was glad it was dark there behind the office; I could tell by the way my ears burned that my face was red again. I sort of stammered a "much obliged," and put the biscuits inside my shirt. With a quick swing up, I pulled the buckskin around and spurred him in the flanks.

Well, even as I done it I knew I shouldn't have. I'd been showing off for Mary Alice, acting the bold and carefree range rider, when my attention should have been on the gelding. When I turned him out on the street and hooked him in the withers he naturally enough took offense: he let out a squeal and swallered his head, and the war began.

I'd been caught off guard and off balance, and the first thing I done was lose my right-hand stirrup and most of my cockiness. The buckskin jumped for the moon; I slammed hard against the saddle's cantle, then sailed above the forks. I grabbed leather without shame, being grateful once again for the darkness. Somehow I managed to hang and rattle as the gelding pitched again, and I stabbed the breeze with my toe as I tried to find that floppin' offside stirrup. I got lucky and caught it, then lost it, and found it again, while I bounced all over that little buckskin horse from croup to withers.

He commenced warming to his work about that time, driving his feet down in a stiff-legged chop that rattled windows across the street and snapped my head like the popper on a whip. Then his hindquarters came down under him, and I was throwed forward against his poll as his head snapped back and collided with my nose. My backbone hurt from tail to neck, but the pain in my nose took my mind off of that. My eyes watered so bad I couldn't have saw anything had it been broad daylight. I'd turned loose of the rigging at last and I swiped at my peepers with my free hand in an effort to clear them and see where I was bound, even if I didn't seem able to control it much.

When finally I was able to make out my surroundings I was surprised to find I hadn't gone all that far. Wilkes and Mary Alice stood at the corral gate, watching the show—such as it was—and I was astride the little buckskin a hundred yards away, facing the road south. My Colt Dragoon had near beat me to death during the short ruckus, but I hadn't lost it and I still had my hat.

I still had Mary Alice's bundle, too, and I took it out of my shirt, held it high, and grinned at her. Well, of course the buckskin took that occasion to renew his wild fandango. I grabbed leather again, throwing pride—and the biscuits—to the winds. Them flaky morsels was raining down like hail, that fool horse was running and bucking south on the road out of town, and I guess I lost my temper some. I took a deep seat and commenced to punish him with my spurs, at which point he throwed a tantrum of his own. We swept on down the road like a chunk in the rapids, with him squealing and pitching and me reared back, riding loose and hooking as we went.

I just set up there with a leg on each side and my mind in the middle, listening to the music of my spurs and making hair fly, until the little horse showed me he wasn't as dumb as he'd let on: he stopped his frog-walking and settled into a smooth, ground-covering run.

I felt pretty good; I was headed back to Dry Creek on a better horse than I rode when I'd left there, with a twenty-dollar gold piece in my pocket and memories of a pretty girl who'd given me biscuits and called me a gentleman. The only melancholy thoughts I had right then were that I was getting farther away from her with every mile I rode, and that some town dog was going to

strike it rich when he found those baking powder biscuits of hers a-laying in the street.

The little buckskin ran flat-out for nearly a mile, then
slowed to a steady, quick-stepping trot. He was
breathing hard, but was not winded, and I was pleased
to find him a smooth-gaited saddler now that we'd had
our waltz and kicked the frost out. He spooked a little
when we crossed the bridge at Careless Creek and he
heard the planks rumble hollow beneath him, but he
didn't balk or shy and I touched his neck with my free
hand and told him I was proud of him.

Dawn had stained the sky dusty rose by the time I hit
Dry Creek, and the Brimstone mountains over east
bulked dark and sharp-edged against the growing light.
It had been a long day, and I was middling tuckered. I
had rode the twenty miles between Dry Creek and
Shenanigan twice in the past twenty-four hours, and my
eyelids had took on a will of their own. They kept a-
closing on me no matter how I struggled to keep them
open, and I wanted sleep more than I did food, to show
you how wore-down I was.

Still, I was grateful; the ride back to Dry Creek had
been cooler aplenty than it had been a-going, and the
little buckskin horse was a pleasure to ride after the
rough-gaited roan.

The town of Dry Creek wasn't much, just a double
handful of sun-bleached buildings scattered every
whichaway along a crooked street, and the town was
still asleep as I rode in. A lantern glowed smoky orange

at the Livery Barn and I figured Old Walt, my boss and the owner of the stable, would still be up. I found him in the office and told him I'd be boarding the buckskin for a day or two. I said I'd be bunking in the loft. Walt allowed that was fine, long as I took care of my own horse and paid for what feed the buckskin used.

I slipped my saddle off and walked the little gelding for a spell to cool him out, rubbed him down good with a grain sack, and put him in a stall. Then I clumb up to the loft and slept like a January bear.

For the next few days I just hung around town, thinking maybe the one-eyed Mexican bandit called *El Borrachon* might come back in, but he never did. I don't know what I thought I'd do if I saw him anyway, maybe say, "Howdy there, mister outlaw. I wonder, could you direct me to the hideout of the Starkweather gang?" As luck would have it, that was a decision I never had to make.

I put a set of shoes on the buckskin, did a little work at the stable, and asked around some. Nobody had seen the big Mexican or his Spanish Barb; at least they told me they hadn't. Walt said the last time he'd seen the Mex was when I'd bought the twenty-five dollar roan from him, and the barkeep over at the Oasis said he wished he *would* come in, him being such a good customer and all, but that he hadn't laid eyes on him in almost two weeks.

As a last resort, I set down and gave the matter some serious thought. During the time I'd worked at Walt's

Livery Barn the man called *El Borrachon* had been in town at least once, and sometimes twice, a week. If he'd been holed up with the Starkweather gang somewhere, that meant their hideout was likely no more than a day's ride out of Dry Creek, probably someplace up in the Brimstone mountains. I'd rode all over that country with Pa when we were running wild horses, and I knew the canyons and rimrocks of that range like an old maid knows her parlor. The more I thought about that country, the more convinced I was that if there was one place those boys were most likely to be it would be the old M Cross line camp up above Brimstone Creek.

Rufus Cain had brought cattle into that country back in '64 when there wasn't a soul living anywhere in the valley, and since that time he'd built his M Cross ranch into the biggest spread around. From the beginning, Cain had used the west slope of the Brimstones as his summer range. He'd had a cabin and corrals built, and his line riders had rode herd on his beef in some of the highest and lonesomest country anywhere. But Cain had quit that range the previous year and moved his cattle south, leaving the cabin to the pack rats and squirrels. And maybe to the Starkweather gang.

Truth is, Cain's riders hadn't used the camp all that much even before; it was high, lonesome, and hard to reach, even in good weather. The cabin and corrals stood back in thick timber underneath a rocky ridge that dropped off into Sheep Canyon on the north side. To the south, a steep, narrow trail led down a sheer rock wall to Brimstone Creek. A good spring ran just west of the cabin, and to the east a snow-fed stream trickled out of a break in the rocks. It had been my Pa who showed me the place. "That there, Merlin," he'd said, "is what I would call a rustler's delight."

Only two trails led into the camp: the narrow track up the canyon wall, and a wider trail to the east that wound its way through aspen groves and lodgepole pine from Brimstone Basin on the east side.

Sure, the Starkweather gang could be other places, but I couldn't think of a more likely hideout, especially not within a day's ride of Dry Creek. I decided I'd go on up there and do some scouting.

Sheriff Wilkes had made it clear that if he didn't hear from me inside a week or so, he'd be coming for me. Of course, that didn't necessarily mean he'd *find* me, but just the same I didn't like the idea of him dogging my trail. I fancied his daughter all right, but I hadn't been real fond of his The next morning I sauntered into the telegraph office and had the agent send Wilkes a message saying I was still looking for game and thought I knew of a place where the hunting might be good. I said I'd let him know when I found out, signed my name, and paid the telegrapher.

At Bender's store I picked up some bacon, beans, bread, and coffee, and I bought a rusty old Henry .44 rifle with a scarred stock for twelve dollars. The bore and the action looked to be all right, and like Pa always said, it ain't how a thing looks but how it works. Old Bender was a sharp trader, but I must have seemed pathetic and wistful enough to soften his heart because he throwed in a scabbard and a box of shells at no charge.

I ran a few cartridges through the Henry out back of the barn, enough to know that whatever I shot at and missed would be my fault alone, and by noon I had forked the buckskin and was headed for the mountains. I don't know whether I was more excited or worried, but it did occur to me that sometimes the only thing worse than not finding what you're looking for is *finding* it.

I rode east out of town across the sagebrush flat that led to the faded blue mass of the Brimstones. The day was hot, and a following wind from the west kept the pungent smell of crushed sage in my nostrils as I traveled. The buckskin zig-zagged his way through the dry and twisted brush in his steady, ground-eating trot, his ears working and his head high as we covered the distance. When a sage hen blowed out in front of us in a frantic flurry of stubby wings, sailed low, and vanished over a cutbank, I noted with approval that the little horse neither spooked nor turned a hair.

I had believed the gelding would be steady and reliable under saddle but I had not been certain, so I'd made no decision regarding which trail to take. But now, having found him alert and trustworthy, I made up my mind that we would go up Brimstone Creek and climb the canyon wall by way of the narrow trail instead of the wider but more distant eastern trail.

As I rode, I saw again in memory the face and form of Mary Alice Wilkes, with her honey-colored hair and her bright flash of a smile. She came cleanly to my mind as I thought of her in the same way an image comes in focus through field glasses, soft and blurred at first, then sharp and clear.

The workings of memory are strange. I could recall my Pa's voice just the way it had sounded when he was alive, but I couldn't remember his face for the life of me, and we had been close. What I could recollect of my mother's face was faint and sort of misty, soft and kind but very sad, and I wondered how come memory was the way it was.

Old Walt had told me once that as a man gets older his memory tends to play tricks on him. He said recent events were sometimes hard to bring to mind while a face or happening from thirty or forty years ago might be recalled in sharp detail. Said he couldn't remember what he'd et for breakfast that morning, but he could clearly recall a dog he had when he wasn't but five years old.

There didn't seem to be any pattern to the way *my* memory worked, but I was glad that Mary Alice was a part of it. I surely did hanker to see her again, and even as I breathed in the sharp scent of sage, I remembered the way she had smelled of lilac that evening at the jail, and the way it had made me feel.

I'd left the plains behind me and had moved into the foothills below Brimstone Canyon when the buckskin commenced to favor his nigh front foot, and I drawed rein to look at it. I figured he'd maybe picked up a rock, and sure enough when I lifted his foot there was a small stone stuck betwixt his hoof and the shoe. I had pried it free with my knife and was about to get back up on him when I saw the riders. There were two of them, about a mile back, and I'll admit that the sudden way they pulled off the trail and slipped into the trees when they saw me looking their way troubled me a good deal more than somewhat.

I had heard old-timers say that a man should always keep an eye on his back trail, and while that seemed a sound enough idea I'd never felt the need to practice it much. Oh, I could see where it might be necessary for outlaws, gunmen, and the like, but I wasn't on the dodge nor hunted and I never saw much point in looking at where I'd been—until now.

Who *were* those fellers? Were they following me, or just riding the same trail?

Over the next mile or so I rode loose and watchful, and twice I caught a glimpse of those boys coming on. The feller in the lead rode a flashy Appaloosa and set his horse like he'd been grafted onto it, while the gent behind him was a tall, slim jasper on a black, long-legged Morgan. They seemed closer than when I first spotted them, probably because I'd been spending so much time looking back instead of where I was going.

The air close to the creek was cooler now, but even so sweat stung my eyes and trickled down inside my shirt, and my neck felt raw from rubbing on my collar as I watched behind me. My mouth was dry and my hands were wet, which is one hell of a combination when you think about it, and all in all I felt about as tense as stretched wire.

The trail ahead circled to the right around a sideling hill and through an aspen grove, and as soon as I came around I kicked the buckskin into a fast run across the hillside and on up into the trees. When I was well inside the grove I reined up and hit the ground running, pulling my rifle as I quit the saddle.

The pounding of my heart was loud in my ears as I jacked a shell into the Henry's chamber and drew a shaky bead on the spot where the trail turned the corner.

I knelt there, my rifle barrel steadied against an aspen tree, and listened hard, straining to hear horses coming, but all I could make out was my own breathing and the sounds of the mountains. Above me, the dollar-sized leaves pattered and shimmered in the breeze. Down below, I could hear Brimstone creek chuckle over its rocky bed. Somewhere back in the pines, a squirrel scolded loud and raucous, and from way off in the distance I heard a raven call.

I held my breath and listened for the riders, waiting for the sound of a hoof striking rock or the jingle of bit or spur, but there was nothing, no sound at all except for my own heartbeat.

And then, cold as a sheepdog's nose, I felt the gun barrel on the back of my neck and my heart like to quit beating altogether.

"Just put the rifle down, son, and stand up slow with your hands high," the voice behind me said. I dropped that Henry like it was white-hot.

THREE

Out of the Frying Pan

"All right, son, you can turn around now," said the voice, and I did, holding my hands hat-high and empty. The first thing I saw was what looked to be a full-blooded Indian of about my age or maybe a little older, holding a Spencer carbine easy in his hands. He was lean and withy, with strong white teeth and eyes blacker than midnight in a mineshaft. Beneath his flat-brimmed hat his hair was shoulder-long and loose, except for two thin braids in front, and he grinned a hard, thin smile as he lifted my Dragoon from its leather.

Beyond him, sitting on an aspen log, sat the man who'd spoke. He looked to be somewhere in his fifties, maybe six-three or four in height, and lean and gangling as a sandhill crane. He wore a belted Colt with yellowed ivory grips and a high-crowned, wide-brimmed hat, and his hair and handlebar moustache were silver-white, the way snow sometimes is, or the moon.

He studied me now, like a man reading a book, and when he was through I had the uneasy feeling there wasn't much about me he didn't know.

"Set yourself and rest easy," he said, "I just need a few minutes of your time, Merlin Fanshaw."

"I see you know my name," I said, "I reckon you have the advantage of me, sir."

38

The old gent smiled. "Why, yes," he said, "I suppose I do, in every way."

He moved his hands from the lapels of his vest down onto his bony knees, and it was then that I saw the glitter of a nickel-plated badge on the left-hand side of his vest. I glanced again at the Indian, and saw with some surprise that he was wearing one, too. "Dang," I thought, "Seems like everyone I *meet* these days is some kind of lawman."

I hunkered down on my boot-heels and thumbed back my hat. The Indian squatted behind me with the Spencer across his thighs and watched me through half-closed eyes.

"My name is Chance Ridgeway," the old gent said, "and I'm United States Marshal for this territory. That noble savage behind you there goes by the name of Luther Little Wolf. Luther was a bloodthirsty redskin varmint when first we met, but I reformed him. Now he don't hardly massacre anybody no more, except maybe once or twice a week. Made him a full deputy last June, which has confused *his* people some and plum' *infuriated* most of *mine*. But I like the boy—he don't interrupt me when I'm talkin' and he's a good listener.

"Anyway, Merlin, I follered you from Dry Creek because I need to ask you a few questions. You reckon that'd be all right, son?"

"You bet," says I, "ask away."

"Thank you kindly," he says, "I appreciate your cooperation. One thing, though: I need truthful, *honest* answers. Now then, are you acquainted with the Sheriff of Progress County, one Mister Androcles Wilkes?"

"Uh, no, sir," says I, "I can't say that I am."

The old gent sort of sighed in a wistful kind of way, glanced over past me, and raised an eyebrow.

Something hit me hard and high in the middle of my back and sent me sprawling. I tried to throw my hands out to block my fall, but didn't make it and I wound up with my face in the dirt, stunned and blindsided, trying to catch my breath. My hat had come off and lay almost at Ridgeway's feet, and from the corner of my eye I could see the deputy standing over me with that Spencer, grinning like a wolf in a rabbit pen.

Ridgeway bent over, picked up my hat, creased it with his fingers, and looked thoughtful. "Merlin, Merlin," he said, shaking his head, "I told you I need *truthful* answers. Now let me ask you again . . ."

"All right," I choked, spitting topsoil like a gopher, "I have met Sheriff Wilkes. He jailed me last week in Shenanigan for ridin' a stolen horse."

"That's better, son," Ridgeway beamed. Gently, he placed my hat back on my head and wiped his fingers on a big bandanna. "I *knew* you fellers were acquainted," he said. "Like to know how I knew?"

This time he didn't wait for my answer, but went on in the same pleasant tone he'd used all along. "You see, the telegraph operator at Dry Creek shows me copies of all his incomin' and outgoin' messages, includin' *yours,* Merlin. You know, the one about you lookin' for game and knowin' a place where the huntin' might be good?

"Well, let me make a wild guess here. I figure Andy

40

Wilkes is lookin' for Original George Starkweather and thinks *you* can help find him. From the message you sent, *you* must think so, *too.*"

Ridgeway looked pleasant and kindly as an elder at a baptism. "Now then," he said, "why don't you just tell me all about it, Merlin?"

I felt my gut go tight, and I remembered Wilkes's mention of me breaking rocks at the territorial pen.

"No disrespect meant, marshal," I said slowly, with a glance back at Luther, "but I'm not sure I can *do* that. Sheriff Wilkes told me . . ."

Ridgeway reared back on his log, his eyes wide and his smile still open and friendly. And then his face changed and his cold blue eyes took on a flinty look.

"Why, bless you, son," he said, "you need to change your way of thinkin'. It ain't Sheriff Wilkes you have to *worry* about just now."

It wasn't so much that I was scared, though I guess I was a little, but dealing with the law has always seemed to me like setting in a poker game with only three cards against a dealer who plays with six and makes up his own rules to boot. The way I saw it, a United States Marshal and a deputy was a higher hand than a county sheriff and a pretty girl. I told Ridgeway dang near everything I knew. I told him about buying the roan from El *Borrachon,* about Wilkes and the Shenanigan jail, and about my idea the Starkweather gang might be holed up at the line camp. The one thing I *didn't* tell him about was Mary Alice. The way I saw it, she was none of his business, and I figured to keep such feelings and

41

memories of her as I had strictly to myself.

When I'd finally told him all I figured to, I shut up and waited. I must have done all right because that hard-eyed deputy didn't knock me down again and Ridgeway himself just sat there like a burrowin' owl in a dog town, looking wise and thoughtful.

"I appreciate your candor, son," he said, "and I reckon it's only fair for me to lay my cards on the table as well.

"About a month ago, Original George Starkweather and his boys stole an Army payroll over south of Fort Savage. Killed the paymaster, got off with more than $40,000 of Uncle Sam's cash, and scattered like quail.

"Well, sir, that event naturally fell under my jurisdiction, seein' as I carry the federal law hereabouts, so Luther and me commenced lookin' into the matter.

"To make a long story short, I have reason to believe that Sheriff Androcles Wilkes told Original George when and where the shipment was to be, and that them two were in cahoots on the robbery. It also appears that George double-crossed Wilkes and kept all the money, which I reckon has caused the good sheriff considerable distress. I have no doubt that he would like to learn the whereabouts of Original George and the boys, not so that he can apprehend the outlaws like he told you, but so he can locate the stolen money.

"I believe George has buried the payroll and is holed up with his gang somewheres. You may be assured, Merlin, that I have a great interest in learnin' the location of both the money and the bandits.

"I'd consider it a personal favor if you'd go on ahead and look for George and the boys like you were goin' to, only before you report to Wilkes you let me know first. You reckon you can do that?"

"Can I ask you somethin', marshal?"

"Surely."

"Well, it seems like finding them owlhoots is *your* business, not mine. Why don't *you* and your deputy ride on up there?"

"I doubt we'd be all that welcome. Besides, those boys almost certainly outnumber us, and I believe we can assume they hold the high ground. I did not reach my mature years by ridin' willy-nilly into ambushes."

I felt like I'd been roped head and heels and was stretched out waiting for the iron. All I ever meant to do was find myself a riding job with some cow outfit or maybe sign on as a bronc buster somewhere, but two different lawmen now had their own ideas about my future and I felt helpless as a hummin' bird in a whirl-wind.

"I don't suppose I have much choice, do I?" I asked.

"A man *always* has a choice, Merlin," Ridgeway said, and I swear he looked hurt that I even asked the question, "I was just hopin' you could do me this little favor."

"Well. How would I get word to you?"

"Through the telegraph office in Dry Creek is one way. Any message that goes through there I'll see. Or contact me at my office in Silver City."

"Well," I said, "Well. I'll do what I can, marshal."

"That's all in the world I'm askin', son," he smiled.

Ridgeway stood, stretched, and stuck his hand out. I got to my feet, too, and took his hand. Now that we were both standing I could see how tall the old boy really was, and I felt like a kid as I looked up into them ice-blue eyes. I could see Luther leading the Appaloosa and the Morgan down from the trees, and I heard the buckskin nicker from up where I'd tied him.

Ridgeway pulled himself into the saddle with a grunt and looked down at me. Luther handed my Dragoon back, slid the Spencer into its scabbard, and swung up onto his spotted pony like a cat.

"Uh . . . marshal," I said, "are you *sure* Sheriff Wilkes was in on that robbery?"

"I don't know as I can prove it just yet in a court of law, but yes, I'm sure, son. Why do you ask?"

"Well, I was just thinking it'll be hard on his daughter when you take him in."

"His *daughter?* Why bless you, son, Wilkes don't have a daughter. He ain't ever been married, far as I know."

I watched for a long time as they rode back down the trail. Then I went and untied the buckskin, wondering if day still follered night and whether two and two still added up to four.

I've never liked to admit that I didn't know things, but right then it seemed to me that all I knew for sure was that I didn't know much, so I tried to focus on the little I did know.

From the many trips I'd made with Pa, I could see the

44

whole trail up to the line camp in my mind's eye. It followed close by the willows along the creek for maybe three miles before it turned back in a sharp switchback and began its climb up through sliderock and timber. Some four or five miles farther on, it broke out onto a granite face maybe two hundred feet above the creek. From there, the track narrowed and crawled upwards across the canyon wall by way of a narrow ledge that caused a man to sweat and make promises to the Almighty. At the top, the trail moved into heavy timber once more and snaked up between the pines and across a long meadow to the cabin.

I figured I could make it, all right, but there was one thing that bothered me. For a considerable distance I'd be visible against the cliff and an easy target for a rifleman on the other side. If those boys were up there and had a guard out, and if they were as goosey as I figured they'd be, my trip up the trail could become about as hairy as a barbershop floor. The other trail, the one to the east, was wider and safer, but it was nearly ten miles longer. Besides, there was no guarantee the outlaws wouldn't be covering it, too; chances were they'd watch it even closer because it *was* the easier way.

I watered Buck and myself down at the creek, tightened my cinch, and swung up into the saddle. "All right, little Buck," says I, "let's go on up and see how much it takes for a trail to spook you."

Well, as it turned out it was me and not my horse that spooked. All the way up the trail I imagined myself being watched through a gunsight, and by the time we quit the timber and drew near the narrow shelf that led out across the canyon wall I was jumpy as a grasshopper on a griddle. I reckon the buckskin could feel my edginess, because he commenced to tense up, too, and just as we were fixing to move out onto the ledge he snorted and shied at a chipmunk like it was king of the grizzlies.

Directly, after he'd got over his scare some, I touched him with my spurs and he stepped out slow, head down and blowing his nose at the trail. I reined up and tried to calm him, patting his neck and calling him "Little Buck" and such. I knowed he had caught some of his fear from me, and I cussed myself because of it. Giving him plenty of rein, I let him pick his own way out onto the trail, and we took it slow and easy while the sweat crawled out from under my hat and my throat went dry as dust.

Up ahead I could see that the trail narrowed to a point where there could be no turning around or turning back, so I slid down off the little buckskin and led him on ahead. My foot touched down maybe two feet from the edge and kicked a rock off into space that seemed to fall forever before I heard it hit, faint and far away. I tried not to think of the shooter that might be across from me. I tried not to look down, but of course I did from time to time, and each time wished I hadn't. Far below ran the creek, twisting its way in a shining ribbon through the now shadowed canyon, and once I even looked down on an eagle as it soared silently above the dark trees.

I don't know how long it took to reach the timber at the far side of the canyon and leave the chancy trail behind, but it seemed like fifty years at least. I wouldn't have been surprised to find my hair had gone white as Ridgeway's. My knees shook as I led the little horse through an opening between some fallen boulders and on to a level, shady place amid the trees. I just stood there, a-holding on to the saddle horn 'til my breathing came back to normal, and then I set foot in the stirrup and went to get back in the saddle.

Of a sudden, I noticed the buckskin's ears. He had turned his head and fixed his attention on something behind me. His head was held high, his nostrils flared and his brown eyes staring. The voice came from behind me, too—ugly, flat and hard.

"You came a long way up a mountain just to *die,* kid."

I turned around slow, my left hand still on the horn and my right high and well clear of my pistol. The gent who'd spoke stood not twenty feet away, and of course he was pointing a firearm at me like everybody else seemed to be doing these days. My first thought was that I was tired of all the attention, but my second was that I'd never seen a harder-looking customer.

From his belt buckle north he was barrel-chested and wide-shouldered, and his big-muscled arms stretched the cloth of a dirty red shirt. Under a battered and sweat-stained hat his eyes were close-set and beady as a snake's, and his yellow teeth were framed by big lips and beard. He wore a half-breed sash beneath his pistol belt, and south of that he was bow-legged and squat all the way down to his raggedy mule-ear boots.

I've thought about it plenty since that day and I'm still not sure what came over me, or why. I believe I just had a bellyful of being pushed around and scared all the time, and I pure and simple went a touch loco. I throwed my shoulders back and puffed my chest out, looked mister hardcase right in his beady eyes, and tried to match his tone of voice.

"Who the hell do you think you're a-threatenin', fuzz-face?" I snapped, "It'd take a heap more than a coon-footed whey-bellied tub o' guts like *you* to put me in the ground."

He pooched out his lips and his eyes opened wider, probably to get a better look at this strange feller with the death wish, but I could see that he sure hadn't expected me to turn hostile on him.

"What's more," I said, "you better point that saddle gun somewheres else and right now before I poke it up your ass and improve your posture." His jaw dropped open from pure surprise, and then I got *real* creative. I took a step towards him and said, "I'm the Bodacious Kid, and I was thinkin' I might join your outfit 'til I got a good look at *you*. I already told you once, mister, take that rifle off me."

I believe to this day it was the surprise of it all that saved my bacon. Fuzz-face squinted his eyes, rubbed his hairy jaw, and broke into a big, yellow smile. He even lowered the saddle gun.

"You're crazier'n a sheepherder, kid," he said, "but you're a feisty whelp. 'Bodacious Kid', huh?"

48

"The same. You heard of me?"

"Can't say I have. Who you up here to see?"

I played the only card I had. "I'm lookin' for *El Borrachon*," I said, "that one-eyed, bean-eatin' boozer sold me a stolen horse, and the Progress County Sheriff throwed me in the crowbar hotel."

"You aim to fight the big Mes'kin over a stole horse?"

"Hell, no. I busted out and stole a better one. I just wanted to let him know the joke's on him."

"Well, he's up at camp, all right. He's even halfway sober, for a change. I'll take you on in, 'Bodacious,' but you'd better be who you claim to be, and he'd damn well better *know you*."

"Let's go, then," says I, "you ain't waiting on me."

I used to go to church with my Pa sometimes, mostly when he was missing Mother and sorry about his drinking, or when he'd got in some fool jackpot and scared himself. I recall the preacher used to talk a lot about prayer, but the only time I messed with it much was when, like Pa, I'd got myself in a bad mess and was spooked. Anyway, while Fuzz-face and me rode over to the camp I took up praying again.

What struck me first as we came up to the cabin at the edge of the meadow was the quality of the horses. Two stood under saddle at a hitchrack in front and three more grazed on stake ropes out in the meadow, and I don't believe I ever saw finer mounts anywhere. They were big, strong animals, some of them thoroughbreds, built for staying power and speed, and it came to me

49

that riding a good horse wasn't a matter of vanity for an outlaw, but a pure necessity.

There were three hard-eyed gents lounging out front when we reined up, and if anything they were even tougher-looking than Fuzz-face. I set my jaw and put on my fiercest expression as we stepped down, but I had the feeling I still looked like a lamb in a coyote den.

One of the boys, a big-eared ranny wearing two pistols and a knife, leaned against the wall with his arms crossed and a quid of tobacco bulging his cheek. He tried to talk around the chaw, found he couldn't, and spat a brown stream five feet away. "What the hell you got there, Kiowa," he said, "you kidnap that baby child away from its Ma?"

Well, I knew it was either paddle or sink, so I pushed out into deep water. "I ain't no child," says I, tight and mean as I knew how, "I'm the Bodacious Kid and I kill lippy old fools like you for practice."

He stiffened like I'd hit him and he came off that wall reaching for his irons, but my Dragoon was already out and centered on his middle so he threw a check-rein on his temper and pulled up short.

I could see he was impressed; he figured I'd beat his draw, but of course I hadn't. The truth is I never was even middling fast, but I'd begun my move before he started his, and the man who starts first always has the edge. Nobody moved for a second or two, and it was so quiet I could have heard a mouse pee on cotton. Then the feller grinned, took his hands off his pistols, and stuck a grimy paw out at me.

50

"Hell, kid, I was just rawhidin' you a mite," he said, "didn't mean to rile you none."

I flipped my six-shooter over to my left hand while we shook, but I kept it ready because my new acquaintance carried those twin lead-chuckers and I wasn't all that sure what *his* left hand might be doing. His grin got even wider when he saw my move; as tobacco juice droozled out a corner of his mouth, he raised his big left paw up shoulder high. "Name's Collyer, Kid—Mace Collyer," he said, "and I can see you didn't just fall off the punkin wagon. Please t' meetcha."

We'd shook hands, but I knew that didn't make us pardners. Those owlhoots studied me like a pack of town dogs sizing up a stray cat, and I knew if I turned my back or lost my nerve even for a second I'd go up in smoke and be heard from no more.

Every now and then I do get lucky, though, and this time Dame Fortune came stumblin' out the cabin's open door in the form of Emiliano Vasquez, better known to one and all as *El Borrachon.*

He looked the same as I remembered him, from his ample belly to his big sombrero and the black patch over his eye, and he jangled off the stoop in his Chihuahua spurs, saw me, and throwed his arms at the sky.

"Chico! Que pasa?" he boomed, "What you doin' here, kid?"

I was so glad to see the old bandit I could have kissed him. "I came to buy another horse from you," I grinned, "Sheriff Wilkes took the last one you sold me."

His expression was a perfect mix of innocence, outrage, and sympathy. "That som'bitch sheriff took you *caballo?*" he said, "*Ai, que lastima!* That som'bitch sheriff, he is *un ladrone*—he is a thief."

"You're tellin' me," I said, "but I got even with him— I broke out of his damn *calabozo* and stole me another one."

His big belly shook with laughter, and that gold tooth flashed just the way I remembered it.

"*Que bueno,*" he said, "you done good, chico."

He flung a big arm around my shoulders and turned toward them assembled hardcases. "Hey, *compañeros,*" he boomed, "This *hombre es mi amigo*—he is my friend."

It was like a ripple went through those boys; you could see the suspicion ease and the stiffness go out of them. Before long there was hand-shaking and back-slapping all around, and *El Borrachon* came up with a quart bottle of tequila which was passed around and sampled pretty free. Even Mace shook my hand again, but I caught a look in his eyes that reminded me I'd made him look small and had rode roughshod over his pride. He didn't strike me at all as being the forgiving kind.

FOUR

And Into the Fire

I was starting to feel the tequila. There was a fireball just below my brisket that kept trying to climb back up my throat, and I kept swallering and trying to hold it back. Somewhere in all the hilarity we finished the first bottle and *El Borrachon* broke out a second one, but a little voice in my head said, "You'd best stop drinking now, Merlin," and I replied, "Too late, do-gooder. Where was you and your dang advice an hour ago?"

Finally, my one-eyed *compadre* gave the boys what was left of the cactus drippin's and took me by the arm.

"*Venga aqui, chico!* Come on, kid," he bellered, pulling me off into the trees beyond the cabin, "I got to show you my new horse."

Behind us, the boys had killed the *pulque* juice and were trying to do the same to the bottle, throwing it in the air and firing their pistols at it.

"*Es el garañon* . . . a stud horse," *El Borrachon* said, as he towed me toward a corral set back in the timber, "*Es muy caballo . . . muy rapido. Tiene los cojones grandes.*"

I kept stumbling along after him, fighting the effects of the tequila and feeling the need to air my paunch, when all of a sudden he jerked me around to face him. "All right, 'Bodacious,' or whatever the hell your name is," he said, cold sober and with hardly a trace of his Mexican accent, "who *are* you, and what are you *doin'* here?"

Well, I don't mind telling you I sobered up fast. *El Borrachon* gripped my shoulders and looked hard into my face.

"You know me," I said, "I'm Merlin Fanshaw, from Dry Creek. I used to take care of your horse at the Livery Barn. You sold me that roan—"

"That ain't what I mean. Damn it, why are you here and why are you wearing Ridgeway's mark?"

"Who . . . what mark? I don't know what you're drivin' at. I'm—"

"Don't give me that 'Bodacious' foolishness! I saw your big entrance back yonder. It's a wonder those boys didn't cut you down on sight. If I hadn't showed up when I did—

"And you know damn well what mark I'm talkin' about . . . that two-fingered blue smudge on your hat. U.S. Marshal Chance Ridgeway put it there."

I snatched my hat off and stared. Sure enough, high on the crown, just below the crease, was a blue stain like a deer track. And then I remembered Ridgeway fingering my hat back there in the aspen grove, and the way he wiped his fingers with his bandanna.

"We don't have a whole lot of time, Kid, so listen up," he went on, glancing nervously back toward the cabin, "I'm Ridgeway's inside man with this wolf pack, and he put that mark on you so I'd know he'd sent you. We'll talk more later, but for now just follow my lead and watch your ass. If those *hombres* get wise to us we'll both be coyote food."

As we walked back, *El Borrachon*—or whoever he really was—looked sideways at me and grinned. " 'Bodacious Kid', huh?" he said, "That's pretty good, Merlin—pretty damn bodacious, in fact."

By the time we got back to the cabin he'd become the same good-natured Mexican bandit he'd seemed to be before. Some of the boys were standing or leaning

54

against the wall, smoking and talking, but Mace Collyer and a yellow-haired gent with a broken nose were sitting cross-legged on the grass, playing mumblety-peg with their belt knives. Goldilocks looked me over through half-closed eyes and flipped his frog stabber off his elbow and stuck it in the ground, but Mace stared as I passed like a wolf looking at a cottontail. I knew that whatever else I might do I must never let him get behind me.

I pulled my saddle off Little Buck and watered him at the spring east of the cabin, then rubbed him down and hobbled him in good grass. As I said before, I was still kid enough then to be hungry most of the time, and as I came back I could see smoke drifting from the cabin's stovepipe and I caught the smell of beef stew a-simmering.

Five men, including *El Borrachon,* sat cross-legged outside, wolfing down stew and biscuits as I ambled up, and for just a second there I thought of Mary Alice and of the biscuits I'd had to leave on the street in Shenanigan. I didn't see Fuzz-face—the one Mace had called 'Kiowa'—and I guessed he'd gone back to guard the trail again. I still hadn't laid eyes on the gang's leader, Original George. I wondered where he was, but nobody had mentioned him, and I didn't figure it was my place to ask. *El Borrachon* gave me a quick glance with his good eye, and maybe he winked—it's hard to tell with a one-eyed man—before he went back to work on his chuck.

I stepped into the cabin and looked around. There

were two double-decker bunks and a single toward the back wall, and a six-foot plank table with a bench on each side near the front. Just inside the door was a big old cookstove, and I knew for dang sure it hadn't been brought up over the same trail I came in on. Next to the stove stood a rough-sawn counter, which held a stack of tin plates, cups, and eating tools. A feller who turned out to be the outfit's cook came in, and he nodded when he saw me. Squat and bandy-legged, the gent had red hair and bright blue eyes, and he smoked a short-stemmed clay pipe as he tended his Dutch ovens.

"Get yourself a cup and plate, boy-O," he said, "and I'll dish you up a portion of this bleedin' ambrosia." His grin growed wider as I held out a battered tin plate. "I'm Shanty O'Kane," he said, "and I do the feedin' for these plug-uglies. I've also killed eight men, but divil a one with me cookery."

I grinned back at him, and done as he directed. As I said before, I like to eat.

The shadows slid cool and dark across the meadow as the sun dropped behind the ridge and the sky turned to glory. The yellow-haired gent caught up his horse and rode off at a fast trot to where the trail broke out on top. A short time later, Kiowa came riding back and I knew he'd been relieved of his guard duty.

I'd wolfed down two helpings of stew and was setting in the grass drinking my coffee as I watched Kiowa picket his horse and walk back toward the cabin. He glanced my way as he passed and went inside, and I

56

nodded and raised my cup in greeting, but he paid me no mind. Directly, he came back out and carried his plate, cup, and eatin' irons over a piece where he set down by himself under a tree.

The other boys had mostly gone inside the cabin and were playing cards by lantern light, but I was just glad to be by myself and have some time to think.

It had been quite a day. First, I had run up against a U.S. Marshal who told me the Progress County Sheriff was crooked as a dog's hind leg, and that the man's daughter *wasn't* his daughter, even though both the man and the girl *said* she was. Then I'd rode up a dang precipice into an outlaw camp where I had feared for my life and still did. I had pulled my gun on a badman and had said my howdies to a bandit I knew who turned out not to be a bandit but some kind of lawman. It was enough to confuse even a thinking man, and I had never been one of those.

I had seen bedrolls on all the bunks, so figured I'd do my sleepin' outside. I was about to roll out my blankets and turn in for the evening when I first laid eyes on Original George, the bandit chief. He came riding across the meadow on a leggy thoroughbred stud, and the sun's last rays lit him up like an actor in a stage play. He was dressed all in black, and the sunlight flashed bright off the metal of bit, spur, and six-gun as he came. Shanty O'Kane stepped out, dried his hands on his flour sack apron, and said in a soft voice, "Ah, 'tis himself, back from his meditations."

57

Original George drew rein and looked me over like a pawnbroker studies a diamond ring. He was near six feet tall, with strong, white teeth, and his hair and beard were a sort of roan, going to white. He was brown as an old saddle, and there was a long, jagged scar down his left cheek like a lightning bolt. As he raised up in the stirrups with his hands resting on the horn, I could see he wore two ivory-handled pistols and a Bowie knife under his coat. I had seen more tough-looking men in that one day than I'd seen in my whole life previous, but Original George Starkweather looked to be the curly wolf. There was a quality about him that put me in mind of a crouching lion or a coiled rattler, and as I met his gaze it was like lookin' down the barrels of a shotgun.

His voice was deep and raspy. "A new face among the old and familiar," he said, "who the hell are you, young sir?"

"I—I'm Merlin Fanshaw," I said, "from over Dry Creek way. Some call me the Bodacious Kid."

His eyes never left my face as he eased himself slowly down off the thoroughbred. "Merlin," he said, "a good name, Merlin. He was the old-timer who rode herd on young Arthur before the kid got into the king business and set up his own gang."

He took a thick, well-worn book from his saddle bag and said, "Read about them old boys from Camelot in this book. I like to read. Been settin' up on a ridge all day a-readin'."

Kiowa had walked over as George had come up, and

he took the reins of the thoroughbred and led the animal away toward the corral behind the cabin. The bandit chief continued to size me up while the Irish cook brought him out a plate of stew. "Now then, Merlin," he said, "How'd you come to find us and why are you here?"

"Well, sir, I knew about this old line camp from huntin' mustangs with my Pa," I told him, "and I thought it might be a good place to hide out. Seems you thought so, too."

"That's true enough," he said, forking stew into his mouth, "Who would you be hidin' out *from,* son?"

"Sheriff Wilkes, in Shenanigan. He jailed me over a stolen horse, but I broke out and stole me another one."

George chuckled. "I bet old Androcles was not amused by that," he said, "I do hope for your sake that you didn't lead him here."

"No, sir, I never. Anyway, I don't believe he wants me bad enough to get off his fat ass and ride after me himself."

"No," he said, looking thoughtful, "not *you.*" He finished the last of his stew and handed the empty plate back to the cook. "We'll talk more tomorrow, Merlin. For now, I bid you good evenin'."

The way he said it didn't leave much doubt our conversation was over. I bade him good night, scraped out a hip hole under a big tree, and crawled into my blankets. I laid there with my head on my saddle and my pistol close at hand as I watched the stars come out. Looking back toward the cabin, I could see George had lit up a stogie and was talking with Shanty and Kiowa, and I wondered what tomorrow would bring. I didn't wonder long, though; sleep fell on me like a pile of sand, and the next thing I knew it was morning.

When I first woke up, it took me a minute or so to remember where I was. I laid there and shivered in my blankets, wishing I had more of them, until I finally nerved myself up enough to roll out. The air was chilly that high in the mountains, and the grass was drippin' wet with frosty dew as I pulled my britches on and tried—without much luck—to keep my teeth from chattering.

Beyond the peaks to the north the Dipper had swung around and was pritnear level just above the ridge, while to the east the dark had faded and the Morning Star blazed bright. Across the meadow Little Buck grazed happy as a butcher's dog on the tall forage. He raised his head and studied me awhile, then went back to feeding.

My boots were stiff and cold, but I yanked and tugged 'til they slid into place, then made my way through the wet grass to the spring and washed up in the icy water. Through the trees, I could see some of the boys at the cabin starting to stir. The orange glow at the window and the smoke rising from the chimney told me O'Kane had the lantern lit and the stove going. I started back to roll my bed, and was almost to the big tree where I'd slept when I saw someone bending over and peering toward my blankets. My heart commenced pounding, and I altogether forgot how cold I was. Taking hold of my pistol with my thumb on the hammer, I set my feet and spoke up loud, hoping my voice wouldn't break. "Lookin' for something?" I asked, and the figure jerked upright and froze.

"Dammit, Kid, you spooked me!" the man said, and I saw it was Mace Collyer, "I just came out to wake you up for breakfast."

"When you go to wake a man up," I said, "you ought to make a little noise, Mace. Goin' quiet like you do makes it seem like you're tryin' to sneak up on him, and some fellers might take offense at that."

"Is that what you think?" he said, "Hell fire, Kid! A man tries to do you a favor, and . . ."

"I appreciate the thought, Mace, but you needn't trouble in future. I'm an early riser and a light sleeper, and I tend to get kind of *sudden* when I'm surprised."

He looked for all the world like he wanted to draw on me, but he saw I had the drop on him again. He turned and stalked away, back toward the cabin. "Hell," he huffed, "I don't give a damn if you starve, Kid."

Well, I didn't starve, not nearly. O'Kane had cooked up beans, bacon, and cornbread, and I et my fill and then some. After I'd finished I hunkered down outside with a cup of coffee and let the morning sun take the chill off me. I had felt like a bug in a chickenhouse when I'd first rode into camp, but that morning three of the boys said howdy. Even Kiowa gave me a short nod. I didn't see *El Borrachon,* and I figured it must be his time to guard the trail.

Original George came out looking grumpy as a wet eagle and went off by his lonesome with nary a word to anyone. Since none of the boys spoke to him, either, I figured that must be his regular habit.

My Pa had been grouchy in the mornings 'til he got some coffee in him, but then he generally sweetened up and took real delight in the day. I figured George might be like that, though I wasn't sure how much sweeter his disposition *ever* got. As for me, I guess I'd have to say I'm pretty even-tempered, and not like the feller in the joke who said his wife was even-tempered—"mad all the time." I'm just sort of naturally good-natured, at least *most* days.

I drank the last of my coffee, throwed out the dregs, and got to my feet.

I felt better all around after the grub and the night's shut-eye. Knowing I had anyway one feller in camp who'd side me should I come to a tight spot eased my mind considerable. I went on inside the cabin, and, without a word to O'Kane, rolled up my sleeves and commenced washing the dishes.

I'd finished my scullery duties and had just stepped outside to dump the wash water when I heard the commotion back at the corrals. It sounded like most all the outfit was there, and I could hear the boys laughing and ragging one another the way men do when they're stirred up and raising hell.

I reckon I'm as curious as the next feller, so I moseyed on back through the trees and found the boys at a round corral, whoopin' and hollerin' like Saturday night come early. The corral had been built for working broncs. It must have been seven foot high, with a well-worn snubbing post in its center. Mace Collyer was standing inside, his face flushed and his eyes bugged out, as he hung onto a skittish little mouse-colored gelding. The horse kept backing up and tossing its head while Mace hung onto the headstall and whupped on the animal with a rawhide quirt.

Mace was bare-headed and corral dirt was on his clothes and in his hair, so it wasn't hard to see he'd been thrown, probably more than once. It also wasn't hard to see that things weren't likely to improve much for him anytime soon, the way he was treating that horse. The little gelding was scared, mostly, and the lashing it was getting from that quirt was doing precious little to calm it. I purely hate to see a man mistreat a horse, and I wanted to tell Mace to back off and go easy, but I knew he already hated my guts and any word from me was likely to make matters worse instead of better.

The boys kept hoorawing him, laughing and jeering, and I knew that wasn't helping his state of mind, either. Nobody likes to be laughed at, and Mace seemed more thin-skinned than most. I judged him to be a man ruled by his pride and his anger, and I wondered how he'd lived as long as he had.

Shanty O'Kane had come up beside me, his face nearly as dark as Mace's. "Damn your eyes, Mace Collyer, stop abusin' that hawrse!" he bellowed, "If you can't get up on the bloody beast and ride it like a man, turn it out!"

63

Mace flashed a sideways glance at Shanty and struck the little horse again, just for spite. "Shut your mouth, you belly-robbin' mick," he snapped, "this ain't none of your business!"

The gunshot was loud and laid a sudden hush on us all. The boys froze like statues, and some of them grabbed for their irons by instinct. When I turned my head there stood Original George himself, a long-barreled Colt pointed at the sky and smoking. He walked over to the corral gate and stepped inside.

"Well?" he said, "I thought you told me you could ride that horse, Mace."

Mace still held the little gelding by the headstall, but he dropped his eyes and sort of scuffed the dirt with the toe of his boot. "Figured I could, Cap'n," he muttered, "but the sonofabitch is crazy wild. He's throwed me twice this mornin.' I don't reckon the loco bastard can *be* rode."

"You don't, huh? Any of you other boys figure *you* can ride that animal?"

O'Kane frowned, his face still red and his blue eyes flashing fire. "Sure, and I could meself was I but five years younger," he said, "that damn Mace is scared of the bloody animal, that's all."

"Well, you *ain't* five years younger," said George, "so I guess we won't know whether you could or not, will we?"

The bandit chief holstered his Colt and favored us with his mad eagle stare. "I'll ask again. Is there a man here thinks he can ride that horse?"

The boys looked a mite sheepish over all, and most of them didn't meet George's gaze. Kiowa and the yellow-haired hombre stepped down off the corral fence and stood ground-hitched, while the rest of us just sort of kept still and listened to the grass grow.

"What about you, Merlin?" George asked, "The Mex told me you and your old man used to break mustangs and sell 'em to the cow outfits. Can *you* ride that horse?"

Well, Hell. There I stood, meek and mild and trying to mind my own business, not even hoorawing Mace like the others, and then George went and put the question to me face to face. I mean, I had some pride *myself*.

The truth is, I figured I *could.* ride the gelding. Mace had been scared, and the little horse knew it, but the pony didn't look like an outlaw to me.

"Yes, sir," I allowed, "I believe that I can."

George smiled then, like a gambler holding aces full who'd got some fool to call his hand. "I read in the book where young Arthur pulled that big sword out of the rock when them other old boys couldn't," he said, "let's see can you do likewise, Merlin."

I closed my eyes for a second, and of a sudden my Pa's face came to me clear and sharp for the first time since he'd died. He was looking at me the way he used to when I'd done something stupid, like tell an outlaw chief I could ride a horse I knew nothing about. He was shaking his head in wonder, but he was *smiling,* the way he did when he was proud of me. I opened my eyes and felt, rather than saw, the gaze of every man at the corral fixed on me, but I put my mind on the mouse-colored gelding and the job at hand.

"I'll ride my own saddle," says I, "it's back at the cabin."

George smiled. He turned to the yellow-haired ranny and said, "Fetch the kid's rig, Pike. Bring his shaps, too."

I opened the corral gate and stepped inside, surprised at how calm I felt.

I could see the whites of the gelding's eyes as he watched me walk around him. He kept shifting his feet in a jerky quick-step, his nostrils flared and his ears following my every move. I saw the welts from the quirt and the bloody spur tracks and I felt a rage that dang near blinded me. I saw rage in Mace's eyes, too, hot and glowing like embers in a breeze. He gave me a look of pure hate as he handed me the reins and leaned stiffly back against the corral.

The headstall was a hackamore with horsehair reins and *mecate*. I tied the little horse short to the snubbin' post and slipped the saddle off. The gelding quivered as I touched him again, but I just rubbed his neck and shoulders with a gentle, steady stroke and talked to him soft and easy.

"Everything's all right, little horse," I told him, "Easy now, pretty little horse."

Running mustangs and breaking broncs with my Pa had been my whole life since I was just a button. I'd learned young that every horse is different and needs his own special handling. Some bronc fighters never seem to savvy that truth. They work every animal the same, which not only don't get the job done, it makes for spoiled horses besides. The little gelding had been mistreated and abused, and while I didn't believe he was ruined, I expected he'd give me quite a ride.

The yellow-haired hombre George had called Pike came bow-legging back with my saddle and shaps. I nodded my thanks and slipped into my leggings. I thought about rigging myself a bucking roll for the saddle's fork, but decided to ride slick—more of that damn pride, I suppose.

I'd learned from experience that the last thing a bronc stomper needs is three pounds of iron a-hammering his hip and caressing his kidneys, so I took off my Dragoon Colt and gave it to George to hold for me.

The mouse-colored gelding had calmed somewhat, but he still rolled his eyes and quivered as I eased the rig up onto his back. I took my time, doing everything slow and easy, cinching up with a steady pull.

"You want somebody to ear him down for you?" George asked.

"No thanks," I said, "if we're a-going to dance, I need to romance him by myself."

I untied the gelding, stepped up close to his shoulder, and caught a handful of mane together with the reins atop his neck. Then, with my right hand gripping the horn, I set foot in the stirrup and swung into the saddle just as the little horse broke in two and went to chinning the moon.

FIVE
Broncs, Bullets, and Buccaneers

The little horse blew up like a black-powder bomb, jumping high, hard, and crooked, then coming down stiff-legged with a jolt that rattled my teeth and troubled my mind. The gelding was quick and strong, and at first I had some doubt about my ability to remain a-horseback.

For the first few jumps he mostly bucked on a dime, going straight up like a trout after a skeeter and coming down like a boulder off a cliff. The dirt clods flew and the little horse squealed his fear and fury, but I was still on him and getting the feel of his rhythm. He'd get his legs all bunched under him and leap for the treetops, and I'd set forward and spur back toward the cantle while I fanned him with my hat. Then he'd bog his head and poke his front feet in the ground while I'd lean back and hook him in the shoulders, which made him even madder.

About then is when he changed his tactics and swapped ends, spinning and throwing himself to the right, but I was ready for him. I leaned into the spin with my weight hard on the off stirrup. Then he reversed himself, going left, and I switched right along with him as we went on a-dancing our fandango.

I knew the boys were watching, and I thought I even heard somebody holler "Ride him, Kid" but I can't swear to that. All I could see was a tip-tilted blur of sky, trees, and dirt, with a mouse-colored horse between my legs and his mane a-whipping like a flag in a gale. Of a sudden he took to sunfishing, throwing his belly at the sky with his shoulder pritnear on the ground while I hung, rattled, and stuck to him like a bug to flypaper. He commenced to run and buck then, and we circled that pole corral about three times before he made a blind charge straight at the thick snubbing post in the center and hit it head on.

Down we went all in a tangle, and I stepped free while he rolled over and found his feet again. By the time he was up and running I was back in the saddle and sticking as close to him as his hide. I whopped him on his off side with my hat, spurring him every jump he made. Directly his bucking grew less and finally stopped altogether.

His breath came in deep, racking gasps and the sweat rolled down his sides like snowmelt in a chinook, but I never let him rest. I reined him about, kicked him into a loose trot around the corral, then rode him back the other way. The boys were grinning as we circled, and Shanty O'Kane was yelling, "Good on you, boy-O— *that's* the way to ride a hawrse!"

Original George leaned against the corral gate, a faint smile on his face as he watched me draw rein and step down. Mace Collyer glared at me, his eyes hot and his jaw a-quiver. I remember thinking at the time that I'd never seen a man so close to losing control. I know now that I should have kept an eye on him, but at the time I was too swole up with myself and too busy grand-standing to have any sense.

I heard Shanty holler, "Watch out, Kid" and I spun around to see what he was yelling about, which I guess is what saved my life. Mace had pulled his pistol and fired point-blank at my head from no more than five feet away! I heard the shot, loud and ringing, and felt burnt powder hit my face as I made a grab for my Dragoon and then remembered I didn't have it.

"Damn you!" Mace screamed, his voice shrill as a woman's, "I've had a bellyful of you showin' me up! You're cold meat, you wet-eared pup!" He thumbed the hammer back to fire again.

That's when Original George knocked him down. He clubbed him hard back of his neck, and kicked him in the belly. Mace dropped the gun and grabbed his middle, stunned and fighting for breath, but still crazy, wild-eyed mad. George picked up the pistol and jerked the man to his feet and held him at arm's length against the corral.

"You always was a yellow bastard," George said in a matter-of-fact tone, "but you tore it this time. I won't have a damn back-shooter in the outfit."

His hand darted down, lifted Mace's second gun from its holster, and held it out to me. "This gutless bastard tried to dry-gulch you, Merlin. Shoot the som'bitch."

Well, I laughed, short and nervous, but I laughed. Of course, I figured George was joking. Then I looked closer at those hard, mad eagle eyes and at the serious faces of the other boys and I knew he wasn't. I felt a

70

chill run through me like I'd been dropped through the ice of a high mountain lake. My belly turned a somersault.

"L-Lordy, George," I said, "I couldn't do that . . . he ain't even armed!"

"Neither was you, kid," he said, "but that didn't stop *him*."

"Lordy! N-No, sir, I just can't . . ."

George shrugged, roll-cocked the Colt, and pushed Mace out away from him. He said, "That's all right, son, I *can*," and shot him between the eyes.

I'll never forget that moment, no matter how long I live. Every detail is burned on my memory like a brand. I remember to this day the smells and the sights—the air fresh, cool, and piney, the earth rich and yeasty from the sun, the pungent, sulphur smell of gunsmoke. I recall how sharp and clear everything appeared—the texture of the tree bark, the dappled light and shadow on the silver-gray corral poles, and the dull green of tree branches. Most of all, I remember the way Original George stood, with his legs wide apart and the smoking pistol dull metal in his hand.

Mace sort of rocked back on his heels when the bullet hit him, and a pink mist blossomed out behind his head in the morning sunlight. The roar of the shot racketed off the trees, and white smoke drifted loose and lacy on the morning air. Then Mace slumped forward and fell like a sack of rocks, face-down into the loose, black dirt of the horse corral.

I remember the silence afterward. My knees felt

weak. I wanted to puke. Everything had happened so fast. One minute Mace was standing there staring at me with hate in his eyes, and the next he was dead on his face in the dirt.

Somehow it all put me in mind of Pa and the morning he'd died. He had grinned that old grin of his as he swung up on the crazy black stud, and the next thing I knew the horse had carried him off the rimrock and they were both dead at the bottom.

Some folks seem to think dying comes slow and stately to people in their beds. They talk of the Death Angel and of people "passing away" and "giving up the ghost," but that's not the way I've seen it. Except for my mother, the dying I've seen has been sudden and hard, and the dearly departed didn't give *up* the ghost so much as they had it jerked *from* them.

Original George handed my belt and pistol back and opened the corral gate. He put his hand on Pike's shoulder and said, "You and Clete bury the som'bitch, or leastways drag him off downwind somewheres. You can have his guns and his boots."

He turned to me and smiled like nothing had happened. "That was a fine ride, Merlin," he said, "walk on up to the cabin with me."

I shouldered my saddle and walked alongside him through the pines and toward the sunlit meadow beyond. As we drew near the cabin, George stopped and lit up a stogie. I could feel him watching me from the corner of his eye. I tried my best to look hard and cold the way he did, but I reckon he saw through me.

"You ain't ever seen a man shot before, have you, Merlin?" he asked.

"No, sir," I replied, "not like *that*. I seen a cowhand kill a gambler over a faro game once, but that was a fight, not a . . ."

"Not an *execution*," George said calmly, "Yes, I reckon there *is* a difference. But don't you go to grievin' old Mace. Damfool just had too much mustard; he brought it on himself. This here's a tough outfit, kid, and I'm top dog. Sometimes that means I've got to take measures.

"We're sort of like them old-time pirates I read about who sailed the high seas, except we travel the high *country* and go horseback instead of on one o' them there galleons. Men like Blackbeard, Kidd, and Morgan led some real hardcases in their day, and they had to be even harder to do it. That's the same way it is here.

"I like you, Merlin, but I ain't quite sure why you want to join this bold band o' buccaneers.

"I told you. I broke out of the Progress County Jail and stole a horse. Sheriff Wilkes is on my back-trail."

"He's on mine, too, son. Androcles Wilkes and me have what you might call a *history*. Point is, you ain't near as *depraved* as the rest of us, but you sure as hell will be if you stay on.

"Now you can saddle up your buckskin and head out right now, with no questions asked and no hard feelin's. Or you can stay. But if you stay, I'll expect you to make a hand and do what I tell you, *when* I tell you. Savvy?"

Most of the time the choices we make don't seem to

73

change things much. I mean, if I go into a hash house and have sourdough cakes and bacon instead of biscuits and red-eye gravy I'm pretty much the same feller when I come out, either way. But there are times when the trail forks and a man makes a decision, and everything changes forever. I knew this was one of those times.

On the one hand, two different lawmen had put pressure on me to help them locate Original George and his boys, and neither one had just *asked* me.

Wilkes had threatened me with prison and had lied to me about Mary Alice being his daughter—according to Ridgeway, anyway. Ridgeway had follered me, cornered me, and told me Wilkes was crooked. He'd had his Indian deputy knock me down, and he had, like Wilkes, used the power of his office to threaten me and force me to do his will.

George, on the other hand, had took me in without threat or promise, and had even killed one of his own men for trying to ambush me.

My Pa had taught me to be honest in all my dealings and had cautioned me not to ride the owlhoot trail, but I could recall some times selling and trading horses when Pa hadn't altogether been on the level himself. In fact, there had been one or two occasions when Pa's honesty level was a few bubbles off the plumb, to put it mild. Well, the old man wasn't around no more, and I had to make my own decisions now. One thing I *did* know was that I'd had a bellyful of being pushed and threatened.

"I reckon I'll throw in with you and the boys," I said, "if you'll have me."

George smiled, his teeth white and even as piano keys. He stuck out his hand and I shook it. "Consider yourself *had,*" he said.

He squinted one-eyed at the sun as if he was checking it for accuracy. "Time to relieve the Mex from guard duty," he said, "take your rifle and go on down there, Merlin."

I saddled Little Buck and headed on out across the meadow. Even in late August the wildflowers up there were plentiful, tiny blooms of purple, white, and blue, and they seemed to be everywhere in the tall grass, but I couldn't really appreciate them. I kept seeing Mace Collyer laying dead in the round corral and remembering the way George looked when he shot him, like he was swatting a fly. In my mind I heard the shot again and saw Mace fall, and as I did so a great cloud blocked the sun and a fast-moving shadow swept over the grass like the Death Angel going home.

El Borrachon had been sitting on a boulder overlooking the trail, but he got to his feet as I rode up. *"Hola, chico,"* he said, "are you alone?"

I stepped down and loosened Buck's cinch. "Far as I know," I told him, "George sent me down to relieve you."

"I'd be *more* relieved if you weren't here at all," he said, looking nervously back toward the meadow, "what were those shots I heard awhile back?"

"Mace Collyer tried to backshoot me, and George

killed him. That's the bobtail version of the story, anyway."

"So *El Jefe* finally snuffed old Mace's candle. He's been hunting an excuse for quite a spell—looks like you gave him one."

He tipped his big *sombrero* back and studied me. "Well, I'm glad it was you he sent," he said, "there's a lot you need to know."

He pulled out a pint bottle of tequila and offered it to me. "Have a drink, *compadre*," he said, "if anyone's watching we're just passing the time of day."

He sure didn't have to ask me twice. I took the bottle and choked down nearly half the contents before I came gasping up for air. "Didn't mean to hog your *mezcal*," I told him when I could finally speak again, "but this mornin's festivities have left me just a tad shaky."

"That's a good sign," he said, "at least you've got enough sense to be spooked."

He sat back down on his boulder with his rifle across his knees and took a healthy swig from the bottle himself.

"All right," he said, "like I told you, I'm Marshal Chance Ridgeway's inside man with the gang. Now I need you to lay all your cards on the table, *chico*. I need to know how you met the marshal and what you're doin' up here in this rattler's den."

"Well," I said, "it all started with that roan horse you sold me. I rode it over to Shenanigan, and Sheriff Wilkes said it was stolen and throwed me in the pokey.

"Later on, he turned me loose and sent me back to

76

Dry Creek in the hope I'd see you again and find out where the gang was holed up. If I did, I was supposed to let him know, and he'd move in with a posse and round up the gang.

"I hung around Dry Creek for a time but you never showed, so I set out looking for the hideout on my own. Marshal Ridgeway got wind of my efforts through a telegram I sent Wilkes, and he jumped me on my way here with that cheerful Indian deputy of his.

"Ridgeway told me about the payroll robbery and said that Wilkes was in on it. Said he wanted to find Original George and the boys, as well as the stolen money, and sent me on my way. If I learned anything I was to let him know before I told Wilkes by way of the telegraph office at Dry Creek."

I went on to tell him about my riding the bronc and about George killing Mace, and I pretty well done what he'd asked me to—laid all my cards on the table, even if one or two of them was face-down.

I hadn't said anything to Ridgeway about Mary Alice, and I didn't bring her up this time, either. I still hadn't worked out how I felt about her, and I didn't know who she really was, anyway. I knew she had big brown eyes and honey-colored hair, and that she smelled of lilac, but that's about all I did know for sure. Ridgeway had told me who she *wasn't*, but I had no idea who she *was*.

All that palaver had made my throat dry, so I asked him if I could have another pull at his tequila bottle, and he handed it over.

"All right," he said, "now listen close and I'll fill you

in on the rest of it. Wilkes is one of those lawmen who has always spent more time in the shade than in the sunlight, which is to say that he's crooked as a snake track. He gets himself re-elected sheriff because he knows where the bodies are buried and whose closets have skeletons in Progress County. Also, he generally runs unopposed in the local elections because those who would run against him get bought off, run off, or just disappear.

"I was his deputy for awhile, before I took up with George and the boys, and I bought that horse I sold you from him. That's how he spotted you, and figured you knew me. But I'm getting ahead of myself.

"Just over a month ago, Wilkes learned that $40,000 in gold—a double payroll for the soldiers at Fort Savage—was coming to Shenanigan by train, and that it would be held at the local bank until troops from the fort showed up to escort the paymaster and the money.

"Two days later, an army ambulance from the fort and two outriders hit town and the paymaster loaded up the *dinero* and headed out. They were six miles from town when George and the gang hit 'em and took the payroll. The paymaster, driver, and one of the troopers were killed outright. The other soldier was pretty well shot up, but lived to tell about the robbery. He described Original George and some of the boys well enough for Ridgeway to know who'd done the deed.

"When the paymaster and escort didn't show up at the fort, the commander sent a detail out and they found the bodies and the wounded out-rider. They also tried to run

George and the boys to ground, but the gang split up and the troops lost 'em.

"I'd gone on a drunk over in Silver City and had been jailed for robbing a jewelry store. Ridgeway learned I was there and came to see me. He knew I used to run with George, so he offered me a deal. I could go to State Pen for ten years, or become his inside man with the Starkweather gang. Didn't take me long to decide. Ridgeway spread the story that I'd killed a bartender at Silver City, and had gone on the dodge. Truth was, the barkeep had died from drinkin' his own merchandise but he *was* dead, he *was* buried, and he sure as hell wasn't tending bar no more.

"I ran into Kiowa at the saloon in Dry Creek about a week later, and he brought me back here to the hideout. Turned out old George was glad to see me. He'd lost a man when they stole the payroll, so he was short-handed. Anyway, he took me on."

"How does Wilkes tie in to all this?" I asked.

"I'm gettin' to that, *chico*. Ridgeway believes Wilkes told George about the payroll, and that they were in on the robbery together. He thinks George double-crossed the good sheriff, and that Wilkes wants to find him now, not for the reward, like he told you, or even for the glory, but to get his share of that Army money.

"Well, that's the long and the short of it, *compadre*. I just wanted you to know what you're dealin' with."

"How do I know you won't quit Ridgeway and sell me out to George?" I asked.

He smiled, and that gold tooth caught sunlight.

"Caray, chico," he said, "how do I know you won't sell *me* out? I guess the answer is I'm more scared of Ridgeway than I am of *El Jefe.* George can kill me, but he's not likely to lock me up in a little room and throw away the key, like Ridgeway is. There ain't a helluva lot of tequila in the Territorial Pen."

He got to his feet and handed me what was left of the cactus squeezin's. "I better get back to camp before the boys start thinkin' you and me are *novios*—you know, sweethearts," he said, *"Cuidado, chico. Vaya con Dios."*

"You, too," I told him, and I meant it. We were both walking a slippery log, and whoever it was who first said "between a rock and a hard place" must have had us in mind. The big Mex bent low and took the hobbles off his Spanish Barb and slid his rifle into the saddle scabbard.

"By the by," said I, "I can't keep on addressin' you as *El Borrachon,* and even 'Emiliano' is quite a mouthful. What should I call you?"

He swung into the saddle and grinned as he turned to take the trail back to the cabin. *"Amigo* will do nicely," he said.

SIX

Life among the Merry Men

I hobbled Little Buck in good grass, slipped his bridle off, and looped the headstall and reins over the saddlehorn. I knew the sun would be scorching the plains and valley down below, but up the mountain where I was it felt mighty good. I perched there on my boulder and soaked the heat deep into my bones.

After the events of the morning I was glad just to be alone for a spell, and I sat there with my old Henry rifle in my lap and tried to corral my scattered thoughts. I'd get them rounded up, bunched, and headed for the gate and they'd break back on me at the last minute and scatter. Nothing was as clear-cut and simple as I'd thought, or wanted it to be, and the waters of my ponderings had turned muddy to where I couldn't see bottom at all.

The more I studied on things, the more I felt like a pup who'd taken to chasing its tail. I was going around in circles, without result and to no avail, and after awhile I wasn't even sure of the things I was *sure* of.

I'd always figured to be upright in my dealings, and so far I mostly had been, but when Original George had offered me the chance to join his outfit I was surprised to find I actually *wanted* to. Oh, I knew the old wolf was a murderer and a thieving outlaw who no doubt deserved prison or death, and yet I found myself liking him and even hankering after his good opinion.

And what about Wilkes and Ridgeway, who were lawmen, sworn to be watchdogs of decency? They had threatened me and used me with scant regard for my feelings or rights, and at least one of them had lied to me besides. Now I was no greenhorn; even at eighteen I knew the difference betwixt a badge and a halo. But right then it seemed to me the line between upright and evil was as fine as frog hair. I wished I had paid more mind to the preacher during my sometime visits to church.

The sun was still a hand's breadth above the west ridge when a gun-hand name of Jigger St. Clare came over to relieve me from guard duty, but my belly had long since informed me it was suppertime. Seeing Mace killed that morning had took away my appetite—forever, I believed at the time—but here it was only late afternoon of the same day and already I was hungry again. I told myself, "Merlin, it sure didn't take you long to become a hardened desperado."

Jigger had sandy hair and freckles, and his big ears stood out like the handles on a sugar bowl. He had buck teeth and a foolish grin, and when I'd first seen him he'd struck me as being about half simple. Nothing I'd observed since then had caused me to change my mind, but he did have a sort of secret, sly look about his eyes that made me think he was smarter than he looked. He would have had to be.

He drawed rein and sat his horse all elbows and knees like the big old farm boy he probably had been. Squinting against the late afternoon sun, he studied me with that slack-jawed smirk of his.

"Clete Potter shot a deer 's'afternoon, Kid," he said slowly, "we-uns got venison for vittles 's'evenin'."

"Glad to hear it, Jigger," I told him, "I'm so hungry I could eat the gut-pile."

Jigger stepped down and stood there looking puzzled—but grinning, if you can picture that. "Aw, Kid," he said, "you wouldn't want to eat no gut-pile. Could make you sick."

It was all I could do to keep from laughing as I put the bridle back on Little Buck and took his hobbles off. "Why, thanks, Jigger," I told him, "I never would've thought of that," and then I swung up and rode off a-chuckling across the meadow on the trail that led to the venison vittles.

Just like Jigger had said, O'Kane had cooked up a mess of mule deer steaks, along with onions, biscuits and gravy, and the smell of that grub led me into camp by the nose. When I finally quit forking it in that evening I had come near foundering myself. I sat there at the plank table drinking coffee and feeling grateful, with a full belly and an easy mind.

By the time the week had passed I finally knew all the boys by name, and I'd begun to feel they were more at ease around me than when I'd first rode in. There was Original George, of course, *El Borrachon,* and the cook, Shanty O'Kane. Then there was Pike Fletcher, the yellow-haired ranny who'd fetched my saddle that morning; Kiowa, with his barrel chest and black beard; Clete Potter, who was somewhere in his fifties and the old man of the outfit; Jigger St. Clare, who was down guarding the trail; Poddy Medford, who was watching the other trail, and last but not least, myself, the famous Bodacious Kid, who had within a few short days become cook's helper, well-known glutton, and the gang's top man with a knife and fork.

I was helping O'Kane with the dishes when Original George pulled a dog-eared deck of cards from the cupboard and tried to shuffle them. I say "tried" because it was plain those pasteboards had seen plenty of use, and, like the boys, had lost considerable of their stiffness.

"How about a few hands of poker, fellers?" George asked, "I feel lucky tonight."

Clete muttered, "You feel lucky *every* night, Chief," and except for Shanty and me the boys all set down around the table, only I noticed they looked more like they was going to a funeral than a card game. I was about to set down myself, when Shanty took me by the arm and led me outside.

"Take my advice, Boy-O, and steer clear of that so-called game o' chance," he whispered, "for there's divil a chance you'll win.

"Our fine captain cheats, you see, and the men all know it, but he insists they play, so what are the poor lads to do?"

"You mean they know he cheats but they play anyway?" I said, louder than I meant to, "Why, that don't make any sense."

"Whisht, lad, are you daft?" Shanty said, "Keep your voice down." He filled his clay pipe with tobacco from a leather pouch and tamped it thoughtfully. "Well, now," he said, "it just *might* make sense if a man cared to remain *alive*. The captain likes poker, you see, but he doesn't like to lose. So he wins, and he takes offense if the lads refuse to play."

"Damn," I said, "How do *you* get out of playing?"

He struck a match with his thumbnail and lit his pipe. "I plead total ignorance of the game in all its aspects," he said, "and the captain has long since grown tired of explainin' its rules to me."

From inside the cabin came the raspy voice of our leader. "Another full house, boys," he bellered, "Did you ever see such a lucky streak?"

I looked at Shanty, and he looked back at me like an owl on a branch. "I believe I'll just go see to my horse and turn in early," I told him.

"May your dreams be pleasant, and may you find sweet rest underneath your lucky star," he said. I wished I could speak Irish.

Pa and me were riding flat-out in the pink light of morning, pushing a dozen mustangs down a long ridge toward our trap in the box canyon beyond. A savvy old broomtail mare led the bunch, and she swept on through the cedars and greasewood with her head held high as she ran. The wind of our passage made my eyes water and pulled at my hat 'til the bonnet strings dug deep into my jaw, and the big bay rimrocker I rode gave me his all, loving the chase as much as I did.

Pa thundered up alongside me with dirt clods a-flying and smiled his big smile, but then I seen it wasn't Pa at all, but Original George. I looked ahead again and all the running horses were gone except for the lead mare, which now left the ground like an eagle and ran smoothly through the air and up into the sky. My horse and George's did the same, still following, and then I saw that Mary Alice sat sidesaddle on the flying mare with her hair a-blowing free as she smiled back over her shoulder at me.

She was wearing her white cotton dress and she rode the mare in an easy rocking motion, beckoning like she wanted me to come to her. Then somehow I had pulled ahead; I could almost reach out and touch her when I glanced across at George. He had his pistol out and pointed at Mary Alice, but she just smiled and held her hands out at her sides. Then George fired the gun like a man swatting a fly, a pink mist bloomed out behind her head, and I woke up hollering, "No!"

I was setting straight up in my blankets, out under the stars, and I was soaked in sweat and a-quivering. The echo of my voice was still in my ears and I feared I had woke up the whole outfit. For a moment I held my breath, listening for I don't know what, and tried to sort out fact from fancy. But nobody came out of the cabin or spoke, so I finally figured I hadn't been heard and took to breathing again.

I don't generally have dreams, or if I do, I don't usually recall them come morning, but this one had been clear as glass and it had spooked me to a fare-thee-well. My hands were still shaking as I dressed and pulled my boots on, but by the time I'd walked through the wet grass to the spring to drink I was back to myself again. The stars were a bright scatter across the sky. From the way the Dipper and Orion set I judged the time to be about four.

Little Buck was awake and grazing, and he nickered

a soft greeting when he saw me walk up to him. I threw my arm across his withers and buried my face in his neck while I stroked him and talked low and easy to him, the way horses like. After awhile I saw lantern glow in the cabin window, and I knowed that Shanty was building the morning meal while the boys were getting up. I could hardly wait for sunup.

The day dawned clear and bright, with nary a cloud in the sky, and the sunlight and morning chuck took away the last cobwebs of my dream. Some of the boys had gone back to the corrals and some were tending their horses out in the meadow, moving their picket-pins and such, while I put an edge on the axe and split some kindling for the cookstove.

George sat just outside the cabin door with his first stogie of the day, reading a book, and Shanty came out, lit up his pipe, and sat down beside him. "We're runnin' low on supplies, captain," he said, "we'll need to be sendin' someone down to the valley soon."

George closed his book and studied the Irishman's face.

"We've rode together quite a spell now, Shanty," he said, "and I know when there's somethin' on your mind. Spill it."

"Well, now, captain," Shanty said, "I was just thinkin' that the boys may be gettin' a bit restless, what with there bein' nothin' much to do here save hole up and lay low. You may wish to put 'em to work before they get into mischief."

"Do you *know* something, or are you just supposin'?"

"Why, *supposin'*, I suppose," Shanty said with a quick smile, "Mace was the first to lose it, but he'll not be the last. There's already been a bit of grumblin' about you not dividin' that payroll money. I think we need to pull another job, George, and let the lads kick up their heels a bit."

"You think so, do you?"

"That I do."

"So do I. That's why I've decided to move on down to Rampage. We've been here too long."

He turned to me. "Round the boys up for me, Merlin," he said, "All of 'em. Tell 'em I want to see 'em here pronto."

I bridled Little Buck and swung up on him bareback, more to see how he'd take to it than anything. He threw his head up, rolled his eyes, and kept his ears busy for awhile, but as time passed and nothing bad happened, he settled down. I reckon he figured being rode without a saddle was just one more of my strange notions, and that he could live with it. Or maybe he figured I'd *forgot* the saddle, I don't know.

Anyway, I rode by the corrals and spoke to the fellers there first, so by the time I'd gone out and fetched back the guards, most of the boys had gathered in a semicircle around Original George.

"Boys," he said, "I believe it's time we kicked over the traces and had ourselves a little fun. Since that payroll job we've been holed up here, waitin' for the dust to settle, but I don't like to stay any one place too long. I believe we need to saddle up and move on."

Kiowa looked thoughtful, or maybe he just had a belly ache. He sort of squinched up his eyes, frowned, and scratched his scraggly beard. "Does that mean we're gonna dig up the money and make the split now, Cap'n?" he asked.

"Not yet. There's too many lawmen waitin' for us to do just that," George said, "No, we'll leave that Army cash set awhile longer.

"But we are holdin' close to a hundred head of M-Cross steers down in the lower pasture, and I believe it's time we moved 'em out and cashed 'em in."

He pointed at Kiowa with the stogie in his right hand. "I want you, Clete, Pike, and the Mex to drive 'em down the east trail and deliver 'em to Slippery Mayfair at Rampage. Tell the old skinflint I expect top dollar, and that I'll be along directly. Shanty and Poddy will follow behind you boys with the packhorses and the kitchen mule.

"I've got me some business to tend to in Dry Creek, so I'll be goin' down the canyon trail. Merlin and Jigger will ride with me. We should meet you boys over in Rampage in a day or two."

By noon the Fairweather gang had pretty well cleared out of their old hideout, except of course for the late Mace, who had as I told you become a dearly departed. I can't swear to it, but just as we were leaving camp I think I caught the sick, sweet stench of his mortal remains a-wafting on the breeze, and I suspicioned he'd been buried in haste, or not at all.

When we came to the narrow ledge that spanned the canyon wall Original George, Jigger, and me got down and led our horses across, just as I'd done when I came up. The trail hadn't improved any with the passage of time, and leading the ponies seemed a good precaution. Horses are big, strong, hard-working animals, but they have little teeny brains and you never know when one of them might take the notion that maybe he can fly.

Jigger led a sorry-looking pinto that appeared to be made out of spare parts from different horses. He kind of hummed to himself as he walked along, picking his nose and grinning like he was five cards short of a deck. I couldn't figure out for the life of me how he'd become part of George's gang and came to the conclusion he must have some kind of hidden talents—well hidden.

George himself walked ahead of me, leading his thoroughbred, and I inched my way along behind him, sweating like a field hand and trying not to look down at the silver thread of Brimstone Creek some two hundred feet below. I was dead certain that *I* couldn't fly.

Finally, we came to the last of the rocky shelf and led our horses off onto the grassy slopes and timber beyond. I wiped my hands on my pants and commenced to breathe again, trying to hide my quivering legs by standing close to Little Buck and pretending to check the cinch on my saddle. George leaned against his hot-blood stud and lit up a stogie, and jigger stood spraddle-legged and grinning while he took a leak and his patchwork pony did likewise.

"Glad that part of the trail's over, Merlin?" George asked.

"Aw, hell, no," said I, "I could've gone prob'ly ten feet further before I died of fright altogether."

"A little fear's good for a man," he said, letting cigar smoke drift out through his nose, "gives tone to the blood."

I mounted Buck, set myself in the saddle, and looked at him. "If that's so, I reckon my blood's got more tone right now than a cathouse piano."

His laugh was short and raspy, like a file on metal. "That's a good one, Merlin," he said, "You do have a way with words, son."

Jigger buttoned his pants and sniggered just as if he savvied the joke. "Uh . . . yeah, Kid," he snorted, "that was a good one. Haw, haw."

When the trail broke out onto Brimstone Creek we watered the horses and drank some ourselves, then mounted up again and rode on down through the dappled sun and shadow toward the sagebrush flats. George had dropped back and now rode alongside me while Jigger led the way with his hat throwed back and singing what sure sounded like "Mary Had A Little Lamb."

George flicked the ash off his stogie and studied me with his crazy eagle eyes. "You ever hear tell of Robin Hood and his Merry Men, Merlin?" he asked.

"That old-time English desperado? The feller who was top gun with a bow and arrow? Yeah, some. Schoolteacher told me about him when I was just a button."

"Well, sir," he said, "old Robin and his gang was a lot like us. They was outlaws, too, and they stole off'n bankers, cattle barons, railroad men, and such same as we do. Like us, they kept one jump ahead of the law, which in their day was Prince John and the Sheriff of Nottingham instead of the U.S. Marshal and the Sheriff of Progress County.

"Only mistake I can see that old Rob made was that damn fool business of givin' the money he stole to the poor, but I don't believe he really done that. I figure some book writer made that part up, like they done with Jesse and Frank James.

"Anyway, one reason I like readin' books, even *with* all the lies, is that it seems like Robin and King Arthur and Blackbeard and them Viking hardcases all had a lot in common with us. Way I see it, we're in the same business whether we wear iron pants and pack a sword or shaps and a Colt's six-shooter. When I read their stories and see how they done things I sometimes learn somethin' that helps me run my own outfit."

George drew deep on his cigar, and the tip went cherry red. The thin smoke drifted back past his ears as he leaned on his saddle horn and studied the ash.

"Now you take loyalty, for instance," he went on, "an outlaw has to be loyal to the gang he rides with. If he ain't, he's a threat to every man in the outfit. So when a feller turns out to be disloyal, or a spy, or a sneakin' yeller-bellied, gut-eatin' traitor, a leader has to take *measures*. You can see that, can't you, Merlin?"

George fixed them cold yellow eyes on me and waited. I recalled the way he'd gunned Mace, and I felt a chill run up my back even though the weather was passing hot. Did George know about Wilkes sending me, or about my meeting with Ridgeway? Had someone overheard me talking to *El Borrachon?* Was George warning me, or just talking to pass the time? I wasn't sure, and I wasn't even sure myself where I stood on the subject of loyalty right then.

"Hell, yes, George," I said, "I can sure see that. Goes without sayin', don't it?" I reckon I sounded casual enough, but my mouth was dry as dust, and right then I couldn't have spit for a hundred-dollar bill.

SEVEN
Shoot-out at Dry Creek and Other Delights

The town of Dry Creek slept in the sun like a cat on a carpet as George, Jigger, and me rode in. The day was another scorcher, and heat waves rippled and shimmered on the sun-baked street as we passed the dark storefronts. A sleepy-eyed hound crossed our path at a slow trot, tongue lolling, and collapsed loosely in the scant shade on the other side. Only dogs look happy in the heat, I thought, they always look like they're laughing.

I had caught the spicy smell of chili cooking the minute we turned our horses onto Dry Creek's main, and only, street. The aroma came a-drifting out of the south on some vagrant breeze, and it drawed me to its source like a stray cat to a fish fry.

I already knew that source to be the Oasis Saloon, where Elmo the barkeep was letting a part-time sheepherder and full-time drunk named Ignacio work off his debt by cooking. I have no idea whether Ignacio was a good mutton puncher or not, but I'd et his chili the first day he worked for Elmo, and I knew for a fact he could cook. I was downright tickled when Original George said he believed we'd just stop for a spell at the Oasis.

There didn't seem to be hardly anyone out and about. I could hear the blacksmith working a shoe on his anvil down by Walt's Livery, and over on the shady side of the street a blanket Indian dozed on the bench outside Bender's Store. Other than that Dry Creek looked like a ghost town during the off season.

Four saddlehorses were asleep on their feet at the hitchrack in front of the Oasis, and George gave them a thoughtful look as we rode past. "No point in callin' attention to ourselves," he said, "we'll just slip in the back way."

We left our horses in the alley behind the saloon and went in through the kitchen. Ignacio sat on a high stool by the open door in a dirty apron and watched us pass by, his eyes like two burned holes in a blanket and his nose the color of raw liver.

The saloon was dark and mostly empty, except for four hard-eyed drifters at a table near the front window who stopped their drinking long enough to give us the once-over as we came in.

Elmo, the barkeep, grinned when he seen us and was about to offer a greeting, but caught himself when Original George shook his head and put a finger to his lips. We set our elbows on the bar and George shook hands with Elmo.

"Good to see you again," George said in his raspy whisper, "any law dogs been sniffin' round here lately?"

"No, sir," said Elmo, whispering in reply, "not even Filmore, the Town Clown. He's gone fishin'. It's good to see you again, too, George."

"I believe we'll each have us a bowl of your chili and a cold beer," George said, "we'll just set ourselves at that table by the kitchen."

"You bet," says Elmo. "Comin' right up."

The four hardcases kept a-staring at us, and George nodded to them as we carried our beers past their table. Of course, Jigger had to go and play the fool, as usual. He stuck his thumbs in his armpits and strutted by with his rear end stuck out and his head bobbing like a barn-yard rooster. "Cock-a-doodle-doo!" he says, "Howdy-do to you!" and giggled like a damned idiot. I was so embarrassed I could've slid through a crack in the floor, but the biggest of the four drifters just sort of curled his lip in a sneer and turned back to his pardners. We moved on over to our table and set down.

Jigger sat there looking pleased with himself and nudged my arm. "Good joke, huh, Kid?" he grinned, "Cock-a-doodle-doo! Howdy-do to you!"

"Yeah, Jigger," I said, "that's about as funny as smallpox. Now shut up and drink your beer."

About that time Elmo brought us our chili, and I forgot all about Jigger's foolishness as I commenced to consume that steamin' grub.

Ignacio knowed his chili, all right. It was a larrupin' blend of red chiles and beef, with nary a bean nor tomater in sight, and hotter than the Devil's dishwater. I was so busy chuckin' it in and washin' it down with that cold beer that I never seen them four fellers get up and leave, but all of a sudden I looked up and noticed they was gone. Both George and Jigger had stopped eating and were sitting quiet, their eyes on the swing doors that faced out onto the street,

"Freeze, boys, or be blowed plum' to hell!" The voice from behind us was low, almost a growl, but it fell on my ears like a thunderclap. I realized them drifters had circled around outside and come in cat-footed and quiet through the kitchen. I had a mouthful of chili, but I never thought to chew nor swaller; I just froze, not so much because the man told me to but because it seemed like the thing to do.

"All right," the voice said, "now stand an' face me, with your hands high and well away from your irons."

I slid my chair back and stood up, and saw George do the same. He kind of uncoiled, turning slow as he come to his feet, and there they were, all four of them fellers, with their pistols drawed and pointed towards the general vicinity of our bellies. It was the big man who'd done the talking. His eyes sort of widened as he studied George's face, and then he grinned that twisted sneer he'd showed us before. "By thunder," he crowed, "it is you—Original George Starkweather! Why, they's a thousand dollar bounty on you, dead or alive. This here is our lucky day, boys!"

George grinned, and his crazy eyes glowed. "Could be," he said, "but then there's all kinds of luck, ain't there?"

The big feller went tense and brought his pistol to full cock. "Hey, dummy," he said, looking past me, "Stand up!"

Out of the corner of my eye I could see Jigger still setting at the table with his back to the drifters. He put his hands on the table top and got to his feet, kicking his chair back as he did so. "Cock-a-doodle-do!" he says, "the hell with *you!*" and right then I learned what Jigger's hidden talent was. He made a quick bow to the right, then jerked back left and spun, his guns belching fire, smoke, and lead. The sound of the shots ran together in an awful roar, and I saw the big man smashed back against the wall like a rag doll, then fall to the floor with a clatter.

Jigger got the second man, too, his bullet taking him high in the chest and slamming him out from under his hat. The other two hardcases were firing now, and I pulled my Dragoon just as a slug tore a furrow down the table top and smashed a beer stein to smithereens.

I felt a hard blow to my thigh and a hot, burning pain like I'd been seared by a brand. George fired point-blank at the third man, and through the haze I saw the drifter go down with his arms windmilling and his pistol flying free before he hit the floor face first.

Everything was confused and crazy and the thick, bitter smoke was everywhere. The fourth man ducked and moved my way as both Jigger and George fired at him, and I cocked and fired my pistol and was plum' astonished to see him jerk, stagger, and drop—he had just stumbled into my bullet, pure and simple.

And then, sudden and more shocking somehow than the noise had been, came the stillness. Elmo slowly rose up from behind the bar like a turtle from a pond, his face the sick white of a snake's belly and his eyes wide and staring. The smoke drifted in a filmy haze out into the light from the window, and I could hear the trickle of spilled beer dripping off the table.

Suddenly, I felt light-headed and my legs decided not to hold me up, so I set down in a chair and laid my six-gun on the table. My right thigh felt numb, and when I reached down to touch it my hand came back bloody. "Lordy," I thought, "I've been shot."

The big feller Jigger had gunned lay on the floor just out from the wall, and now he commenced to moan and look wall-eyed at us while he tried to get his legs under him. George stepped over, his long-barreled Colt in his hand, and stood astraddle of him. He looked down and said, "Dumb som'bitch. You boys should've come in a-shootin.' It was all that palaver got you killed." And he shot him in the head.

Which is when I doubled over where I set and throwed up the chili, beer, and whatever else I'd et that day. Jigger was happily going through the dead men's pockets and a-humming "Mary Had a Little Lamb." George worked the rod on his pistol as he kicked the empties out, and reloaded.

Elmo came out from behind the bar, his eyes wide as saucers. He kept shifting his weight, taking little short nervous steps up and down without going anywhere. "Oh, my," he whimpered, "oh, my." He looked like he was going to faint, while I *felt* like I was going to, but somehow neither of us did.

My thigh was bleeding pretty free and was commencing to throb some, but I had no idea how bad I'd been hit. I fished my jackknife out of my pocket and cut the bloody cloth away, but I still couldn't see much. And then all at once the truth came to me clear as a bell—I had shot *myself!* When I'd pulled my Dragoon during the skirmish I had got previous on the trigger and put a bullet through my own leg. There just ain't any way I can tell you how humiliated and foolish I felt—I just wanted to crawl into a hole and wailer there in my shame and disgrace.

George came over to where I sat and took a long, savvy look at my wound. His eyebrows went up and a quick grin crossed his leathery face before he pulled rein on his expression and changed it back to serious.

"That's *two* men you shot today, Merlin," he said in a

raspy whisper I hoped nobody else heard, "I told you you'd get to be depraved like the rest of us."

He turned to Elmo, who still did his funny little going nowhere dance, and pointed to the bottles behind the bar. "Them boys put a bullet through the Kid's leg," George said, "fetch me a bottle of whiskey and a clean rag, right by-god now!"

Elmo broke out of his trance and scurried off to do as George had told him, bringing back a full bottle of Confederate Dew and some clean bar towels. I shed my gun belt, pulled my pants and drawers down, and while I tried to think of more pleasant matters—like being scalped alive with a soup spoon—George probed around some and poured whiskey into the wound. I did not pass out, but I will admit both of them actions captured my full and immediate attention.

"You're lucky, Kid," said George, "the slug went straight through, like crap through a turkey. Missed the artery and the bone. It'll smart some for awhile, but you'll be good as new in no time."

He tore up a bar towel, plugged the holes, and wrapped the leg in a manner that told me he'd done this more than a few times. When he handed me the whiskey bottle, I didn't need to be coaxed. I took a long pull on the Confederate Dew, came up for air, and took an even longer one.

"Here, now," George grinned, taking the bottle back, "save a little o' that sheepherder's delight for your doctor. You know what they say, 'Physician, heal your own self.'"

"Lordy," I said, remembering the fourth man, "I—I *killed* a feller, George!"

George wiped his mouth on his sleeve and handed the bottle to Jigger.

"Yes, you surely did, Merlin," he said, "but don't you go to grievin' over the likes of him. When it comes to bullets, I have found it truly is better to give than to receive."

Elmo didn't usually drink whiskey, but he must have decided our little disagreement with the four drifters was a special occasion or something because he was swilling down the hard stuff like old Ignacio on his best day. "Need to steady my nerves," he mumbled, although I figured if he kept a-going like he was his nerves would be so steady he couldn't move.

George strolled over to him and laid three double eagles on the bar, one by one. "There's sixty dollars in gold there, Elmo," he said, "I hope that'll take care of the mess and see them boys get planted up at the bone orchard."

Just seeing that money seemed to complete the steadying of Elmo's nerves. He corked the bottle and gave the cash his full attention. The color even came back to his face.

"Hell, George," he said, "there's no need for that. I'd have took care of it for nothing. We're friends, ain't we?" But he had already scooped up the coins and put them in his pocket.

George took a sealed envelope from his coat and placed it on the bar, then put down two more double eagles. "Yes, we are, Elmo," he allowed, "that's why I know I can ask you to do me another little favor.

"I need you to take that letter to the Shenanigan Bank and deliver it personal to Ollie Langford. You know him, don't you?"

Elmo picked up the envelope, but his eyes were on the gold. "The banker? Sure, I know who he is. I'll have a man ride over there with it this very afternoon."

Fast as a sidewinder's strike, George grabbed Elmo by the collar and jerked him halfway across the bar. "You ain't a-listenin' to me," he said, "I want you to take it to him your own self." His face was only inches away from the barkeep's, and his eyes had that loco stare again. "Unless," he said in that harsh, husky voice of his, "you figure it's too much trouble."

I could see Elmo's nerves had gone unsteady again. His face lost its new-found color, and his toothy smile was a plea for mercy. "N-No trouble at all, George," he said, "what I m-meant was *I'll* ride over with it this very afternoon."

"That's what I thought you meant. Have Langford write me out an answer, and then you fetch it to me over at Rampage. We'll be there for a week or so."

Jigger had a pistol in each hand, and he'd already started toward the back door. The numbness had wore off and my leg had commenced to hurt in earnest, but I found I could hobble along after a fashion, and I turned to foller him. George came up and put a hand on my shoulder. "How you doin', Kid?" he asked, "How's the leg?"

102

"Well," says I, "I don't expect I'm goin' to *enjoy* it all that much, but I reckon I can ride all right."

"Let's do it then," he said.

The street was mostly empty as we rode through town, but I knew that behind the closed windows and doors there was eyes a-watching us. The Indian was gone, blanket and all, from the bench in front of Bender's, but old Ambrose, Dry Creek's undertaker, watched us ride by from the open door of the funeral parlor. I figured he'd heard the gunfire and smelled himself a potential opportunity for commerce. Little did either of us know when I was making him payments on my Pa's funeral that I would later go on to become a famous desperado with the Starkweather gang and shoottwo men in a saloon fight, one of which was me.

Jigger led the way on his jigsaw horse as we left town and spurred off across the sagebrush flats. By now I had come to believe the center of all creation was the hole in my thigh. It pained me a good deal more than somewhat, but I was determined not to let on. In the first place, I had a little pride left even if I had been dumb enough to plug myself, and in the second place I reckoned my stupidity had canceled whatever right I may have had to complain.

On top of everything else, I was hungry again. I was a constant marvel to myself.

George loped out ahead of us as we left town, and minutes later we crossed Careless Creek and headed due north. We kept the horses at a flat run for the first five miles, then eased them back to a fast, ground-covering trot. I tried everything I knew to take my mind off my leg. I thought about the good times running mustangs with Pa, about elk grazing in high country meadows, about Mary Alice and the soft breathy sound of her voice. I thought about the man I'd shot back there in Dry Creek, and I wondered did he have a wife or maybe kids. I thought about dying, about being alive one minute and forever dead the next, and I mostly managed to keep the hurt at bay, sometimes for minutes at a time.

The sun had dropped low in the western sky when George pulled his thoroughbred back even with Little Buck and put a hand on my shoulder. "How you makin' it, Bodacious?" he asked.

"Fine, George," I lied, "If I was doing any better I'd have myself a runaway." Oh, I was a tough one, all right.

Well, I knew Original George Starkweather could read men even better than he could his books on pirates, round-table knights, and Robin Hood, so I knew he seen through my bluff easy. My voice had sounded tight and strained, even to me, and I was dripping sweat. It sure didn't require no mind reader to know I was a-hurting.

"Glad you're doin' so well," George said, and then he proceeded to tell me all about our destination, whether to instruct or distract me I don't know to this day, but I reckon probably both.

He told me that Rampage, a place decent folks did not

104

frequent, lay twenty miles north of Dry Creek, in the twisted breaks and badlands the other side of the Big Porcupine River. George said people spoke of it, if they mentioned it at all, as a town where outlaws, tinhorn gamblers, and whores done all sorts of wicked and interesting things and where even the boldest peace officer dared not enter. The truth, he said, was that Rampage wasn't a town at all.

According to George, Rampage had once been the headquarters of a dry-land ranch, but it had been abandoned when the gent who owned it found it a heap more dry land than ranch. A year or so later, George said, saloon-keeper and gambler Slippery Mayfair moved in and took the place over. Mayfair had turned the rambling two-story ranch house into a saloon, with rooms upstairs where the whores plied their trade. Downstairs, George said, there was a big, common room where a desperado could drink himself into a stupor, get killed over a bad woman, or lose his ill-gotten gains to a cold-eyed cardsharp—all in the name of good, clean fun.

George told me there was a sod-roofed store where a man could buy tobacco, ammunition, and such at about six times their true value, and a big, ramshackle barn with a loft for sleeping and corrals out back for saddle-horses and stolen livestock. There was also a small blacksmith shop, a log bunkhouse, and a weed-grown burial patch on a low hill where the occasional fool-hardy deputy or unlucky bandit could rest 'til judgment day amidst the greasewood and prickly pear.

"Like I said, the entire pleasure resort is owned and

operated by a sad-eyed villain with a numb conscience name of Slippery Mayfair," George went on, "Old Slippery is slicker than a greased hog and twice as fat, but he pays top dollar for stolen stock, and he provides a place where the boys can let off steam.

"Him and me have us an understanding. Slippery knows I need him, and he also knows I'll kill him if I have to, so we tend to get along fine."

I vaguely recall crossing the Big Porcupine River, sometime after full dark. Shortly after that, we finally caught sight of Rampage. A half moon hung like a broken dinner plate above the scatter of dark buildings that loomed up against the night sky. Orange light showed in the windows of the two story house, and from inside came drunken laughter and the tinny jangle of a piano. Somewhere off in the darkness a horse whinnied a greeting, and George's stud answered it.

My leg felt numb. I could feel wetness all down my breeches and inside my boot, and I knew my thigh was bleeding again. I had a death grip on the saddle horn and I was setting Little Buck mostly by instinct. I don't believe I've ever felt as bone-tired as I did that night. I seemed to move in a strange world where everything had slowed down to maybe one-quarter speed.

I heard George say, "We're here, Merlin. Welcome to Camelot", but his words sounded hollow and far away, like they were coming from a deep and distant cave.

I opened my mouth and tried to ask, "Already?" but nothing came out.

I felt the reins slip through my fingers and fall to the ground, and then I slid from the saddle and did likewise. I do not recall striking the earth.

EIGHT

First Day at Rampage

I came awake with effort from a long way off, like a man climbing out of a deep well with an anvil on his back. My mouth was bone-dry, with a dirty brown taste that caused me to wonder if I'd shared supper with a coyote. Knowing the *way* I like to eat, it wouldn't have surprised me none to find out I had.

I was laying in a feather bed that smelled powerful strong of rose perfume, and I could feel sunlight from somewhere a-shining warm upon my face. For a while, I just laid there, trying to recollect how I came to be wherever I was, but I didn't feel ready to open my eyes right then, so I didn't.

Then I felt the throbbing hurt in my thigh, and everything came back to me in a rush of remembering.

I recalled the bitter smoke and gunfire at the Oasis, and my lightning speed as I cleverly shot myself through the leg. I remembered the ride out of Dry Creek through the sagebrush to the badlands of the Big Porcupine, and coming into Rampage in the dark.

Mostly, I recalled the man I'd gunned during the fracas and the fact I hadn't even had a good look at him, neither before nor after my bullet took his life. I wondered how I was going to recognize the feller when I got down to Hell (I was fairly certain at the time we were both a-going there) but I decided if I didn't spot him he'd most likely look *me* up.

It was then I heard the sound of a door opening, and knew I was no longer alone. I sat up and opened my eyes and there stood Shanty O'Kane, grinning around the stem of his old clay pipe and carrying a covered tray and a coffee pot.

"Top o' the mornin' to you, Boy-O," said he, "are you after sleepin' your young life away, or would you care to return now to the land o' the livin'?"

I took a quick look around. There was lace curtains on the window, fancy wallpaper, and a painted bowl and pitcher with towels on an oak commode. A clock and a banquet lamp was on the table next to the bed, and a bootjack set on the carpet by the wardrobe. A sheet-iron heating stove crouched like a bulldog near the front wall, and there was an easy chair with a silk pillow on it and all manner of women's fumadiddle and foofaraw. I knew then I was in the room of one of them horizontal workers, and I wondered how I came to be there. Shanty stood a-grinning down at me with his back to the window, and the sunshine from behind him made it look like his red hair was afire.

I grinned back at him. "Good to see you again, Shanty," I said, "Is that grub you're a-carryin' or is my nose a dang liar?"

"'Tis grub indeed," he said, whisking the dish towel off the tray with a flourish, "a healthy samplin' o' the

108

Three B's—biscuits, beans, and bacon—but then I don't suppose a bold young outlaw like yourself would be hungry at all."

"The day I ain't hungry will be the day I die," I said, reaching for the vittles, "and even on that day I'll be hungry right up to when the moment comes."

An old chair with a green velvet seat stood near the bed, and Shanty pulled it over and sat down. He struck a sulphur match on the sole of his brogan, lit up his pipe, and puffed contentedly while he watched me eat.

"Jigger and the captain carried you into the bar last evenin'," he said, "after you demonstrated your amazin' new method for gettin' down off a hawrse.

"I was deep in conversation, you might say, with an old friend named Jackrabbit Annie when the captain called me. Himself and the Jigger brought you up here, and Annie and me managed to clean you up a bit, change your bandage, and tuck you into bed. *Her* bed."

"You undressed me in front of a *woman?* And *washed* me?"

Shanty's blue eyes twinkled, and his bushy eyebrows clumb higher on his brow like a pair of fuzzy red caterpillars. "The truth is," he said, "*she* undressed you in front of *me*. But don't be alarmed, Boy-O, Jackrabbit Annie has a doctor's own knowledge of male anatomy, and the woman has the very soul of a healer."

My ears felt hot, and I knew I was blushing like a schoolgirl. "Well," I said, all huffy, "I 'preciate Miss Annie's hospitality, and yours, but the smell of that rose perfume is makin' me sick as a poisoned pup, and I

109

need me some air. Tell her I said, 'much obliged'."

I had swung my legs off the side of the bed in a move to get up and out of there when I seen my drawers were missing and that I was buck nekkid from the waist down. "Dang, Shanty!" I said, a-clutching the bedsheet around my hips, "what happened to my clothes?"

Just then the door opened again and a big red-headed lady I took to be Jackrabbit Annie walked in with a bundle in her arms. "We had to cut 'em off your pink little arse, kid," she said, "when we tended to your bullet wound."

She put the bundle on the bed and smiled at me. "These here drawers and breeches belonged to Buck-tooth Betty's beloved, young Romeo Flores, 'til they hung him over at Silver City," she said, "now I figure they're in the public domain."

"Uh, th-thank you, ma'am," I stammered, trying to catch up to my dignity, "but I d-do not require no d-dead man's d-drawers."

"Why the hell not?" she said, "Romeo sure won't be needin' 'em no more. Fact is, them breeches was sewed by a tailor from Mexico City, and they're a big improvement over them rags you was wearin', if you ast me."

I seen I had hurt her feelings, which I sure hadn't meant to, so I threw a half-hitch on my tongue and backed off.

"I'm sorry, ma'am," I told her, "I appreciate your kindness, and Betty's, too. Thanks for the duds. Now if you'll just turn your back a minute, I'll put 'em on."

"You bet, kid. And I won't peek, neither. Might be drove stark loco with lust if I do, and it just ain't worth the risk. Hell, I might even start *givin'* it away."

Then she and Shanty commenced laughin' like fools, and I slipped into Romeo's pants and fell to blushin' again.

When I got outside the room I leaned against the wall, pulled my boots on, and belted my Colt Dragoon. I seen that I was in a long hallway, and I limped past some doors to a stairway going down. My leg still hurt plenty, but not as bad as I'd expected, and Romeo's breeches fit like they was made for me. I remember they was black wool, with silver buttons all down the sides, and they flared out at the bottom to show a flash of red in the Mexican style. I was still a poor excuse for a desperado, but leastways I was beginning to look the part.

My pride told me not to use the handrail on my way downstairs, but my hurt leg said if I didn't it wouldn't be a-going, so I took hold and started on down. By the time I'd reached bottom I had begun to sweat, and I felt light-headed and shaky, so I hung on to the banister and looked the place over.

The room was big, with windows and a door up front and a long bar down one side. Kiowa, Clete, and Pike set at a table, playing poker with a long-faced tinhorn. Tobacco smoke hung thick overhead in shifting layers like a pattern I seen once in a marble tombstone. Original George was at another table down by the piano, talking to a fat man with eyes like a bloodhound and a belly like a brood mare in foal.

"Hey, Kid!" George bellered, "Come on over here and meet Slippery Mayfair, the feller who runs this murderers' monastery. The old tightwad might even buy you a drink."

"I don't buy drinks, I sell them," said Slippery.

I tried my best to swagger across the room like a proper outlaw, but it's hard to swagger when you're a cripple, and my prideful strut turned into a sort of pathetic shuffle.

"Shake hands with the landlord, Kid," said George, "his right name's Obadiah J. Mayfair, but even his momma calls him 'Slippery'. He's so slick he has to sand his chubby hips just to keep his pants on."

I had never seen a man so fat. He sort of oozed over the sides of a big, special built chair, and I figured he'd produce right at 200 pounds of pure leaf lard if a man was to render him down.

There was a bottle of Tennessee sour mash whiskey on the table, and George pulled the cork and refilled his glass. I seen his hand shake as he did so, and I figured he'd already had his today share and part of tomorrow's. He squinted at his roly-poly companion, and said, "This here's young Merlin Fanshaw, Slippery—better known as the Bodacious Kid. Merlin is my new *pistolero*."

George grinned his wicked grin and winked at me. "Got hisself shot in the leg durin' that little dust-up I told you about," he said, and then his grin got wider, "but he sure as hell put a bullet through the man who *did* it, didn'cha, Kid?"

Slippery studied me with his hound-dog eyes and nodded, but he didn't offer his hand. "Bodacious," said he in a deep, serious voice, "welcome to Rampage."

The bartender was a nervous-looking cuss with a bad wig and sideburns that looked like they'd been drawed on with an ink pen. George twisted in his chair, reared back, and fixed his wild eagle's eye upon him. "Fetch us another glass over here, Leonard," he bellered, "your slippery old boss is a-buyin' young Merlin a drink."

The barkeep swung up the pass-through at the end of the bar and padded over with the glass. Slippery Mayfair looked bored and half-asleep as he pondered the fingernails of his right hand. "Well," the barkeep huffed, "he never said nothin' to *me* about it."

George grinned a drunken grin, grasped the bartender by the lapels of his vest, and exhaled a breath on him that made the man's eyes water. "That'sh because he din't *know* he was buyin'," George explained.

I eased into a chair across from George and Slippery, and if my leg could have spoke for itself I believe it would have purred out of pure gratitude, like a kitten in a cream can.

George applied his full concentration to pouring me a drink of that Tennessee sippin' whiskey, and by chance he even got some of it in my glass. "Here's how," he said, touching my glass with his own, "You was *good* back there at Dry Creek, Merlin."

Well, I *wasn't* good back there, I knew that. I had gunned one of them fellers, sure, but it had happened through dumb luck after I had already shot myself. I was grateful to Original George, though. He had knowed about my mishap from the first but he had kept my secret, and I appreciated it more than I could say.

I gave salute to George and to Slippery with my glass and swallered the contents. The sour mash was good whiskey for sure, and it slid down smooth as oil, hitting bottom and spreading its warmth out from my belly like ripples on a summer pond.

"Old Slippery here was kind enough to buy them steers we drove down," George said, "and he was, as usual, the very soul of generosity. Paid almost a fifth of what they're worth."

He pulled a buckskin poke from his coat pocket and poured four double eagles out onto the table. "Already gave the other boys their share, Merlin," he said, "but you ain't had yours yet."

"Haven't been with the outfit long enough to be in for a share," I said.

"Makes no never mind," George said, "you ride with me, you get a share. Them gold pieces are yours, Merlin.

"Spend 'em on booze, cards, or them painted bawds upstairs—whatever suits you. Walk proud an' tall, Kid—you're a high-ridin' raider with the Starkweather gang."

"I'm much obliged, cap'n," I said, "but I believe I'd just like to go see to my horse right now."

I got to my feet, shook George's hand, and turned to Slippery Mayfair. "Pleased t' meet you, Mr. Mayfair," I said.

"A pleasure to make *your* acquaintance, Bodacious," he said in that serious way he had, and this time he shook my hand.

I had moved off toward the front door when I heard George call after me, "By the way, Merlin, how's your wound?"

"*What* wound?" says I, and went on outside.

The sunlight like to blinded me after the dark of the bar room, and I squinched up my eyes and waited 'til they equalized some before moving on toward the barn. Poddy Medford lay sprawled near the hitchrack with his mouth open, and at first I thought he was dead. But then he let out a sort of strangled belch and rolled over, and I seen he was merely dead drunk and sleeping it off.

The day was hot and muggy, and without a breath of wind. Big old fleecy thunderheads floated by overhead, teasing the parched country with the promise of rain, but as usual they lied. I figured moisture wouldn't hit the badlands until November, and it was only the last part of August.

Jigger St. Clare was off beyond the sod-roofed store, shooting at bottles and cans in a dry wash. I could hear the pop-pop-pop of his pistols like the tearing of threads in a blanket. When he seen me, he grinned his foolish, slack-jawed grin and holstered his guns. Then, with a whoop and a flourish, he drawed them out and spun them back into the leather again, all quicker than the eye could foller. He took off his hat and howdied me, and his image shimmered and danced amid the heat waves. I howdied him in return, and he went back to his shooting once again.

There didn't seem to be anybody tending the store, and it looked closed.

As I watched Jigger burn powder it occurred to me that I should stock up on cartridges and put in a little practice myself, now that I had embraced the outlaw vocation. Not only was skill with weapons necessary to the conduct of our business dealings, it was also a bedrock form of life insurance. Anyway, that's how it seemed to me at the time.

I had resolved to keep working my wounded leg so it wouldn't stiffen up on me, which was another reason I decided to hobble on down to the barn. I set forth with my customary confidence, but was wet with sweat and hurting aplenty by the time I got there, and I was more than ready to set down somewhere.

The barn was big and solid-built of square-hewn cottonwood logs, and the sun had bleached the wood to a soft, powder gray. The roof had seen better days; its shingles were mostly gone now, leaving wide gaps where mud swallows flew in and out in a busy flutter of sickle-shaped wings and tiny bodies as shiny-black as gunmetal.

Inside, I walked past George's thoroughbred and Jigger's amazing patchwork steed and found Little Buck in a stall toward the rear. He raised his head, sniffing the air, and whinnied when he caught my scent. I believe he was glad to see me. I know I was glad to see him.

I found a curry comb and gave the little horse a good going over until I had combed the dried sweat and mud from his coat and had took the tangles out of his mane and tail. My leg was hurting like fire by the time I was done, so I poured him a can of oats, set down on an empty nail keg, and just talked to him, low and easy.

Ever since I was just a button I had told my deepest thoughts and secrets to horses, and if that seems peculiar to you, so be it. Horses are good listeners, they never shame a man or give him advice, and there is something solid and steady about even the dumbest of the breed. Anyway, I commenced to talk to the buckskin there in that barn, and he et his oats and listened, or leastways he seemed to.

Pa and me had got ourselves lost one time while hunting elk in thick timber on the west slope of the Brimstones, and we like to have never found our way out. Pa said we wasn't lost but only temporarily confused, and that may have been true for him but I don't mind telling you I was sure lost, and scared to boot.

When the sun went down it got darker than the inside of a buffalo, so we made camp as best we could among some deadfall and one of us slept like a baby, guess which. Yes, that's right, I laid there all night, wide-eyed and listening for mountain lions, grizzly bears, maneating squirrels and such, but all I heard was my Pa a-snoring. Come morning, we found a game trail that took us up to a high ridge where we could see the whole country spread out below us for fifty miles or more, and we found the landmarks that took us on home.

Pa was always a great one at finding lessons for living in ordinary happenings, and of course he found one that time. He said, "Merlin, there will be times in your life when you'll lose your way and be temporarily confused, just like we was down yonder in that canyon. You'll be too closed in by timber and shadows to see your way clear, and you won't know where or who you are.

"When those times come, think back to now and get some distance in your mind. Find yourself a place where you can see the whole picture and look for landmarks, so to speak, and you'll know what you need to do and how to get home."

That was about as flowery as my Pa ever talked. Now I have to tell you that not all of his teachings worked out, or even made sense. Sometimes Pa would say things he didn't really believe himself just because they sounded good, or because he'd read them in a book somewhere. One time he told me that if you caught a skunk by the tail and lifted his hind feet off the ground he couldn't spray you, and you was safe at least 'til you put him down again. When I asked if he'd ever tried it himself he grinned and said, "Hell, no. I ain't *that* crazy!"

Well, you can understand that occasions such as that caused me to sometimes question Pa's fatherly wisdom, but I never forgot his words about getting some distance in order to see the whole picture. His words have never failed me in a lifetime of getting lost and finding myself again.

Anyway, I set there on my keg and talked while Little Buck switched flies and munched away at his oat ration. What I talked about, mostly, was the twists and turns my life had took over the past few weeks. I tried to catch aholt of where I'd been, where I was now, and where the trail was leading me.

I had not set out to be an outlaw, nor a peace officer, neither. All I had intended to do was find me a riding job with some cow outfit, or maybe sign on to ride the rough string. Meeting Androcles Wilkes had changed all that, meeting Marshal Ridgeway had changed things some more, and the final change had come when I told Original George I'd ride with his gang.

Now I had killed a man in a gun battle and had took payment in gold as a member of an outlaw band, and I wasn't sure how I felt about it.

"You horses are lucky," I told Buck, "a horse is just a horse, plain and simple, and far as I know he don't worry much about the right and wrong of things.

"A man is different. Preachers say we have something called a conscience inside us to guide us, and I reckon that's a fact. I have done good things and felt good, and I've done bad things and felt plum' miserable and guilty."

Except it don't always work that way. By everything I know of conscience, killing that feller in Dry Creek should have made me feel bad, but it didn't. I was *glad* it was him that was dead, and me that was alive. Maybe George was right; maybe I *had* become depraved.

And what *about* George? Did *his* conscience bother

him? And if it did, did it bother him about the same things mine did? Was one man's conscience different from another's? And if it was, what did that say about right and wrong?

I seen Little Buck yawn and spraddle out his hind legs. I jumped up and scampered back just as he let go a yellow stream that splashed and spattered the stall's floor but for a mercy missed my new Mexican pants.

"Well, thanks for listening," I told him, and for maybe the ten thousandth time in my young life I wished I was smarter.

NINE

Healing up and Heading out

During the next few weeks August crossed the border into September, and the weather turned even hotter. Them big old puffy clouds still drifted by overhead from time to time, sliding patches of fast-moving shade across the breaks, but they had given up all pretense of bringing rain. It was as if they was bored with their game and didn't even bother to tease the dusty badlands any more. The land itself seemed to know the moisture wasn't coming. It had been fooled too many times before, and now it just sulled there under the sun and got drier by the day.

The wound in my thigh had mostly quit hurting and had commenced to itch considerable, so I figured I was on the mend. I don't mind telling you I was plenty relieved. I knew that a bullet tended to carry bits of cloth, leather and what-not into a man, and that the real danger from a gunshot wound often came later through blood poisoning and gangrene. Jackrabbit Annie told me she had run some of Slippery's Tennessee whiskey through my thigh with a turkey baster the night I came to Rampage, and I reckon that had sterilized things pretty well. From what samples of Slippery's whiskey I had consumed I believe it could have *dissolved* cloth and leather, if it didn't cauterize the wound altogether.

Anyway, my leg was healing, and I figured I was lucky to have got off so light. Had the slug struck bone, or my knee, or had it cut an artery, I knew matters would have been a heap more serious. As things turned out, the worst damage was to my pride, which no doubt needed some comeuppance anyhow. In any case, I do not recommend self-inflicted bullet wounds, nor any other kind neither.

While the gang was in Rampage I mostly tended to be early to bed and early to rise. I would saddle the buckskin just before dawn and ride the rough country around Rampage, at times going as far as the Big Porcupine River before returning. At noon, I'd take on some grub and catch me a brief *siesta* during the heat of the day, after which I'd usually practice shooting for an hour or so with Jigger St. Clare. The other boys didn't seem to like Jigger much, and I believe they was scared of him because he was such a wizard with a six-gun. He seemed pleased to have my company and he showed me things about handling a short gun I never knew were possible.

Thinking about it now, it strikes me as curious the way I came to like Jigger after almost despising him at first meeting. I suppose it was because of what we'd gone through together back there at Dry Creek, and because we were close to the same age. He still wore that stupid grin, his big ears still stuck out, and I knew now his sly, cold eyes were those of a born killer, but Jigger was a man I'd rode with and fought beside, and somehow that made all the difference.

The other boys—Kiowa, Clete, Pike, and Poddy—spent their afternoons losing money to the horse-faced cardsharp, getting as drunk as humanly possible, and fighting among themselves. They spent their evenings—and their money—a-wallering around upstairs with them giggling, granite-eyed chippies, and they devoted their mornings to healing up from the night before.

Of course, some of them soiled doves made up to me, and there was one night when Bucktooth Betty got all teary-eyed and sloppy and offered me a free ride, probably because seeing me wearing the late Romeo Flores' breeches made her sentimental or something. Truth is, I never went with any of them ceiling experts, even though there was a time or two I had the inclination. Mostly, I just blushed, stammered, and left them laughing.

I've thought about it since, and I still ain't sure why I stayed on the riverbank instead of jumping into the swimmin' hole, so to speak, but I believe it was partly because I wasn't sure I could *swim,* if you take my meaning. Oh, I knew *how* to swim, I reckon, it's just that I hadn't ever actually been in the *water.*

Then there was the other thing. I'd be standing there with my hat in my hand, talking to one of them sporting women and thinking maybe I *would* take the plunge, when all of a sudden and clear as a bell I'd see the face of Mary Alice instead, with her honey-colored hair and her eyes like a newborn fawn, and I'd recall the soft scent of lilac once again.

When those times came, I'd just smile, take my leave, and make my way downstairs and out into the night. I'd stare up at them bright, distant stars and breathe in the cold evening air until I cleared the heavy smell of rose perfume from my nose and my mind. Then I'd think on Mary Alice, and despite my confusion I'd feel a hankering so strong it was a sweet, lonesome ache.

I used to wonder about the ways of them bandits with women. Some of the boys seemed in almost a constant state of lust, like buck deer during the fall rut. Others went to the whores now and again, but spent most of their time at drinking and card-playing. Some, like Original George, didn't seem to much care whether they had a woman or not, but was able to take them or leave them alone. None of them hardcases seemed to care much which bawd he took up with, or limited his attentions to just one woman; none, that is, except Shanty O'Kane. Shanty spent most all of his time with

Jackrabbit Annie while the gang was in Rampage, and I didn't see much of him. It was almost like they was married, which I guess they sort of was, in a temporary kind of way. Leastways I never seen either of them keeping company with any others during our time there.

Original George spent his days playing cribbage and drinking with Slippery Mayfair. George seemed to take pleasure in vexing the fat man, calling him "Moby Dick" from a book he'd been reading about a big, white whale. George taunted Slippery for being cheap, or slick in his business dealings. For his part, Slippery never appeared to get riled or take offense: he just ignored George's badgering and kept on talking serious and polite like he usually did. I reckon they'd been friends a long time, and they just had different ways of showing their friendship.

As always, George did a lot of reading. Sometimes when I was out on Little Buck I'd see him off by himself, setting on a hilltop in the shade of one of them chippies' silk parasols with a book in his hand and a bottle by his side. When he'd see me he'd wave and go back to his reading, and I always waved back and let him be. He tended to hit the bottle pretty steady all through the day, but the whiskey never seemed to bother him all that much. Now and then he'd come out and join Jigger and me at our pistol practice, and the man was a ring-tailed, double-rectified wonder with the Colt's, whether he had a snootfull or not.

Come nightfall, he'd deal poker in the big room with

the boys, and as usual he mostly won. Later, he'd sometimes bed down with one of the whores, usually Bucktooth Betty or the curly-headed one with the moustache everybody called the Belgian Mare, but women didn't seem to mean that much to George one way or the other. If he had any passion, I believe it must have been for money, power, and being top dog. Then, of course, there were his books.

I asked him once how he come to be such a reader, and he said he'd took it up while doing a stretch in the pen for rustling. "Bein' locked up like to drove me plum' loco, Merlin," he said, "I'd get to longing for space and freedom so bad I'd damn near die. Couldn't eat, sleep, or nothin'.

"Then one day an old forger told me about books, and how they'd kept him from goin' crazy. The old boy quoted me a passage he'd read somewhere that began: *'There is no frigate like a book, to take us all to lands away . . .'*

"I commenced reading and found it was true. From then on, iron bars could cage my body, but they couldn't corral my mind."

George loaned me a book about King Arthur and his big book about pirates, and I took to reading for the first time since I'd gone to school. Oh, I tripped and stumbled over some of the big words, but when I'd get plum' bogged down I'd ask George and he'd help me get untangled and lined out again.

I had never liked to read much when I was a kid, but once I got started on the pirate book it was like riding a runaway wagon downhill. Reading about them bucca-neers and their bloody deeds on the high seas surely did make the time pass, and I felt as though I was right there with them. I could fairly hear the cannons roar and smell the smoke, I could see the mainmast toppled by shot and shell, and the flames rise up from dying trea-sure ships. With my fellow freebooters at my side, I ran up the Jolly Roger and swung a cutlass alongside Cap-tain Kidd himself. I led the chase as we boarded rich merchant vessels, kidnapped Spanish ladies with eyes like newborn fawns, and buried chests of gold and jewels on sandy beaches under a tropic moon. What-ever else George did, he sure had got me to reading again, and this time it was because I wanted to.

Now and then I'd come on a passage in the book where the writer had fancied up the story with words I didn't know, and I'd lose the trail for awhile. In the pirate book the author wrote of a sea battle he said was "Homeric," and I had no idea what he was driving at. But George told me the word had to do with an old Greek named Homer who wrote about grand doings that were bigger than life. George said that's what the author was saying, and that he was writing *figuratively*. George said most writers wrote figurative from time to time, and some worse than others.

"Well, I don't see why he couldn't just say the battle was a *big 'un*," I huffed, "using them ten dollar words just throws up a dust cloud and causes a man to get sidetracked."

George gave me one of his tolerant looks. "I reckon

he done it for the same reason Shanty adds chili peppers to his stew." he said, "to give it a little spice."

Well, of course when he compared the feller's writing style to vittles the whole thing came clear to me, and from then on I came to look forward to places where the author throwed in some *figuratives*.

Those weeks in the badlands passed smooth enough, I guess. I was grateful for the chance to let my leg heal, but by the beginning of the third week I began to notice a few dark clouds a-looming up on the horizon of our possibilities (not *real* clouds, of course, I'm talking *figuratively*).

For one thing, I could see that the boys were getting restless. They had pretty well run out of money, and it seemed to me they had enjoyed just about all the debauchery they could stand. Kiowa John and Clete Potter got into a scuffle one day at the barn over whether brown or black was the better color for a horse, and Clete nearly bit Kiowa's left ear off. For his part, Kiowa knocked out three of Clete's teeth and busted his nose. They would have gone to their pistols, but George walked in and said he'd kill the first man to pull a gun, so they didn't.

For another thing, I hadn't seen *El Borrachon* since we left the line camp, and I couldn't find anyone else who had, either. I wondered if he'd taken word of our new location to Ridgeway, or if he'd maybe just gone off on a drunk somewhere, but the days turned into weeks and still he never showed up.

When I asked George about it, he didn't seem worried much. "Oh," he said, "I suppose he'll turn up, sooner or later." And so I quit asking, but I still wondered.

Then I noticed George was growing edgy, too. He quit playing cards with Slippery, and he seemed to go off inside himself somewhere to a place that was his alone. He got all quiet and tense, and when I spoke to him he'd either growl and snap like a trapped wolf or just say nothing at all. He even quit reading his books, and I'd see him sometimes a-staring into the distance with his jaw set and his cold, eagle eyes blazing like there was a fire inside him. All the boys walked wide of him, including me. Being around him at all was like being near a black powder bomb with the fuse lit.

Except for some pistol practice with Jigger, I didn't spend much time with the other boys while we were all there at Rampage. I mostly took care of my horse, split firewood for the cookstove, and spent the days reading the books George lent me.

I was usually the first one up of a morning, rolling out of my blankets while it was still dark. I'd wash up, roll my bed, and foller the lantern light to the kitchen of the main house where Slippery's Chinese cook would be waiting with fresh coffee and vittles. We didn't palaver much at such times; neither of us seemed able to savvy the other's lingo. The cook would grin and gabble away in what I supposed was Chinese while I et my breakfast and told him in English how good everything was. Then I'd scrape my plate, stack it on the counter by the back door, and go on back to the barn where I slept.

A hundred feet below the barn stood a sun-bleached outhouse on the edge of a dry wash, and it was my habit to go there each day after morning chuck and meditate for a time. The outhouse was a one-hole hooter, and it leaned backward at a crazy angle which gave me a sort of uncertain feeling 'til I got used to it. It had plank sides and a door, but no roof at all, which meant it would be miserable inside when it rained. Of course, that wasn't a big problem around Rampage, because it hardly ever did—rain, I mean. Looking on the bright side, the open top offered a fine view of the clouds and sky, and the sides and door gave a man privacy from all except the occasional high-flying bird.

Just inside the front door, at the top of the wall, was a paper-gray wasp's nest, and I liked to watch them hard-working hornets fly off and come back with caterpillars, spiders, and other such groceries. Like I done with George and the boys, I gave them wasps space aplenty, and I hoped they wouldn't bother me.

Anyway, I was perched there at my usual angle one morning, reading about Blackbeard the pirate and listening to the drone of the hornets, when I heard somebody coming. It sounded like two men walking together and talking low, and I was about to holler that I'd be out in a minute when I recognized George's voice, and then Shanty O'Kane's.

"Reckon this is far enough, Shanty," I heard George say, "just wanted to make sure we weren't overheard."

I wanted to call out and let them know I was in the

privy, but there was something in the sound of George's voice that made me hesitate. I heard the footsteps stop, and then he spoke again.

"Either that damn Elmo never took my note to Langford, or somethin's gone wrong. I should've had an answer from that nickel-nursin' high roller a week ago."

"Sure, and the lads are gettin' restless, Cap'n," Shanty said, "they're startin' to mutter about that Army payroll again—and about gettin' their share."

"That's why I need word from Shenanigan," George said, "the boys need a diversion. What they don't know is they ain't *gettin'* none of that gover'ment money, now or *ever. You* and *me* are splittin' that eighty thousand between us."

George's voice sounded tense. I knowed I was hearing things I wasn't supposed to, but I'd waited too long to speak up and now I was too curious not to listen.

"Ollie Langford started dippin' into his depositors' cash almost a year ago," George continued, "and the bank examiner is arrivin' on the tenth of September, six days from now. Ollie needs a bank robbery real bad."

"Why ever did the fool man take up embezzlin' in the first place, Cap'n? Bad investments? Or did he fancy he was a gambler?"

"Oldest story since Samson got a haircut. The good banker's been supportin' a wife in the manner to which she'd got accustomed, and he's keepin' a fancy woman on the side.

"Our old friend Sheriff Wilkes found out about Ollie's sins and sold him some silence on the easy payment plan. The deal was pay up or have his missiz, and the whole damn town, find out."

"And so he paid, of course. They always do."

"Yeah. Anyway, when Ollie got word the bank examiner was on his way, he found himself betwixt the hammer and the anvil. That's when he came to me and asked for a bank robbery."

"That would be the diversion for the lads you spoke of?"

"Right. The boys get to pull a bank job, Ollie gets off the hook with the examiner, and we get to stick it to Androcles Wilkes one more time. But I've got to be sure everything's set. Somehow, I have to get in touch with Ollie, and soon."

"Well, you'd be daft to go in there yourself, cap'n— Wilkes and his deputies would spot you in a second."

"That's a fact. And he'd recognize the other boys, too. But there may be a way. What if I was to send young Merlin?"

Well, I don't mind telling you that hearing George speak my name got my full and complete attention. I froze, not moving a muscle; I dang near quit breathing. Them wasps were working in and out of their nest, and some of the feisty little varmints were flying wide circles near my face. "Please, Lord," I thought, "don't let 'em sting me now."

Then it was Shanty's voice that sounded tense. "I don't know, George," he said, "he's a good-hearted lad, but he's green as new grass. You'd be takin' a helluva chance."

131

"I've took chances before," George replied, "and anyway, I ain't got all that many options. All the fool kid has to do is find Langford, keep out of Wilkes's way, and get himself back here. How hard could *that* be?"

I held my breath. For what seemed a long time there was silence. Then George spoke again. "That's what we'll do, Shanty. Find Merlin for me, and tell him I want to see him back at the house."

"Find him I will," Shanty said, "And may the Saints ride with the lad when he goes."

"If I had the Saints ridin' for me, I wouldn't need the damn Kid," George said.

Well, I had been caught with my pants down, and no mistake. I just sat there with my new Mexican breeches around my ankles and tried not to breathe. I could hear my heart pounding in my ears, and I figured George and Shanty must surely be able to hear it, too. I quit worrying about the hornets; now I just hoped neither man would decide he needed to use the privy. ("Well, howdy, cap'n. I was just settin' here a-spyin' on your private conversation. Sure did sound interestin', yes, sir.")

After what seemed like a long time, I decided they really had gone, and I took up breathing again. My feet had gone to sleep, and they sort of tingled like they'd been soaked in sheep dip. I pulled my pants up, tucked in my shirt-tail, and belted on my Dragoon again, then I slowly eased the door open. George and Shanty were gone, all right; except for them hard-working wasps there was neither man nor critter anywhere in sight.

It didn't take me long to let myself get found. I walked into the big bar room and high-heeled it over to where Leonard the barkeep was admiring himself in a hand mirror, trying to see if his drawed-on sideburns was even. I ordered a beer, and when he slid it down the bar to me, I gave him four bits and told him to put the change toward a decent wig.

George sat at his favorite table with Shanty, and they both looked up when I came in. "Merlin," George called out, "Come set with us."

I put my fingers on my chest and raised up my eyebrows all innocent like I couldn't believe he was talking to me.

"Yeah, Kid," George said, sliding out a vacant chair with his foot, "Fetch your beer and come on over."

I walked across the floor and put my stein on the table as I eased into the chair. "Much obliged, cap'n," I said, "seems like you're feelin' better."

He showed his strong, white teeth in a broad smile. "I surely am, son," said he, "How's your leg?"

I have to admit I was enjoying myself. I knew I was being romanced, and I knew why. It was like knowing the other feller's hand in a poker game. I hadn't missed the way he'd called me "son," neither.

Twenty minutes earlier it had been "fool kid" and "damn kid," but George wanted something of me now, so all of a sudden he was dripping charm like hot molasses.

"Doin' good, Cap'n," I said, "almost as good as new."

"Glad to hear it, son."

George thumbnailed a sulphur match and lit up one of his long black stogies. He puffed on it until the tip was glowing cherry red and the smoke hung in clouds above the table, studying me all the while with that hard, steady gaze of his.

"Back when King Arthur headed up the Round Table Gang over to Camelot, he sometimes sent one of his top hands off on a special job called a *quest*. He'd pick some old boy he knowed he could trust, a man he figured would get the job done, and send him off to rescue a maiden, butcher a dragon, or somethin'.

"Well, I've got what you might call a quest for *you,* son, if you figure you can handle it."

Even knowing the old wolf was selling me a bill of goods didn't keep me from wanting his good opinion. It was like he'd showed me how to do a card trick, then went ahead and done the trick and fooled me anyway.

"Sure, George," I told him, "I'm your man."

Thirty minutes later I was on the road to Shenanigan.

TEN

Old Acquaintance

The trail snaked south out of Rampage and dropped off through the many-colored breaks and hills of the badlands to the banks of the Big Porcupine. The river in

134

late summer was muddy and wide, but not deep, and I reined the buckskin up only briefly at its edge before urging him out into the water and across.

A dozen gnarled cottonwood trees huddled together on the far bank like forlorn swimmers reluctant to take the water, and the little horse splashed over and into their meager shade, hooves clacking on the gravel as he left the river. Then I touched him with my spurs and he swept up a dry wash and out onto the dusty road that led to Shenanigan.

Little Buck clipped along in his smooth, clean-footed trot, looking this way and that with his head high and his ears working, and I knew he was as glad to be out and going again as I was myself.

George had made it plain what he wanted me to do. I was to ride into Shenanigan without being seen by Sheriff Wilkes or his deputies, locate banker Langford, and tell him the boys would be along to raid his bank Friday next if George didn't hear from him before then. Then I was to carry word back to Rampage. George hadn't explained the why of what he called my "quest," but I had overheard his talk with Shanty, so knew more than I should have, and maybe more than was good for me.

I carried a canteen, of course. It was twenty miles to Shenanigan, and almost ten before I'd reach decent water. My blanket roll was tied behind the cantle, and my saddlebags held fried bacon rolled up in leftover hotcakes from breakfast, as well as a tin of peaches and some beef jerky. There was a pretty good spring at Ten

Mile, and I figured I'd noon there and water the buckskin before riding on. I knew it would likely be sundown or later before I hit town, so figured I'd make camp on the banks of Careless Creek that evening, then slip into Shenanigan at first light and be there when the bank opened.

It felt good to be horseback again and riding the country. I took Buck off the winding road and cut across due south, keeping to the ridges as much as I could. I had learned to watch my backtrail, and I pulled up now and again to study where I'd been, but the only sign of movement in all that big country was a golden eagle circling high overhead and a pair of coyotes hunting far off to the west. I figured none of them posed much of a threat to me.

I felt light-hearted, yet somehow impatient and restless at the same time. I caught myself pushing the buckskin faster than was needful, and I drew rein to let him catch his breath while I tried to figure out why. Then, all at once, I knew. I was headed for Shenanigan, and that's the place I last saw *her.*

Well, at that point I lost all patience with young Merlin Fanshaw, alias the Bodacious Kid, alias me, and I came down on myself hard and vicious as a wolverine on a partridge.

"You dumb, bone-headed ninny," I told myself, " You don't know, and you have no *way* of knowing, whether she's still in town or not. Even if she is, there isn't much chance you'll run into her, especially while you're a-sneaking around on your secret mission. Furthermore,

136

she likely forgot you before you was even out of sight, if she ever remembered you in the first place. And finally, you muddle-headed moon-calf, you don't have a glimmerin' of an idea who she is, or even what her real *name* is."

Oh, I gave myself a tongue-lashing *I'd* never forget, but of course I *did* forget, almost that very moment. Like when someone tells you not to think of a purple bear and then all you can think about is a dang purple bear. I no sooner told myself to quit thinking about Mary Alice than all I could think about was her. I found myself hoping that somehow, some way, I would see her again, and that Destiny, or some other such foolishness, would cause it to happen on this trip.

When I got to Ten Mile there was good grass in the coulees and the spring was running clear. I watered Little Buck and let him graze in his hobbles while I filled my canteen and et some of my cold hotcakes and bacon. My thigh had gone to hurting a little, and my legs felt stiff from the ride, so I stomped around some until they loosened up. Then I tightened the girth on my saddle, mounted Buck, and took the high road to Shenanigan.

The country looked some better as I neared Careless Creek, and the dry breaks and greasewood had given way to rolling grassland and sagebrush flats that seemed to go on for two days past forever. There were a few homesteads out on the edge of the plain, and I saw smoke from their chimneys catch the day's last light as the shadows grew long and the sun slipped down toward the edge of the world.

Nightfall seems to come fast in that country. For just a minute there the heavens were a red blaze of glory and the land itself was dusted over with a soft rose light. Then, almost before I knew it, darkness covered the prairie like a gray blanket and the color bled out of the sky. As I topped a low hill just this side of Careless Creek I could make out the town of Shenanigan over on the other side, and I could already see lamplight in a few of the windows.

There was a stand of cottonwood and willow along the creek about a mile from town in a low spot that must have one time been the old creek bed. I stepped down from the buckskin back in the thick brush, slid my rig off his back, and watched his pleasure as he rolled and wallered in the loose dirt. I figured the little horse was tired enough he wouldn't go anywhere, but I hadn't come this far to take chances. Thirty yards up the creek, I found good grass, put his hobbles on, and rolled out my blankets under a tree.

I made a cold supper of the last of my hotcakes and bacon, et the peaches, and wished I had me some coffee. From across the creek, I could hear the lonesome wail of a train whistle as the southbound chuffed out of the station and slowly picked up speed on its way to Silver City. The evening star came out, bright and growing brighter as the sky got darker, and I laid back against my saddle to rest my eyes.

Next thing I knowed it was morning.

• • •

It was the sun that woke me, or leastways began to. I had slept all right, but was still far from clear-headed. It wasn't until I stumbled down to the creek and splashed water on my face that I became ready to face the day.

Over on the other side of the creek, the town was coming alive, too, and the early risers were already up and doing. From somewhere over there I heard a dog bark, and I watched as a teamster, perched high on the tank wagon, sprinkled water up and down the street to settle the dust. A pair of cowhands tied their horses in front of the Red Rooster Cafe and went inside. My belly growled from pure jealousy.

Little Buck said good mornin' with a soft nicker, and I rubbed him down with a handful of grass, saddled up, and rolled my blankets before I led the little horse to water. When he'd finally drunk his fill, I swung up on him and we splashed across what he'd left of Careless Creek and climbed the steep bank into Shenanigan.

From the angle of the sun I judged the time to be nearly eight o'clock, which meant I had an hour to kill before the bank opened. I believe I would have sold my very soul right then for a cup of coffee and a biscuit, but as much as I wanted to I knew that I dared not show my face in the cafe, or anywheres else I didn't have to.

I could picture them cowboys inside a-wolfin' down hotcakes, ham, beefsteak, eggs, and taters, and drinking hot, steaming coffee by the gallon, and in no time at all I had myself wallerin' in self pity like a spinster on a hay ride.

I knew Wilkes didn't miss much that happened in his town, and I had already seen the inside of his jail, so I swung Buck around in a big circle and rode up a side street to the alley behind the bank. There was a rickety board fence back there, and I tied the buckskin to it and loosened his cinch before checking the loads in my Colt's Dragoon and making my way around to the front of the building and across the street.

Directly across from the bank stood the hotel, and I walked over to the long loafer's bench on the gallery, set down with my back against the wall, and studied the bank.

The Shenanigan Bank occupied the first floor of a two-story building at the corner of Main and Front Streets. It was the only brick structure in town, and it sported a board-and-batten awning above a raised boardwalk.

An outside stairway led to the second floor, and the signs on the upstairs windows declared that a painless dentist and a lawyer had offices there. I suppose the lawyer was painless, too, although the sign never said so.

Anyway, I set there with my hat low over my eyes and waited for banker Langford to arrive.

It must have been nine o'clock straight up, or close to it, when a young feller wearing spectacles and a sack coat moseyed up to the bank and unlocked the front door. I say it must have been nine because even though I did not own a watch, I figured the young feller did, and that it was his job to open up on time.

There was a little more life on the street. Two doors down, a storekeeper came out and swept his sidewalk, an older gent drove by in a side-sprung buggy, and a hollow-eyed gambler came home from a hard night's work and went past me into the hotel. I stayed there on my gallery bench and waited.

Then, maybe ten minutes after the young feller opened the bank, I seen Ollie Langford come strutting up the street like he was his own parade. I had never met the man before, but there wasn't a doubt in my mind it was him. He wore a claw-hammer coat over a high collared shirt and fancy vest, and he walked all puffed up and proud, like a magpie on a manure pile. He didn't go in the front door, as the young feller had done, but unlocked a side door I figured led to his private office, glanced both ways, and proceeded inside. Five minutes later, I follered suit and walked over to the bank.

The young feller with the eyeglasses was counting money behind the counter when I came in. His coat hung on a hook inside the teller's cage, and he wore a green eyeshade and sleeve protectors. "Can I help you?" he asked.

"Why, yes, I believe you can," I told him, "I have a message for your boss."

He took a long minute to study my dusty hat, gunbelt, and my stained shaps with the bullet hole in the thigh. From the way he frowned I figured he didn't like what he saw. "Mister Langford?" he asked, "Is he *expecting* you?"

I took my hat off and whopped it against my leg. A small cloud of trail dust caught sunlight and disappeared. "I don't *believe* so," I grinned, "but I really have no way of knowin.' Might be he's got a crystal ball, or somethin'."

There was a closed door beyond the counter that I figured led to where Langford was denned up. I nodded in that direction and asked, "That his office back yonder?"

A worried look came over the teller and he came out from in back of his counter to stand between me and the door.

"Why, yes," he said, "but if he's not *expecting you* . . ."

"Well," I said, the very soul of reason, "how *could* he be expectin' me if you haven't let him know I'm *here?* Just tell him I bring word from his old Uncle George."

The teller rapped respectfully on the office door and opened it. His voice sounded like he was both afraid to deliver the message and afraid not to.

"There's a . . . gentleman . . . a *cowboy* . . . to see you, Mr. Langford. Says he brings word from your 'old Uncle George.' "

I didn't hear the reply, but I could tell young Four-eyes did, and that it confused him. "Mr. Langford will see you now," he said, "you can go in."

"Much obliged, sonny," I said, and stepped inside.

Langford was sitting at a big oak desk, facing the door, and he stood up as I came in. He was combed and curried like a show horse, and he looked fat, soft, and prosperous. His black hair and mustache was fresh trimmed, and either him or his barber had overdone the bay rum and left him smelling like a petunia patch. I judged him to be in his mid-thirties, and if he had any calluses on him anywhere I figured they was covered by his striped pants.

"I'm Ollie Langford," he said, "You say you have a message for me?"

"That's right. Original George Starkweather sent me. He said to tell you the boys will hit your bank on Friday next if he don't hear from you before then."

It was then I noticed how nervous he was. His eyes sort of jerked back and forth like he'd been set on a cookstove and was starting to feel the heat. I saw little drops of sweat on his forehead and upper lip, and he couldn't seem to keep his hands still. And then, too late, I knew why—*there was someone else in the room, behind the door.* The two sounds I heard next like to spoilt my day before it had hardly begun—the sharp double click of the hammer going back on a Colt's Peacemaker and the cold, merciless drawl of Sheriff Androcles Wilkes!

"Well, howdy there, Merlin Fanshaw," said he, "I *heard* you was in town."

I froze where I stood, and let my eyes find Wilkes on their own. He was slouched back against the wall, watching me like a snake studies a rabbit. His big six-shooter was pointed at my middle but he held it almost casual, like I was too pitiful to take account of, and I sure couldn't blame him for that. But I figured his attitude might give me an edge if I was to make a move he didn't expect. From the corner of my eye, I judged the

143

position of Wilkes, the open door, and myself.

"I know you're snipe-gutted and snake-hipped, kid," Wilkes said, "but I don't believe I could miss you at this range if I tried, and you know I don't aim to try." Covering me with his Colt's Peacemaker, he reached out his left hand to take my Dragoon from its leather.

That's when I threw my shoulder into the heavy oak door and drove it hard against him. He grunted as my weight smashed him back to the wall and jarred the Peacemaker from his hand. I slammed him into the wall again, pulled my own gun, and broke back into the bank, headed for the front door. Suddenly, a big man in a black hat blocked my path; I recognized him as the watermelon-eater I'd saw at the jail, the one I figured was Wilkes's deputy. I raised my pistol as I saw him set himself, but before I could bring it to bear he swung his right fist hard into my middle and I felt a shock and a fierce pain like I'd swallered a fire bomb. The next thing I knew I was down on the floor, looking at a big pair of dusty boots, drooling on the hardwood, and gasping for air like a trout on a riverbank.

The pain rolled through my body in jagged red waves as I laid there a-hugging my midsection and tasting the floor wax. Even my hair hurt, and I wished I could die just for the relief of it. Worst of all, I couldn't seem to get my wind, and I kept gagging and trying to until I thought my head would explode from the pressure. Then, finally, I could breathe again, and I sucked air in like a blacksmith's bellows.

I heard Wilkes's voice, deep and far away, like from

inside a cave, saying, "You're quite a disappointment to me, son. I do believe you've gone back on our agreement and have took to running with the bad 'uns."

I had enough sass left in me to reply, "*You're* the bad 'un, Wilkes."

The big man in the black hat jerked me to my feet by my hair and grinned at me. He had a broad, flat face like a sandstone cliff which featured a broken nose, a gap-toothed smile, and two black beady eyes set close together like the barrels of a shotgun.

"The gent who stopped your runaway just now is my deputy, Faunt Bodeen," Wilkes said. He dabbed at his nose with his bandanna and I saw with some pleasure that I'd bloodied it when I slammed the door on him. He turned to the big man. "Go lock him up, Faunt," he said, "and draw the man his bath."

Faunt's black marble eyes sort of glowed. His snaggle-toothed grin got wider, and there was something about the way he looked at me that sent a chill straight up my backbone. If demons grin, I reckon that's how *they* do it.

Both cells were empty when we got to the jail, and Bodeen throwed me in the first one. He had locked my hands behind me with handcuffs and I backed up 'til I touched the bunk and set down on it. Then he brought a heavy wooden tub that looked like half a rain barrel into the other cell and began filling it up with water, two buckets at a time. I'd hear the pump a-squeaking outside as he filled the buckets, and then he'd carry them past my cell and grin that demon grin as he poured the water into the tub. Every time he passed me his gun barrel eyes would glow, and I came to believe that whatever Androcles Wilkes had in store for me would in no way resemble kind and humane treatment.

Directly, the old he-bull himself showed up. Wilkes sort of shook his head, went into the cell where the tub was, set down on the bunk, and studied me through the bars. Bodeen leaned against the open cell door and chewed on a match. "Fetch him in here, Faunt," Wilkes said.

The big deputy took hold of my arms and half dragged, half carried me into the second cell, where he set me down on my knees in front of the tub. Wilkes put his hands on his thighs and looked thoughtful.

"Faunt here spotted you when you were camped across the creek last evenin.' He slipped across downstream, looked things over, and reported back to me. I didn't recognize you from his description right off, but when he told me about the buckskin horse with my brand on him I figured the prodigal had returned.

"Struck me as curious why you wouldn't ride on in and report to me, and I was forced to conclude that George Starkweather must have made you a better offer. You have no idea how that disappoints me, son.

"Faunt and me watched you ride in this mornin', saw you tie up behind the bank, and cross over to the hotel. I was in the alley when Langford came to work, and when you started for the front door I follered him in the side while Faunt trailed you in the front.

"Now I know all about Ollie's problems with the examiner, and about him askin' George to cover his shortage by robbin' the bank. Ollie sent word through Elmo the barkeep at Dry Creek, who passed it on to George through a hardcase named Kiowa John.

"Then a few weeks ago, George and two of his *pistoleros* gunned four drifters in Elmo's place, and George sent Elmo back with a note for Ollie. All it said was, 'When? Give Elmo your answer. Signed: George.'"

Wilkes took his watch from his vest pocket and commenced to wind it.

"Well, sir," he said, "I asked Elmo where he was to take the answer, but he was scared George would kill him if he told. I said I understood, but that *I'd* kill him if he *didn't*.

"Turned out Elmo was more scared of George than he was of me, and he wouldn't tell. Then, while Faunt was questioning him, the poor feller had a real bad accident and passed away, so you might say old Elmo cheated me out of an answer.

"Now I *will* get George when he comes in Friday, but there will no doubt be shootin', and that will pose a danger to the good people of my town, stray dogs, livestock, and what not. So I would prefer to just go get him where he is."

Wilkes held the watch up to his ear, listened, and looked back at me.

"Anyway, here you come with another message from George, and I am glad to know when he'll be here. But

147

I'd still like you to tell me where he is now, how many men he has ridin' with him, and so forth. You will do that, won't you, son?"

"Go to hell, Androcles," I told him.

He didn't seem to take offense at my rude reply; he just looked sort of weary, and he breathed a long sigh. "I was afraid you'd say that, Merlin," he said.

He looked at Faunt and nodded his head, and the deputy came around behind me and took hold of the back of my head with a grip like a vise. I was impressed by the size of his hand; I felt his thumb back of my left ear and his fingertips over behind my right.

Wilkes held the watch out at arm's length and squinted at its face. "You're gonna bob for apples, son," he said, "except there ain't no apples, so I reckon you'll just bob. We'll start him off at sixty seconds, Faunt . . . I'll tell you when."

Faunt plunged my head into the tub and under water with a sudden, strong push and held me down. I tried to stiffen up and resist, but I might as well have been pushing against a locomotive. Bubbles roared up past my ears and I fought to hold my breath. I could feel the handcuffs cut into my wrists as I struggled, and the pressure began to build behind my eyes. I felt a terrible fear that I was going to drown. I commenced to twist and thrash about with all my might, but it was no use. I strangled, choked, breathed in water, and panicked altogether. Then, suddenly, Faunt let my head up. I exploded back and out of that tub, spraying water and sliding on my knees as I desperately inhaled. Nothing was ever sweeter or more welcome than the air in that dank cell.

I blinked, gagged, and shook water from my eyes and nose. Wilkes sat there on the bunk like a kindly schoolteacher, smiling as if he'd just asked me what two plus two equals.

"I have to be honest with you, Merlin," he said, "it don't get any easier from here on out. We'll try a minute forty-five next. *Where's George?*"

Inside my head I was having another of them conversations with myself that I seem so partial to. Why *didn't* I just tell Wilkes where George was? What was it that made me take the side of a notorious outlaw against the duly elected sheriff of the county? Marshal Ridgeway had told me Wilkes was crooked; well, maybe he was, but that only made him and George the same.

Maybe it was my fool contrary nature, or maybe it was just prideful cussedness, but the way I saw it George had stood up for me like my Pa would have. George had took me in, he'd gunned Mace on my account, and he'd doctored my wound after the shooting affray at Dry Creek. Besides all that—and I know this part don't make no sense at all—I just *liked* George, regardless of all I knew him to be, and I dang sure *didn't* like Wilkes. Feelings don't seem to pay much heed to *should* and *ought to.*

I coughed up water awhile and asked, "George *who?*" Wilkes looked above my head at Faunt, nodded, and I went under again.

Androcles Wilkes was right about one thing: it didn't

get any easier. The fourth time Faunt pushed me down I didn't think I was ever coming up again. My body took over and fought for its life without no help at all from my brain, and I could feel my legs kicking and slipping on the wet stone floor like a frog on ice. That's when I decided if by some miracle I didn't die and they let me up again I would tell Wilkes everything I ever knew about *everybody* . I would even make up what I *didn't* know if it would please him and keep my head out in the fresh air where it belonged. As things turned out I never had to do that; right then I suddenly stopped struggling, passed out, and slid through a red haze into a cozy black pit where I could curl up and rest forever in the silence.

When I came to I was laying face up on the wet cell floor and Bodeen was pushing on my middle with them big hands of his. My throat and lungs felt like they was on fire, and I kept a-retching and coughing up water. I was not, at the moment, glad to be back in the land of the living; right then I just wanted to return to the snug hiding place I'd found in my mind and sleep. Faunt grabbed my arms again and set me back on my knees over the tub. I was surprised to see there was still water in it; I could have swore I had swallered it all.

Wilkes still sat on the bunk, holding his watch, and there was neither kindness nor pity in his eyes, no more than if I was a bug.

"You're a damn fool if you die for George Stark-weather," he said, "you've got your whole life ahead of you, kid."

For a long moment I was quiet. I felt Faunt grip my head again, and I stopped resisting and took to deception.

"All right," I lied, "George is in Dry Creek."

ELEVEN

Much Ado about Something

Wilkes looked up sharply. "Dry Creek?" he asked, "Whereabouts in Dry Creek?"

It is amazing how creative a man can become when he's trying to avoid something unpleasant, like being drowned by a plug ugly in a tub. My brain went from a slow walk to a full gallop.

"You know where the old Parker Hotel is?" I asked.

"Know where it *was*," Wilkes said, "at the edge of town, beyond the Livery Barn. But that building's empty. Abandoned years ago."

"Well, it's not empty now. Original George Starkweather is there, with a dozen men."

Wilkes looked interested in spite of himself. Slowly, he returned his watch to the pocket of his vest. I felt the deputy's grip on my head ease up a little. "How come you didn't let me know sooner, like we agreed?" Wilkes asked.

"I won't lie to you, Sheriff," I said, lying to him, "at first I couldn't get away because I was watched. And later, I guess I came to be like Elmo, more scared of George than of you."

I must have been a sight. I knelt there on the wet floor, my hands locked behind me, drooling spit, and soaking wet from the top down. I'd cut my lip on the edge of the tub during my struggles, and blood was dripping off my chin into the water. Worst of all, I was starting to shiver, from the cold and nerves both, I reckon.

I could see Wilkes wasn't sure whether to believe me or not. It was so quiet in that cell I could hear the ticking of his pocket watch as he studied me. His fingers drummed a slow rhythm on his thigh.

"You know if I ride all the way to Dry Creek and George ain't there, I'm gonna be disappointed, don't you, son?" he said quietly.

"Yes, sir," I told him, "but like you said, I'd be a damn fool to die for George Starkweather. He's there, all right."

Wilkes stood up and walked to the cell door. "He'd *better* be, son," he said, "he had better *be.*"

He looked at Bodeen. "Take the cuffs off him, Faunt, and lock him in the other cell. I'll need you to watch him while I'm gone."

"You ain't gonna ride over to Dry Creek on *his* say-so, are you, Sheriff?" Bodeen said, "Damn pup would say anythin' to save his hide."

"Maybe," Wilkes agreed, "but he knows we'll squeeze him even harder if he's lyin', maybe even snuff his damn candle. I figure it's worth my takin' a look-see."

Bodeen hauled me to my feet and unlocked the hand-cuffs. Getting up sudden like that gave me a sick, woozy feeling, and I came near to passing out, but I managed to stumble along ahead of the big deputy into the first cell and set down on the bed before that happened.

Faunt Bodeen locked the cell door and grinned his scary, gap-toothed grin at me through the bars. "You ain't out of the woods yet, kid," he said, then he turned away and followed Wilkes into the office.

I laid back on the bunk and shut my eyes. I had bought a little time, that's all, maybe two days at the outside. Wilkes would not find George and the boys at Dry Creek, and he would come back to deal with me.

Bodeen had left the office door ajar, and I could hear him talking to Wilkes.

"Why don't you just telegraph the town marshal at Dry Creek and ask him if Starkweather's there?" he asked, "Be a helluva lot easier than ridin' all that way."

"Easier ain't always *better,* Faunt," Wilkes said, "Marshal Fillmore is a damn joke. Starkweather, if he's in Dry Creek, has either bought him off, scared him off, or run him off. Besides, George would be watching the telegraph office. No, I need to take some boys and go see for myself."

"Well, good huntin', then. If you don't find him, we'll get him on Friday when he brings his gang in to rob the bank."

"That's a fact. Original George and his desperados will think they have walked into a hailstorm of lead in that second before we blow the bastards back to hell where they came from." His voice took on a chilly note, and it felt like the temperature dropped twenty degrees as he said, "It ain't my habit to get personal about my work, but I hate that bastard George Starkweather a-goin' and a'comin', and from hell to breakfast."

I heard Wilkes's footfall as he clumped angrily across the office to the door and went out, and I laid there and thought about the way men came to stand against one another. A cardsharp at Dry Creek had told me once that a man's status in the pecking order could be judged by the hatred of his enemies, and I thought if that was so then Original George was Top Dog indeed.

I must have dozed off for awhile because when next I opened my eyes I didn't know where I was or how I got there. But then the events of the day came drifting back and I allowed remembrance to blow through my mind like a cool breeze.

My gut still hurt from where Bodeen had hit me that morning at the bank. As I pondered the way he'd done me, both then and since, I began to take offense. I remembered the way his black eyes had glowed and the way he'd bared his snaggly teeth as he filled the tub, and I recalled his strong grip while he was a-drowning me. The more I thought about them things the more hostile I became. It was bad enough being abused by that big deputy without him having such a good time about it, and I decided right then I'd had a bellyful of being mauled. I told myself I was either the Bodacious Kid or I was a sheep in a shearing pen, and I couldn't find no place on me where I was a-growing wool.

I knew I had to get shut of that county hotel and hit the high places between there and Rampage. George had to be warned that Wilkes and his deputies were waiting for him, and that the boys would be riding headlong into an ambush if they came in on Friday. Through the open door I could hear Wilkes's swivel chair squeak, and I knew that Faunt was setting in it and pretending *he* was the sheriff of Progress County, which I figured he was mean enough to be but not smart enough.

"Faunt!" I bellered, "Get your fat ass in here, you yeller-bellied tub o' guts . . . I've got somethin' to *tell you!*"

I heard the chair creak, and Faunt's big feet hit the floor and carried him to the doorway and through it. That crazy glow was in his eyes again, and the demon grin had come back, too.

"You want to say that again, big mouth?" he said, "I don't believe I quite *heard* you the first time."

"Oh, I guess you heard me all right. It's not your ears that's the problem, it's your feeble brain. You ain't even *half* smart, Faunt.

"I heard you playin' sheriff in there, with your feet up on the desk and all, and I couldn't help but laugh. You wouldn't make a pimple on a real sheriff's ass."

His eyes glowed even brighter, but his grin vanished. He took a step closer to the bars. "What's got into you, kid?" he asked, "You tired of livin'?"

"Hell, no," I taunted, "I just ain't all that impressed by *bulk*. I got this notion I can *whip* your sorry ass, if my

155

hands ain't locked behind me."

Faunt frowned, and I could see the color rise in his meaty face. "You best shut your damn mouth before I come in there and let you try," he said, "I'll squash you like the scrawny little pissant you are."

I slid off the bed, planted my feet wide on the stone floor, and grinned. "Come on ahead, then," says I.

His scowl deepened, and I could see his mind working, like a wolf sniffing for a trap. For a moment I thought he was going to turn and walk away, but then his wicked grin came back and I knew he'd taken the bait.

He shucked his gun and belt, laid them on the gallery table, and lifted the cell key from its peg near the office door. "You're dead meat, kid," he said.

The cell door swung open with a rusty screech as the big man stepped inside and fixed his gun-muzzle eyes upon me. He looked wary but not worried, and my next move both surprised and confused him. I stepped back, dropped to the floor, drawed my knees up, and went to crawfishing like a pup in a dog fight.

"I didn't mean it, deputy," I cried, all high-pitched and whiney, "I was just foolin'! D-Don't hurt me!"

Faunt was almost on top of me, and he looked down at where I was cringing and groveling, and I saw puzzlement cross his face. For just a second, he hesitated, and that turned out to be plenty. I grabbed the bars near the floor and kicked out hard, straight, and nasty.

My boot heel caught Faunt's left knee, and I heard him grunt as it popped and his leg went out from under him. I stomped him in the crotch as he was going down and heard him roar in pain like a mad bear. Quick as a cat, I scrambled to my feet and sidestepped him, and I confess I was remembering the tub and his big hands forcing my head underwater when I clubbed him double-handed into the bars. I followed that with another two-handed chop to the back of his neck, and I saw his eyes glaze as he began to sag toward the floor.

I knew my only chance was to keep out of his reach, and I hit him again and dodged around behind him and through the cell door. He was back on his feet and swearing with rage as I swung the big door shut in his face and turned the key in the lock. He made a wild grab for me, but I danced back out of his reach and grinned at him. "See what I mean?" I said, "If brains was castor oil you couldn't physic a chigger."

I picked up his belt and pistol and ambled over to the office door, where I turned and looked at him. He was gripping the bars so hard his knuckles was white, and he was so mad he was speechless, but I knew he wouldn't stay that way for long.

"I'm taking your six-shooter and whatever else I can think of from the office," I told him, "Wish I could be around to hear you explain this to Wilkes, but I've got places to go."

That's when Bodeen found his voice again. He commenced to cuss and holler until I feared he'd perish of apoplexy, and I don't know to this day what *some* of those things he called me *are*.

I found my old Dragoon with its holster and belt

hanging on a rack in the office, and I strapped it on and felt like my old self once again. Faunt had been eating fried chicken from a basket, and I figured he wouldn't mind sharing so I took what was left and bolted out the front door and onto the street.

First thing I saw when I broke into the sun was a white-haired sodbuster, wearing dashboard overalls, and a hay hat. Behind me, Faunt was ranting and raving even louder than before, and I figured he could be heard in most parts of Progress County, if not the west part of the state.

The farmer went wall-eyed and shaky, and for a minute there I thought he was going to stampede and go to running.

"Sheepherder went crazy this morning up at his camp," I told him, "Had to fetch him down and lock him up inside. Poor devil thinks he's a deputy sheriff."

There were three horses in the corral behind the jail, and as luck would have it one of them was Little Buck. Wilkes hadn't even unsaddled him, but had just loosened the girth and tied him to a corral pole. I swung the gate open, tightened the cinch, mounted the buckskin, and with a whoop and a holler ran the other two horses out toward the tall and uncut.

Buck seemed to sense my mood. I could feel his muscles ripple and bunch beneath me, and at the touch of my spur the little horse lit out for Careless Creek like he was trying to outrun his shadow. The rumble of the bridge planks under his hooves inspired him still further, and I barely had time to fling the cell key out into the creek before we were across and fogging it up the long road to the badlands.

It was past midnight by the time I struck the Big Porcupine. The twisted trees stood dark along the riverbank and moonrise painted the muddy water silver as Little Buck splashed across and loped on toward Rampage. When I rode up to the barn Poddy Medford was standing guard. He throwed down on me with his Winchester and hollered, "Who's there?" and I told him it was me and said I surely would appreciate it if he didn't shoot me. Poddy cussed me and grumbled some about me riding up hard and sudden the way I had, but he put the rifle up and went back inside the barn.

I pulled my rigging off Little Buck and walked him around awhile in the corral to cool him out. His breath came in quick, rattling gasps and he was thick lathered and hot as a stove. I was more pleased than ever with his toughness, heart, and willing nature. We had busted a hole in the breeze all the way from Shenanigan, going from a high lope to a trot and back again, and the little buckskin had gave me everything he had, and borrowed some from tomorrow. Directly, I put him in a stall, rubbed him down, and headed for the main house to report to George.

As I walked up to the front door, Flea Hotel, the mangy dog Slippery Mayfair kept around the place, came out a-barking like he thought I was a bear or a catamount, but I flung a rock at him and he found other things to do.

The lower level of the house was dark, but there was a light on upstairs and I groped my way through the bar and climbed the steps. A smoky lamp lit the upper hallway, and I could see a pencil-thin beam at the threshold of Bucktooth Betty's room. Then the door opened a crack and a wedge of lamplight flowed out into the hall. A deep voice challenged, "Who's there?" and I could not have mistaken George's hoarse rasp.

"It's me, cap'n, it's Merlin," I told him, "I have to talk to you."

The door swung wide, and there he stood. He was bare of foot and chest, wearing only his drawers, and he held one of his long-barreled Colt's in his right hand. "Come in, then," he said, and stepped back into the room.

I purely hate it when I blush, but I don't seem able to do a dang thing about it; I just feel my ears a-growing hot, and I turn beet-red and bashful as a school girl. As I entered the room, I could tell I was blushing again.

George had gone back to the huge old bed and set down on the edge of the mattress, and I seen both Betty and the Belgian Mare was a-laying there with him. I have no idea why I was so flustered; them ladies wasn't exactly *ladies,* after all, and *they* sure didn't seem to be embarrassed. The Belgian Mare did pull a sheet up over her bosoms, though, and Betty gave me a shy smile from behind a pillow and wiggled her dainty fingers at me for a greeting.

"Take a walk somewheres, darlin's," George told them, "I need to talk to Merlin for a minute."

Them sisters of joy slid out of bed and scampered off down the hall like deer, which I admit surprised me some because the Belgian Mare was a heavy-set woman and I never thought she'd be so light on her feet.

George cleared off a chair and bade me set, so I did. He lit up a stogie, leaned back, and fixed me with a steady gaze. "Go ahead, son," he said.

Quick and clear as I knowed how, I gave George the bobtail version of everything that had happened on my trip. Good King George laid back on the bed with his cheroot and his raggedy drawers and listened while Sir Merlin the Bold spake of his quest unto the hamlet of Shenanigan, of his meeting with Sir Ollie the Crooked, of his capture by the Black Knight Wilkes, and of torture most foul by water in the dungeon of Wilkes's castle.

George's eyes lit up when I told him how I'd sent Wilkes on a wild goose chase to Dry Creek and locked Bodeen in his own cell, but when I warned him about the planned ambush he just smiled and closed his eyes.

For what seemed a long time he said nothing, and I sat there and waited. I had never seen George without his shirt, and it was hard at first to match that scarred, sunburnt face with the fish-belly white of his body. His trunk was heavy-matted with black hair going to gray, and was so white it looked like a shirt next to the deep brown of his neck. There were old scars on the right side of his chest I took to be bullet wounds, and a ragged red streak lower down that I figured had been made by a knife. His left forearm sported a blue tattoo of a skull and crossbones, with the words 'No Quarter' underneath, and he had still another scar down near his wrist.

George opened his eyes and studied me carefully for a moment. "You done well, Sir Merlin the Bodacious," he said. He got up from the bed and made his way to a tall dresser near the window, where a bottle of the good Tennessee whiskey stood amid perfume bottles, powder puffs, jewel boxes, and other female truck. George turned his back to me, and I could hear the clink of the bottle on glass. "We need to have a drink to celebrate your successful mission," he said, "then we'll talk about the ambush."

I didn't much feel like a drink. I'd had a long, hard couple of days, and all I wanted was sleep. "Well," I said, "all right, cap'n. Maybe just one."

George turned around, and I saw he held a half-filled glass of the good Tennessee in each hand. He handed me one glass, and raised the other. "Here's how," he said.

"How," I said, and we drank.

The whiskey went down smooth as silk, and as I sat there and felt its heat spread through me I realized how played out I really was. I had rode eighty miles a-horseback over the last two days, I'd been whupped on, dang near drowned, and generally abused. I had got in a few licks of my own and had brought word of Wilkes's trap back to my chief. Of a sudden I felt bone weary and dog tired.

George studied me with his cold, bold stare, but he didn't say a word. He had a peculiar sort of half smile on his face, and I had the feeling he was *waiting* for something. Had I made myself clear? Did he understand that the raid on the Shenanigan bank was doomed? Somehow I had to make sure he *did* know, so I tried again.

"Cap'n," I said, "Wilkes and his deputies . . . the whole town . . . will be *waiting* for you and the boys on Friday. If you ride in there . . ."

"I know, son," George replied softly, "that's why I ain't a-going. I'm sendin' the boys."

The air seemed to have suddenly left the room; I had trouble getting my breath. I tried to get up out of the chair, but I couldn't move, and when I tried to speak, no words came out.

"You see, son," George continued, his voice sounding slowed down and draggy, "the boys have got to be a sort of problem to me, always after me to give them their share of that Army money and all, so I figured I'd let 'em have the Shenanigan bank instead.

"Oh, I suppose some of 'em will maybe die, all right, or wind up in jail, but like I told you before, Merlin, sometimes a leader has to take *measures*."

The room felt hot; I was sweating and shaky. My mouth was dry, and there was a ringing in my ears like crickets on a summer night as I tried again to get on my feet.

"Had to put a little somethin' extra in your whiskey," George went on, "only thing to do short of killin' you,

163

son. I can't have you tellin' the boys and havin' them maybe call off the raid, can I?"

I broke free of the chair at last and sort of tottered on my feet for a second. Then I tilted forward like a toppled tree, and the pattern on Buck-tooth Betty's Oriental rug swooped up and smacked me on the nose.

TWELVE

Going to the Turkey Shoot

I dreamed I was a pirate at the bottom of the sea. I had been made to walk the plank by a bold buccaneer who looked for all the world like Sheriff Wilkes, and I plunged beneath the waves to the very depths of Davy Jones's Locker. I tried to hold my breath as I went down, but drowned, of course, and my poor carcass came to rest amid sunken galleons, chests full of gold doubloons, and dead men who told no tales.

I recall I was mighty scared during the actual drowning, but afterward it was almost peaceful just laying there in the half light amongst the seaweed, watching the fish as they swam past overhead and tried to swaller one another. I thought maybe I'd meet up with a mermaid or something. For what seemed a long while I waited there, but finally I gave up, closed my eyes, and took me a nap.

Next thing I knew I popped off the sea bed like a cork from a bottle and rose up out of the darkness toward the surface, and light. Then, all of a sudden, I broke out into sunlight and the motion stopped.

I squinched my eyes against the brightness, breathed deep, and knew by the misery I felt that I had returned to the land of the living. My mouth was dry as dust, and my tongue felt big as a cow's. I caught a whiff of my own breath, and came near to passing out all over again. It smelled like a blend of hog slop, Limburger cheese, and a trash fire. I believe it could have took old paint off of wood.

There was a dull, thudding ache behind my eyes, and when I tried to move it grew into a pounding hurt that made me go quiet again. My nose seemed to be working all right; I could smell fresh coffee, old whiskey, and the sweet, heavy rose perfume so favored by the strumpets of Rampage.

I lay still, and the memories came drifting back into my mind like ducks lighting on a pond—the ride to Shenanigan, my troubles there, and the long ride back. I remembered Original George and the cold, flat sound of his voice when he said, "sometimes a leader has to take *measures*." And then I remembered the drugged whiskey and the blackness, and I opened my eyes.

The bright sunlight slanting in through the window blinded me for a second or two, and then I saw Buck-tooth Betty. She was wearing a silk wrapper and a troubled expression, and she carried a tray that held a coffee pot and two chipped china cups.

"Welcome back, cowboy," she said, "I was beginnin' to worry about you."

"You had cause," I said thickly, "that snooze potion the cap'n slipped me like to done me in."

"Yeah," she said sadly, "I feel like that was partly my fault. I keep some knockout drops in a little blue bottle on the dresser there in case a customer goes to acting rude. One time I told the captain about 'em."

Betty's dark eyes and buck teeth gave her the comical look of a good-hearted beaver. I reckon she might have been a real beauty if it wasn't for them teeth; poor Betty could have et corn on the cob through a picket fence and never miss a kernel.

She handed me a cup of coffee, and I tried to hold it steady with my shaky hands but wound up spilling some on me and on the bedclothes.

"You've been asleep almost thirty hours," she said, "George gave you more of that stuff than he should have."

"If I had my druthers I druther he wouldn't have drugged me at all," I said, "Where is the good captain today—out tormentin' widows and orphans, or just pullin' the wings off flies?"

"He's gone," Betty said wistfully, "they're *all* gone."

"*Gone?* Gone *where?*"

"I ain't altogether sure," she said, "but they are gone, all but you. Everybody except George and Shanty rode out on the Shenanigan road an hour ago, and *those* two headed off elsewhere maybe a half hour later."

"My head feels like there's bull buffalo fightin' inside it, and I'm not thinkin' too clear, Betty. What day is today?"

"You mean day of the week, darlin'? Why, it's Friday."

I handed my cup back to her, laid back down, and closed my eyes. "Yes," I said, "I guess it would be."

Clear as if I was riding with them, I could see the boys going on down the road. They'd be laughing and joking, or they'd be quiet and tense, but they'd be looking forward to the robbery and the way danger made the air taste sweeter and their hearts beat faster.

They'd be looking forward to the money, too, and to what it would buy them, but mainly it would be the risk and the wild, free way it made them feel. That's the way I felt about running mustangs and riding rough stock. I figured men mostly did whatever it was they done so they could feel alive and in charge of theirselves.

Pike and Kiowa John would be in the lead, follered by Clete and Poddy, and back behind them would be Jigger on his patchwork pony, grinning his slack-jawed grin and maybe singing "Mary had a Little Lamb" to himself as he rode. The boys would be moving slow, going easy on the horses so as to save them for the get-away, and they could have no idea of the fiery Hell that waited for them on the streets of Shenanigan.

Still shaky, I got myself up off the bed and pulled my boots on while Betty scampered downstairs to fetch me some breakfast. I leaned my hands on the window sill and looked out in the direction the boys had gone, but the land lay still and empty of movement under a hot morning sun.

Then another picture came to my mind, this time of Androcles Wilkes, Faunt Bodeen, and all the other deputies and men of Shenanigan as they cleaned and loaded pistols, shotguns, and rifles in preparation for the day's sport, like fellers getting ready for a turkey shoot. *Their* hearts would be beating faster, too, and many would be looking forward to this chance to kill other men and to be upstanding public citizens while they done it. Only they wouldn't *be* upstanding in the strict sense; most of them bold townsfolk would be a-crouching behind cover, and they'd do their killing from ambush.

Betty came back with a plateful of corn bread covered by a dish towel and a pot of baked beans, and I et everything but the towel. By the time I'd follered that up with most of a pot of coffee I had made up my mind. I couldn't let the boys ride into that town and up to that bank like critters to a slaughterhouse without at least trying to warn them. Maybe I wouldn't catch them in time, and maybe they wouldn't listen to me if I did, but I could try; even a steer can try.

I thanked Betty for the vittles and for the use of her bed, and I gave her a kiss on the cheek as I left. I told her that money and me were strangers right then, but that I'd remember her kindness should I ever be solvent again, and that I might come by one day and bring her a pretty.

"You've been a friend, Betty," I told her, "giving me Romeo's pants and all. Much obliged, until you're better paid."

Her dark eyes kind of misted up and she blowed her nose on the dish towel before she spoke. "Don't mention it, darlin'," she said, "if there's anything *else* I can do—on the *house,* of course . ..."

But I was already through the door and on my way downstairs. Danged if I wasn't blushing again.

A man would have thought a freshwater spring unlikely in that badlands country around Rampage, but there was one, and I reckon it was the reason folks had built there in the first place. It flowed out of a hill back of the big house, but someone had long ago piped water over to a trough at the barn and that's where I found Little Buck. He whinnied when he seen me, as if to say, "Where the hell have *you* been?" but he didn't look near as worn down as I thought he would.

I knew it would take hard riding if I hoped to catch up with the boys, and I knew Buck had just made the hard, twenty mile trip twice. But I knew, too, that he was a tough little dickens, and that my thirty-hour nap had gave him a chance to rest up some, too.

The big old barn and corrals were empty now, and the whole shebang looked downright forlorn. Slippery Mayfair owned some good horses, of course, and Jackrabbit Annie had a fair driving team, but they had all been taken out to graze by the wrangler and Buck was the only horse still on the place. "Looks like you're elected, old son," I told him.

I gave him a quick brushing, slid my Navajo blanket up past his withers, and went to pick up my saddle from

169

the rack. It was then I saw the deerskin pouch tied to the horn by its pucker strings, and a note stuck to it with a horseshoe nail.

"Sir Merlin," it read, "Sum fellers just kant hold their likker. Haw Haw. The munny is to keep you eating til you git wurk. You aint cut out to be no dam desperado anyways. Yur frend, sinserly, George."

I thought: For a feller who read as many books as he did, Original George Starkweather couldn't spell worth sic'em.

There was a hundred dollars in gold coin in that pouch. I just looked at the money for a spell, put it in my pants pocket together with the note, and finished saddling Buck. When he heard me say low and quiet, "You bloodthirsty, cold-hearted, likeable bastard," the little horse looked like he thought I was talking to him.

It didn't take Little Buck any time at all to savvy what I wanted of him; I pointed him south, touched his flanks with my hooks, and he took us through the painted hills and washes like a prairie fire in a gale. Once we'd crossed the river, I let the little horse run flat out until I felt him start to labor, then pulled him back to an easy lope that covered the country but allowed him to catch his breath.

The day was not as hot as when we'd come this way before, but I sure never saw no igloos neither. It wasn't long before we were both sweating free. Dust rose up in a plume behind us, and I scanned the country for some sign of the boys, but they were nowhere in sight. I had hoped I might catch up to them at Ten Mile, and I remembered the good grass and water there, but when I rode in all I found was their tracks. They had come and gone, and they were traveling faster than I ever thought they would.

We didn't tarry long ourselves. I waited 'til Buck got his wind and then rode him out at a high lope on the road to Shenanigan once again. Before long, I left the road and took to the ridges, straining to see dust from the boys' horses off in the distance, but saw none. The boys had left the road, too, and I could see by their tracks they were riding hell-for-leather and devil take the hindmost.

I pushed the little horse still harder then, and he gave me all he had, but I knew with a sinking feeling we were too late. By the time we thundered across the bridge outside town I could already hear the first gunshots from over at the bank.

My heart was hammering louder than the gunfire as I spurred Buck up the street past Cherokee Bob's and on toward Main. People were running out of the buildings and along the boardwalks like bees from a hive, and most of them were carrying guns. I seen one feller with soap on his face and a barber's cloth still around his neck trying to run and load a shotgun at the same time. I also seen a barefoot kid of maybe nine or ten cut across the street in front of me with a rusty old flintlock that was bigger than he was.

When I turned the corner onto the square it looked like the last minutes at the Alamo. People were shooting from the windows of the hotel and on top of the roof. It seemed to me that everyone in town except invalid grandmas and babies in their cribs had come to join in the blood-letting.

Over at the bank I saw that Jigger's ill-favored pony was down in the street kicking and dying, and through the smoke I could see Poddy Medford at the hitchrack struggling to hold the other horses. They were rearing and striking in blind panic, and I saw Poddy's own bay take a slug and go down with a scream like a scared woman.

I figured the other boys were still inside the bank, pinned down by the wild shooting outside. I could see bullets splinter the board awning and throw up little clouds of brick dust when they struck the building, and a marksman somewhere who couldn't even have been *trying* shot the glass out of both the upstairs windows.

I pulled my Henry from its saddle scabbard and levered a shell into the chamber. Buck was jittering in the dust with nervous little quicksteps, and his eyes were wide with fear, but he neither blowed up nor cut and run. In the midst of all the clatter and confusion I know it was silly to even think of it, but I was proud of him.

My eyes blurred, and I realized I was crying like a dang kid out of pure bafflement. I held the Henry rifle and my horse, but I had no idea what to do. Who was I going to shoot? What could I do to help the boys? I slid the Henry back into its boot, feeling helpless as a bug on flypaper. All I could do was watch as a sudden volley blew poor Poddy to doll rags and the horses broke loose and took flight.

I managed to catch Kiowa's blue roan as it ran past and held onto its reins with a death grip. Right then the front door opened and Clete Potter came out pushing the banker, Ollie Langford, in front of him for a shield, with the other boys following.

A wagon had been rolled into the street across from the bank, and Sheriff Andy Wilkes stepped out from behind it calm as if he was strolling to church. Cold as ice and plum' deliberate, he set his feet and shot first Langford and then Clete with two blasts from a sawed-off shotgun. Wilkes passed the scattergun to his left hand then and pulled his pistol, just as Kiowa and Pike Fletcher came out.

I screamed like a gutshot cougar and spurred into the fray, pulling the frightened roan behind me. I saw Wilkes look up in surprise as I rode down on him. His face went dark and he tried to bring his pistol to bear, but it was too late. Little Buck's shoulder struck his chest and jarred him off his feet, and the sheriff went down in the dirt underneath the buckskin's hooves.

Pa had told me of Indian warriors who sang their death songs in battle, and I'd always admired their bravery. Well, I *wasn't* brave but scared aplenty, and the death song I heard right then was the angry whip and whine of bullets passing. With one hand guiding Little Buck and the other leading Kiowa's roan, I couldn't even return the fire. When I looked back and saw that Wilkes was back on his feet again and firing at me, I very nearly became discouraged.

I'll never know why I wasn't killed right then and there; the sound of gunfire was a ragged roar all around. I could see smoke and tongues of orange fire stabbing through it, every one of them a-looking for a vital part of me. I crouched low in the saddle, slid to Buck's off side, and pulled the roan on around past the bank as Kiowa swung into his saddle on the fly.

Pike Fletcher was behind him, clutching a money bag to his chest with his left arm while he fired toward the wagon with his right. I saw dust fly as a bullet smacked hard into the bag, and Pike dropped it just as a second slug struck him high in the chest. Stunned, he caught the back of Kiowa's saddle and was trying to get up behind him when a third bullet took him in the head and he fell loose and heavy as a sack of sand to the dusty street.

I spurred the little buckskin around the corner and drove hard for the alley, with Kiowa John close behind me. As we swept past the bank's side door, Jigger St. Clare stepped out, grinning his idiot grin, and said, "Cock a doodle doo! Howdy doodle to you!" I slowed Buck to a near stop, gave Jigger my arm, and lined out again as he swung up behind me. Then we turned into the alley and hightailed it for deliverance and a climate where the air contained less lead. I don't know to this day what it was about chickens and Jigger St. Clare, but there wasn't a doubt in my mind that it was time for us to fly the coop.

We had nearly cleared the alley when I saw the man

with the rifle. He was an old man with white hair and chin whiskers. He had tottered out into our path and was aiming what looked to be an old Confederate musket at us. Behind me, I heard Jigger cock his pistol somewhere near my right ear.

"Don't shoot him, Jigger," I said, "he's just an old man."

"Old man with a *rifle,*" he grunted, "old fool ain't *getting* no *older.*"

I reined Little Buck hard to the left and into somebody's back yard just as Jigger fired, and I heard him swear and knew his shot had gone wild, as I'd intended. Looking back, I could see the old-timer still trying to shoot us, and I had to laugh at the way the heavy barrel wobbled every whichaway as he tried to get us in his sights. A second later, the old musket went off behind us with a belch like a cannon, and I heard the ball whistle somewhere off down the alley.

Buck was zigzagging through somebody's garden, past sheds, trellises, and such, and I reckon I was looking back when I should have been looking ahead because the next thing I knew I rode full-tilt into a clothesline full of wet wash. The little horse bowed his head and slipped on under, but the rope cleared Jigger and me off his back slicker than calf slobbers.

I wasn't hurt; I wanted to laugh, but the wind had been knocked out of me so I laid there a-watching the bedsheets and bloomers above me and tried to catch my breath.

Kiowa had followed us in, but he'd pulled up in time

to miss the laundry. Jigger had lit near me, but I seen he was on his feet again. He glanced at my crumpled form and I don't know if he thought I'd broke my neck or what, but he turned and swung up behind Kiowa on the roan and the two of them rode past me and off toward the city limits.

By the time I heard the riders coming hard up the alley I was able to breathe again. I scrambled to my feet and went to looking for my horse. But he hadn't waited on me, and I really couldn't blame him none. I figured he'd had all the warfare he could use for the moment and had decided to give me my walking papers.

The riders I'd heard rode on past me, and I figured they were after Kiowa and Jigger, but I knew there would be plenty of others coming and that I had to get myself hid, and soon. There was no time for crying over spilt milk, nor loose horses neither, so I took to running and dodging through the neighborhood until I came to the edge of town.

A small, whitewashed house stood at the edge of a sagebrush coulee just ahead, and I done a pretty fair piece of sneaking as I crossed the open ground to the front gate of its fenced yard. Inside, there was rose bushes, hollyhocks, some other flowers I couldn't put a name to, and a pair of young cottonwood trees just getting a foothold on the shade-making business.

The front steps led to a small porch with a hanging swing and a door with a beveled glass window and a brass knob. Going slow and careful, I clumb the front steps, tried the door, and found it unlocked. Drawing a deep breath—and my Colt's Dragoon—I eased it open and slipped inside.

That's when I got another surprise. As I stepped out of the brightness into the dim hallway, I felt the cold muzzle of a pistol at my ear, and heard the hammer go back full with a sharp double click.

"I don't believe I heard you *knock*," said Mary Alice.

THIRTEEN

Apple Pie and Coffee

"Put the pistol on the floor, mister, and turn around slow, with your hands up. And if you think I won't kill you, you're dead wrong."

It was a voice I had heard often in my memory since that long-ago night at the Shenanigan jail; it was her voice, the voice of Mary Alice, and no mistake.

I bent low and laid the Dragoon on the rug, then I straightened with my hands shoulder high and turned to face her. She wore that same white cotton dress I remembered, and the sunlight through the door behind her lit up her hair like a halo in one of them holy pictures. It was Mary Alice, all right, and she was every bit as pretty as I remembered. Even the nickel-plated derringer pistol she was pointing at my brisket did not distract me. Just seeing her again made me feel like I'd been dipped buck naked in warm oil.

"Well, howdy there, biscuit maker," I grinned.

Her brown eyes narrowed, and I saw her frown as she studied me over the twin barrels of the derringer. Then, of a sudden, I saw recognition cross her face.

"Merlin Fanshaw?" she asked, "Is that you?"

"Yes, ma'am," I said, sassy as a coyote pup, "and how is your sweet old daddy, the sheriff?"

She lowered the pistol, and I saw the same spunky look she'd wore that night at the jail. "All right," she said, "you know Andy Wilkes is no kin of mine. He got me to pose as his daughter to help persuade you to spy for him."

"Worked like a charm, too," I said, "Downright amazin' what a person can accomplish if they're willing to *lie* a little. I suppose your name ain't really Mary Alice, neither."

"Oh, it's Mary Alice, all right," she said, "and don't you get snippy with me. Last I heard, you'd quit *pretending* to be an outlaw and had *become* one. I suppose you were part of the bank robbery today, too."

"How'd you know there *was* a bank robbery? It just now *happened*."

"Heard the shooting. Then Tom Dollan and his son rode past here, all a-twitter at the prospect of killing a bank robber, and *they* told me."

"Yeah," I said, "Truth is, I tried to stop it, but I got here late. Next thing I knew I'd lost my horse and was being chased by everyone in town who could lay hands on a firearm."

Mary Alice smiled in that mocking way she had. "So you didn't break into my house to rob me or do me harm, but merely to *hide.* My goodness! I can't tell you how relieved I am."

She cocked her head and studied me for a spell. "All right," she said, "leave those dirty boots by the door and come with me to the kitchen. I'll pour you a cup of coffee while we catch up on old times."

I followed her in my stocking feet past a small bedroom and a tidy parlor to a kitchen on the east side of the house. Like the other rooms, it was neat as a pin, and so clean it fairly gleamed. I hadn't gave it much thought until then, but all at once I came aware to how dirty I was, and I felt like a boar hog at a tea party.

All my recent riding between Shenanigan and Rampage had left me wearing a pound or two of trail dust, and looking down at my feet I could see my socks was near dirty as my boots. I couldn't recall the last time I'd had a bath, unless I was to count the drowning lessons Faunt Bodeen had gave me; I sort of took a sidelong look to see if Mary Alice was keeping upwind of me, but she didn't seem to pay my filthy condition any mind.

She set a cup of coffee before me and sat down across the table with a smile that could have melted snow. The sweet, clean smell of lilacs wafted across from her to me, and I have no idea, nor do I want to know, what aroma of mine drifted the other way.

"So, Merlin Fanshaw," she said, "what have you been up to?"

I knew I tended to stammer some when I got mad, but I hadn't known until that minute, when I looked deep

179

into the warm brown eyes of Mary Alice, that I also done it when in the presence of females. Or anyway that particular one.

"Oh, y-you know," says I, trying to sound self-assured, "m-murder and m-mayhem, looting and a-pillaging—all them outlaw chores. How about you, biscuit maker?"

Her tone didn't change, but she dropped her eyes as she spoke. I was reminded of the way a moving cloud shadow steals the light from a sunny slope.

"Nothing so exciting," she said, "I mostly just stay here at home. Tell me about the robbery."

"Not much to tell. Outlaws hit the bank, and the law was waiting for 'em. Three were killed, two got away, and I lost my horse."

"And took refuge in my house. How do you know I won't turn you in? I could, you know."

"Didn't know it *was* your house. And yeah, I reckon you *could* turn me in. Truth is, I helped them two bandits get away, but I wasn't part of the hold-up myself."

Mary Alice looked at me for what seemed a long time, and them brown eyes like to melted me like butter on a hot rock. Then she favored me with her bright smile, and said, "I believe you, Merlin Fanshaw. There's just a chance I may have company shortly, but I don't know for sure. Either way, you can hide out here until dark. Then you go."

Looking out the kitchen window I could see the shadows on the low hills above the coulee had grown longer, and that sundown would be coming soon.

"That's mighty kind of you, Mary Alice," I told her, "Much obliged," and right then I wished I knew of some way to hold the darkness off forever.

She smiled her quick smile and stood up from the table. "Truth is, I can do even better than that," she said, "There's an apple pie in my pantry that's yours if you want it. You interested?"

"You bet!" I said, "Eating is what I do best, and the memory of your fine baking has sustained me on many a long, lonesome ride."

She laughed then, and the sound was cheery and bright as a meadowlark's song. "Yes," she said, "but I seem to remember you left a few of my biscuits *behind* the last time I saw you."

The pantry was behind a door near the table, and Mary Alice stepped inside and came back with the pie. She cut me a generous wedge, slid it onto a plate, and set it before me. "There you go," she said, "I'll just get the coffeepot and warm . . ."

Mary Alice had froze in mid-sentence, and she was staring out the kitchen window. "It's Sheriff Wilkes!" she said, "He's coming this way . . . he's walking straight for the *back door!*"

I pushed away from the table, and my hand went to where my Colt's Dragoon should have been and found the holster empty. Then I remembered placing my pistol on the rug in the hallway, and I saw Mary Alice still looking at the door, her face drawn and her eyes wide. "Quick," she said, "Take your pie and hide in the pantry!"

The pantry was small and dark, with shelves on each side and a narrow walk space up the middle. I crouched against the far wall, facing the door, and listened to my heart a-hammering. I hunkered there like a fool, with a wedge of pie between my feet and my six-gun out in the vestibule, and mentally kicked myself. I had neglected to close the pantry door all the way, and now I saw Mary Alice come back to the table, with Androcles Wilkes close behind her. For once, I had lost my appetite altogether.

Wilkes had taken his big hat off, and he held it in front of his belly as he watched Mary Alice. I saw her glance in my direction, then look quickly away.

"I was just having some coffee," she said, indicating my cup and saucer, "would you like some, sheriff?"

Wilkes looked sober and official. "No, thank you, Mary Alice," he said, "I don't believe I'd care for none right now."

"No," he said, his voice somber as an undertaker's, "this here's an official visit. I'm afraid I have bad news."

"Please, sheriff," Mary Alice said, taking the chair facing the pantry, "won't you sit down?"

Wilkes pulled out a chair and eased his considerable bulk onto it. He was facing Mary Alice across the table, his back to me. "There's no easy way to tell you this, girl—Ollie's dead. Outlaws gunned him during the raid on the bank."

"Ollie *dead?* Who . . . how . . ."

"It was the Starkweather gang. Original George

wasn't with 'em, but they was his boys, all right, and one of 'em cut Ollie off at the pockets with a sawed-off ten-gauge.

"It was that young horse-thief, Merlin Fanshaw—the one I had in my jail that time. He murdered Ollie. Sorry to say, him and two others got away clean."

Right then I had the clear impression that the sheriff didn't like me very much, but then I can't say I was exactly in love with him, neither.

For a long moment Wilkes was quiet. When he did speak again his voice had an edge to it like rusty metal. "You don't seem all that grief-stricken, girl. Here I tell you your married lover and meal-ticket has done met his maker with his soft belly full of double-ought buck, and you don't even turn a hair. Now why is that?"

"What did you expect, tears?" said Mary Alice, and her soft brown eyes flashed fire, "If you want to know the truth, I'm relieved. Oh, I'm sorry Ollie's dead, but I'm glad that I'm alive. And free at last."

Wilkes's chuckle had a sound like a mean kid tormenting a critter. "Oh, I wouldn't count on *freedom* all that much, was I you, girl," he said, "around Progress County I generally decide who's free and who ain't, and believe me, darlin', you *ain't*. As it happens, I hold the paper on this little house and I own all that's in it, up to and includin' *you*. It's sort of like old Ollie died and left me title deed to his possessions, and you have now changed *hands,* so to speak.

"Now it ain't that you interest me all that much on a *personal* level—I've mostly banked my ruttin' fires and

183

said good riddance to 'em. But I see you as an investment, and I naturally expect some kind of return. To put it brief, you're workin' for *me* now, girl."

"I see. And just what kind of work would that be?"

"Oh, you know—one thing and another. Entertainin' gents here at the house, bein' a hostess of sorts, whatever else comes to mind. You know what I'm talkin' about."

"Oh, yes, I know what you're talking about. Suppose I say no?"

"I think you're *smarter* than that, girl. If you say no, I'll just have to work at changin' your mind, maybe send Faunt Bodeen over to see can *he* tame you some. But there's no call for all this unpleasant talk. I just came by to express my condolences on your loss, and to let you know you'll be took care of in the future."

I had often told myself I would never shoot a man in the back, but I truly believe if I'd had my pistol right then I would have made an exception in the case of Sheriff Androcles Wilkes. As it was, I looked around the pantry shelves for some kind of weapon, but the closest I came to one was a jar of pickles, and I was not convinced that would prove fatal enough for my purposes.

Wilkes stood up from the table, put his Buckeye Stetson back on his head, and walked out of my line of sight. I heard him high-heel it over to the door and open it. Mary Alice sat facing the pantry, her face tight and strained.

"One more thing," I heard Wilkes say, "we found that

buckskin horse young Fanshaw was ridin.' It was loose and grazin' just outside the city limits, so there's a chance the kid's still around town somewheres. You *will* let me know if you happen to see him, won't you, girl?"

Then I heard the door close, and I came out of the pantry and set the pie plate on the table. Mary Alice still sat stiffly in her chair, and I saw her small hand tremble as she lifted the china cup and sipped the coffee.

"That the company you were expecting?" I asked. "I guess you know he's a dang liar, among other things."

Her voice sounded weary and far away. "You mean about you killing Ollie Langford? Oh, I know you didn't do that. And no, he's not the company I expected. I—I didn't really expect *anyone*."

Mary Alice got up and walked over to the stove. Steam rose from the big copper boiler beside the coffee pot, and her eyes seemed sad and a little lost as she looked at it. "I—I thought maybe Ollie would be coming by," she said, "but he doesn't—that is, he didn't—come here very often."

She picked up the coffee pot, refilled the cup, and looked at me, her eyes searching and direct. I found myself unable to meet her gaze, and I looked away, but still I could feel her eyes upon me.

"He mostly went home to his wife," she said, and I could hear pain in her voice, "but I guess he won't be going there any more, *either,* will he?"

I cleared my throat. "No," I said, "I saw him die. One of the outlaws tried to use him for a shield. Wilkes shot

Ollie first, then the outlaw. He didn't even hesitate."

"Poor Ollie. I didn't love him—didn't even like him much, but . . ."

"It's none of my business, Mary Alice."

She went on as if she hadn't heard me, as if she was talking to herself.

"He was out of his depth. Ollie was greedy and weak, and he thought he could hold his own with the big boys, but he knew nothing about men like Wilkes and Original George."

"It's none of my business," I said again.

"I'll tell you about Ollie and me sometime, Merlin," she said, "but not right now. Right now, I have to get away from this town, and away from Androcles Wilkes."

Mary Alice stood, her back to me, staring out her kitchen window. For a minute or so she was quiet, and when at last she spoke again there was sadness in her voice, but determination, too.

"The train to Silver City will be through here about eight-thirty tonight, and I plan to be on board when it leaves. You're welcome to come along."

"Wilkes will be watching for just that kind of move," I said, "He'll spot us both before we get halfway to the depot."

She flashed her sweet, bright smile and took my hand in hers. "No, he won't," she said, "*Trust* me, Merlin."

Well, of course I *did* trust her. Mary Alice had a smile that could light up a graveyard at midnight. As I recall, it also lit up my heart.

• • •

The sun had long since dropped behind the western hills, and the high, thin clouds over Shenanigan had blazed bright, flamed gold, cooled to red, and finally gone to gray like the ashes of a campfire in the sky. Mary Alice drawed the blinds and locked both doors before she lit up a coal oil lamp and dragged a galvanized wash tub over to the stove.

"I'm assuming you've *had* a bath some time in your life," she said, "but I'm taking that on faith, not on the evidence. There's hot water in that copper boiler on the stove, and Ollie's shaving brush, soap, and razor are there on the wash stand. Anyway, make it quick, and don't worry if you mess up the kitchen; it isn't going to matter. While you're doing that, I'll pack a bag and get ready to go myself.

"I *have* had a bath or two in my time," I told her, "it's just that I have lacked the opportunity of late. Anyway, why is it so all-fired important for me to be clean?"

She stopped at the doorway and favored me with her taunting smile. "Well," she said, "for one thing, it will make a fine *disguise*. Nobody around here has ever *seen* you that way."

It was a better bath than Wilkes and Bodeen had gave me, anyway. By the time I got done scouring my handsome young body in that hot, soapy water I had lost all my trail dust and most of my huffiness, and I had took on the shine of a new-minted dollar.

Using Ollie's brush and razor, I shaved my face clean,

cutting myself only three or four times, and I even slicked back my hair and splashed on some bay rum. Mary Alice had laid out some of Ollie's clothes for me, and even though the banker had been considerably thicker about the middle than I was, I rummaged through the pile until I found some duds I figured would do.

When I finally finished dressing I was duded up to a fare-thee-well in a white linen shirt, silk cravat, fancy brocade vest, and a frock coat of black broadcloth. I tried on a pair of the banker's breeches, but without success; I could have smuggled a watermelon in the waistband of them pants. There was nothing for it but to go back to Romeo Flores's Mexican breeches, but I did shake the dust out and brush them as best I could. My raggedy boots, my battered old hat, and my belted six-gun completed my outfit. One look into the mirror above the wash stand told me clear that my disguise fell far short of the mark. Instead of looking like a dirty outlaw, I looked like a cleaned-up outlaw trying to look like somebody else.

Directly, I heard Mary Alice knock sharply on the kitchen door. "I hope you're decent, Merlin Fanshaw," she said, "I think I just heard the train whistle."

"Well, I'm dressed," I said, opening the door, "but I'm not sure I ever *will* be altogether *decent*."

I had known she was pretty, but seeing her dressed up there in the doorway like to have took away my ability to speak. She wore a pale green traveling dress under a coat of darker hue, and a jaunty little hat set low over her warm brown eyes. Lamplight caught in the soft curls of her honey-colored hair, and she smiled her brightest smile as she looked at me as if to say she liked what she saw. I would have took a thousand baths and run through cactus barefoot just to see that look on her face, and in all my years since that evening I don't believe I have forgot a single detail.

"You clean up real good, Merlin Fanshaw," she said, and her voice was like the purr of a kitten.

Mary Alice handed me her traveling bag, picked up the lamp from the kitchen table, and carried it into the vestibule. I threw my shaps and spurs into a carpetbag, together with my trail clothes, and followed her to the front door. "Go ahead and start for the depot," she said, "I'll catch up with you in a moment."

I had gone maybe fifty yards or so when I looked back to see her lift the oil lamp high above her head in the open doorway and dash it to the floor of the parlor. She came running through the gate and caught up to me just as the parlor exploded into fire and billowing smoke. I could hear the crunching sound as the flames commenced to devour the little house, and Mary Alice's voice at my ear.

"I think Sheriff Wilkes will be along when he hears his house is on fire," she said grimly, "but we can't stay around to greet him. You and me have a train to catch."

FOURTEEN
Night Train to Silver City

Mary Alice and me made our way through town by way of the back alleys, keeping well away from the lighted streets. By the time we hit Front Street the town had come alive, and we stood back in the shadows and watched folks heading for the burning house above the coulee the way they had swarmed to the shootout earlier that day.

I was carrying both her traveling bag and my own, but Mary Alice took hers from me and walked on through the darkened side streets like a house afire (if you'll pardon the expression), her eyes straight ahead and her mind fixed firm upon the evening train.

As for me, I reckon I was more curious. I stopped for a minute just beyond Cherokee Bob's and watched the flames light up the night sky behind us. Smoke was rolling and belching toward the heavens, and bright sparks danced upward in flurries while the orange light flickered and lit the street like a giant lantern in a windstorm.

Somebody had commenced ringing the church bell as an alarm, and was doing it with so much enthusiasm I figured the town would need either a new bell or a new bell-ringer by morning. The local dogs were doing what dogs do best, which is to bark at whatever they don't understand, and since them town dogs didn't understand much, there was a heap of barking going on. People were hollering and running around with buckets, and drunks who'd been celebrating the day's blood-letting at their favorite saloon had staggered out to catch the night show. Since the big excitement most days in Shenanigan was watching mud dry in the sun, I figured that particular Friday had to have been one of the town's more eventful twenty-four hours.

Mary Alice had been right about Wilkes turning out for the fire; I stepped back into the shadows and watched as the sheriff came a-scurrying toward the blaze. He had a look on his face that was three parts puzzled and one part grim. I knew his expression would soon change to four parts furious when he seen whose house was a-burning. His plug-ugly deputy Faunt Bodeen follered along behind him with a checkered napkin still tucked in his collar, so I reckoned him and Wilkes had been having themselves a late supper down at the Red Rooster when they'd got the news.

The water wagon came rumbling and sloshing up the street with the driver whupping his team along like one of them old-time chariot racers. Volunteers follered close behind, pushing a pump on a handcart as they made a beeline for the blaze.

All of a sudden the hollow snort of the locomotive's steam whistle cut through the hubbub, and I looked toward the train station just in time to see the conductor give Mary Alice a helping hand into the coach. He picked up the iron step, set it on board, and swung up himself, and when I seen him lean out and signal the engine driver with a wave of his lantern I broke into a lope that would have done a pronghorn proud. The train was chuffing slow but building speed as it left the depot, and as I came alongside I throwed my bag on, took holt of the hand rail, and pulled myself up and inside.

Mary Alice was sitting by the window toward the rear of the car, and when I came a-rambling down the aisle she raised one eyebrow and said, "Glad you could make it, Merlin. I thought maybe you'd decided to stay and help Sheriff Wilkes fight fire."

"No, ma'am," I grinned, sitting down beside her, "Him and me have shared some entertainin' and upliftin' moments, but I still druther be with you." She favored me with her quick, bright smile, and what I felt but *didn't* say was I druther be with her than do *anything*.

We pretty much had the car to ourselves, except for a hardware drummer down the aisle playing solitaire on his sample case and a sleeping cowhand at the far end with his saddle in a sack alongside him. The conductor walked up to where we sat and asked, "Where to, folks?"

I pulled out the deerskin poke George had left me and handed him a double eagle. "Me and the missiz are going to Silver City, pardner," I said. He took two tickets from his vest, punched them, and stuck them in the slot next to the window. "Quite a fire back there," he said, "somebody's house, I suppose."

"I suppose," I said, glancing at Mary Alice, "seems to

have broke out kind of sudden."

"Fire will do that," said he, "you folks have a pleasant trip."

The train picked up speed as it left the lights of Shenanigan behind, and the coach rocked and swayed along the rails like a ship in a gale, but the conductor just sauntered up the aisle with an easy, steady gait and went on into the next car.

"You and the *missiz,* eh?" Mary Alice teased, "when was the wedding?"

The smoky oil lamps overhead were turned low, and the light in the car was dim. I was grateful; I could feel myself blushing like a dern kid, and sitting close beside her the way I was and breathing the fragrance of her lilac perfume made me feel light-headed and, I don't know, kind of *fidgety,* somehow. "Well," I said, sounding more grumpy than I meant to, "it just s-seemed like the thing to s-say at the time."

Mary Alice slipped her arm through mine and sort of nestled close beside me. "It was sweet of you, Merlin Fanshaw," she said.

Then, before I knew it, her head was on my shoulder, and for awhile there I thought she had fell asleep. Outside, the night was black as pitch, and I could see the two of us reflected in the window glass like lovers in a tintype. The wheels rumbled beneath us and clicked over the rails in a steady rhythm, as I held my breath for fear if I breathed too deep or even moved it would all disappear, like a sweet dream with the coming of daylight.

Then, quiet and sad, I heard her say, "I said I'd tell you about Ollie and me sometime. I guess this might as well be that sometime."

"I-I'm not sure I want to *know,* Mary Alice," I said, "I don't *need* to know."

"*I* need to *tell* it," she said, "and I need someone—I need *you*—to *listen.*"

Well, what could I do? I swallered, nodded my head, and listened.

"My true name is Mary Alice Weems," she said, "and I grew up south of Shenanigan on my daddy's horse ranch. My mother ran off with a racehorse man when I wasn't but ten, and I quit school and went to working at home. I cooked, cleaned, did the washing, and took care of the cows and chickens. I helped out around the ranch, too—I built fence, put up hay, worked with the horses, and did whatever else came to hand. We didn't always have enough food, clothes, or other necessaries, but the one thing we *did* have plenty of was hard work.

"The trouble was, daddy had borrowed money on the place from the Shenanigan Bank. It seemed like no matter how hard we worked or how well we did, everything we made went to make our loan payment.

"Then, the spring I turned fifteen, daddy had a Morgan mare fall with him and break his leg and his hip. He was laid up all summer, and I had to take care of him, do his work, and my own, too. Guess you could say the mare fell on *him,* and the *work* fell on *me.*

"To make matters worse, that was the year of the Big Dry. The last rain fell on the fourth of June that year, and we didn't see moisture again 'til the snow came in late November. The range dried up, and so did the water holes. Even the grasshoppers looked thirsty. People not only quit buying horses, they couldn't take care of the ones they already *had*.

"Neither could we. Of course we weren't able to make our payment when the note came due. Ollie Langford came out to look the place over, and he told daddy he was sorry, but the bank would have to foreclose.

"The light left daddy's eyes like someone had blown out a lamp. He slumped in his chair, his shoulders sagged, and he seemed to grow smaller and older as I watched. I remembered how he'd once been: strong, full of laughter and song. I couldn't help myself—I broke down and fell to weeping right there in front of daddy and the banker. I guess I'd held back my tears too long.

"Anyway, next thing I knew Ollie was holding me in his arms and I was crying hot tears all over his fancy brocade vest. There was more moisture right there in our little kitchen than the range had seen all summer."

For a long time Mary Alice was silent, just looking out into the blackness beyond the window. I said nothing, but closed my eyes and listened as the train rattled on and the engine moaned its lonesome wail through the night like a coyote romancing the moon.

My left arm was behind Mary Alice on the red plush seat back, and it had long since fell asleep and gone to tingling. One night back in Rampage, Bucktooth Betty had gave me some French champagne, and my arm felt something like the way that bubbly booze had *tasted,* only more painful by a damsite. Of course, I knew if I took my arm away from her shoulders and moved it around some the circulation would come back and the hurt would stop, but I never even considered it. Some things are *worth* hurting for.

Her voice sounded older when at last she spoke again, older and weary. "By the time I'd stopped bawling," she said, "and had stepped back to dry my eyes, I could see that Ollie looked at me in a different way than he had before, and I thought he might be a prince come to rescue me. He *wasn't,* of course, but there's a lot you don't know at fifteen.

"Well, I can't make a sad story happy, but I can make a long story short. Daddy couldn't sell horses that year, but he *was* able to sell a good-looking daughter, and he did. Ollie Langford extended daddy's loan and gave him enough extra to take on a hired man, and I rode back to town with the banker. He put me up in my own little house, and I became a kept woman before I was even a woman.

"I saw daddy only once after that, a year later. He seemed embarrassed and distant, and he would neither touch me nor look me in the eye. Ollie says—said—he's still on the old home place, but I haven't seen him since."

The hardware drummer looked back at us and smiled like he hankered to make our acquaintance, but I scowled at him and brushed aside the tail of my coat so my holstered six-gun showed. He got real busy minding his own business.

"Ollie was weak and vain, but he was good to me," Mary Alice continued, "I think maybe he even loved me a little. But then everything changed when Androcles Wilkes dealt himself in. Wilkes said he'd make sure Ollie's wife—and the bank's directors—didn't find out about me if Ollie would pay a small 'insurance' fee, and of course Ollie paid. And paid. And *paid,* month after month. Wilkes *raised* the price, and Ollie paid. Then he raised it again, and Ollie started dipping into the *bank's* money.

"Then in June, Wilkes learned that a double Army payroll for Fort Savage would, for the first time ever, be coming through Shenanigan. Always before, the Army had shipped it through Silver City, but word had come through the U.S. Marshal's office that the Starkweather gang was looking to intercept it, so the plans had been changed.

"The money was to come to Shenanigan by train, be held in the vault at the bank, and then transferred under guard by troopers from the fort. The only thing Wilkes and Ollie didn't know was exactly *when* it would arrive.

"The paymaster came to town, inspected the bank, and talked security with Wilkes, but he refused to tell the arrival date of the money. Wilkes and Ollie would be informed in due time, he said.

"But Wilkes had ideas of his own. Apparently, he and Original George had a *history,* of sorts. Sometimes they fought, and sometimes they worked together. This time Wilkes saw the chance to cut himself in on some really big money. If he could somehow find out when the shipment would be moved, he could pass the word on to George and take a share of the proceeds.

"He came to Ollie with his big idea, and Ollie brought it to me. I was to *entertain* the paymaster and find out the date the money would arrive. The paymaster was a sweet, lonely, older man. He told me, of course, I told Ollie, and Ollie told Wilkes. Wilkes then told Original George, and the outlaws hit the escort a few miles from a place called Alkali Springs. They killed the paymaster and two of the troopers, and made off with $40,000 in federal money.

"But George double-crossed Wilkes and disappeared. The good sheriff was fit to be tied; he'd told Ollie that if he'd help him learn the date the payroll would arrive he'd let him off the hook regarding his payments. But then he changed his mind, and Ollie was back on the hook again.

"Later, when he had you in jail and thought you might lead him to George, he had me pose as his daughter to help persuade you. I did as he asked, Merlin, and I'm sorry.

"I haven't been able to get the robbery out of my mind; I felt as though I'd killed those troopers and the paymaster myself. In a way I guess I did. I've done a lot of things the last year or so I'm not proud of.

"Anyway, I told myself that if I ever had a chance to get away from that town and from Androcles Wilkes, I would. Now Ollie is dead, and my chance has come. Thanks for helping, Merlin, and thanks for listening."

She fell silent again, and I shut my eyes and thought about all she had said. Some of what she'd told me I already knew, or had guessed. Some, I hadn't known and was glad to learn, and some of it I didn't *want* to know, or believe. I knew that Mary Alice was the fancy woman George told Shanty about that day I was eavesdropping in the outhouse, and I didn't like thinking about her and Langford that way, so I turned my mind away from it, or leastways *tried* to. She had been the banker's mistress, she had used her wiles to pry information out of a lonesome old codger, and she had helped charm me into working for that badge-wearing sidewinder, Androcles Wilkes.

"What do you reckon you'll do?" I asked her, "where will you go?"

"I don't really know," she said, "just leaving Shenanigan is enough for right now. Later, maybe Denver, or San Francisco—someplace I can make a new start."

Right then the train swung hard around a curve and the force of the turn caught me off guard and pressed me hard against her. I have to admit that as I felt the firm warmth of her body next to mine I wouldn't have gave a damn had she been a blood-sucking vampire, wicked Queen Jezebel, and a axe murderess combined.

Anyway, who was I to judge her? I sported neither halo nor wings, and I sure couldn't play no harp. I had done what I had to, same as her, and I wasn't all that proud of some of *my* doin's. I guess the thing that bothered me most was the way I had let myself be used by Wilkes, Original George, and even Marshal Ridgeway. It seemed all anyone had to do was say they wanted me to do a thing, and I'd wag my tail and scurry around trying to do it. It was like I had a big sign on my back which read, "USE ME, ABUSE ME. I DON'T HAVE A LICK OF SENSE, NOR SELF RESPECT, NEITHER."

Just over an hour had gone by when all at once the train slowed and shuddered, and I felt the couplings jerk all along the line as the engine commenced to labor on the uphill climb that led across the mountainside and down into Silver City. I recalled that the tracks ran through a jumble of boulders and thick timber, looking out over a broad and fertile valley, but the night was dark as the inside of a cow as I stared out the window. I couldn't see a blessed thing.

Mary Alice had gone quiet and off somewhere into her own thoughts, her head laid back on the seat and her eyes closed. I found myself studying her face like it was a holy relic or something. Just looking at her made my throat feel tight, and it seemed to me then that I had seen some *pretty* in my life, but I had not until that moment truly seen *beauty*. I looked at her in the dim light of the smoky overhead lamp and felt dang near overcome by the hankering to hold her close, to bury my face in her soft shining curls, and to kiss the lips that right then were so close to my own.

I had never felt about anyone the way I felt about her,

and it caused me to wonder some. There was no good *reason* for my feelings that I could see; it seemed to me I should despise her, or at least be indifferent, but I could do neither. It was not the first nor the last time in my life when "should" meant nothing, and what I *knew* came up hard against what I *felt*. Once again, my head and my heart had gone to war, and my head, as usual, had lost.

Suddenly the door at the end of the coach opened, and the conductor came through it and started up the aisle toward us. "Silver City next," he said, "next stop, Silver City."

I looked out the window again just as the train swept out around the mountain's face and began its descent. Below lay the lights of Silver City, and in the blackness of the night it looked like the stars had fell to earth and lay spread out and shining all across the valley's floor. Mary Alice had leaned forward and was watching the lights, too, and there was something like wonder on her face.

"Looks like the sky is upside down, don't it?" I said.

"Yes," she said, "like diamonds scattered on black velvet."

I stood and fetched down our bags from the rack over the windows just as the conductor stopped near us and consulted his timepiece by the dull flicker of the lamp.

"Well," he said, "we're thirty minutes late, but we were *forty-five* minutes late last time, so it's almost like we're *early* this evening."

Mary Alice smiled her bright smile at him and I swear

I felt a stab of jealousy gouge me just under my rib cage, like she was only supposed to smile at me. I had it bad, and no mistake.

"My—husband—and I haven't been to Silver City before," she said, "could you recommend lodging in town?"

"Why, yes, ma'am," said he, "the Winslow is the town's best hotel. You folks can hire a hack at the station. Take you right to the door."

"Much obliged," I told him, all serious and trying to sound like a proper husband, "the missiz and me believe in goin' first class when we travel."

I felt better; now she was smiling her bright smile at *me* again.

FIFTEEN
City Lights

Silver City was a town in the process of change. For most of its short, reckless life it had been a booming, hell-for-leather mining camp, and folks had believed it would one day grow up to be a real city. But the silver ore that kept its heart a-pumping had commenced to run thin, and the town had turned to serving the needs of the cowmen and nesters from along the Big Porcupine river and the foothills and prairies beyond the Brimstones.

Since then its growth had slowed some and had tapered off to a more steady pace, but the burg still showed signs of its gaudy, carefree youth. A good many of the buildings were two stories high, with some even taller, made of brick and stone; they stood cheek by jowl with false-front frame and log structures from the early days. Some of the main streets were paved with cobblestones. The town even boasted gas lights and a horse-drawn trolley.

The night Mary Alice and me rolled into Silver City was a warm September evening, and if the town wasn't as lively as it had been in its heyday, it was by no means deserted neither. There were people at the train station, buggies, hacks, and dray wagons parked along the curb, and considerable horseback traffic up and down the streets by riders both drunk and sober. The big engine slid to a stop at the depot in a cloud of steam and belching smoke, and sort of stood there a-quivering with its bell clanging while eight or ten people, including us, stepped down from the passenger cars.

The conductor had told the truth; there were hackney drivers aplenty willing to take us anyplace we wanted to go, and between trying to attract our attention and out-hollering the competition a couple of them nearly came to blows.

I sauntered over to a big red-headed teamster who looked like he could whup most of the other boys and handed him our bags. "Hotel Winslow," said I.

The big feller nodded, tipped his derby hat to Mary Alice, and gave her a hand up into the coach. While he was doing that I fixed him with m toughest outlaw stare just to let him know I wouldn't stand for him taking any liberties with my woman, and then I climbed on up myself.

The hackney coach looked to be a sort of four passenger surrey, and I sat beside Mary Alice in the rear seat while the driver swung his team out onto the cobblestones and away from the depot. A good many of the town's buildings were dark, but we went by two or three saloons and a couple of eating places that were well-lit, where I could hear music and laughter drifting out through the open doors as we clattered past.

Well, sir, I reckoned right then that riding through Silver City with Mary Alice Weems beside me was about the most pleasant thing I had ever done. The evening had cooled some after the heat of the day, but the air was still warm and mild. The iron wheels of the carriage rumbled over the cobbles, and now and then the horses' hooves struck sparks in the darkness as we rattled along. Above the streetlamps moths fluttered and danced, and the soft light washed over us like the beam from a lighthouse as we passed each lamp post, then faded into darkness as we moved on ahead to the next one. I could feel Mary Alice's firm young body right through my coat, shirt, and vest—shoot, I could have felt her through a dang brick *wall*.

My hands were wet, my mouth was dry, and I found I was taking quick, shallow breaths the way I sometimes do when stalking a big mule deer buck. I kept a-glancing sideways at her face, and I wanted to speak up and tell her how downright beautiful she was, but I knew I'd go to stammering if I tried to—my *thoughts* were stammering *already*. I could hear my heart pounding in my ears, and my shirt collar had somehow growed too small for my neck. I was drawn to her like steel dust to a magnet, or like them moths to the light, and the feeling came over me strong and certain that if I didn't take her in my arms and hold her close right that very minute I would surely die.

She turned toward me then, and her warm brown eyes were deep and searching as she studied my face. In the half light her lips looked soft as a butterfly's wing, and I felt her fingers reach out and touch my face. I kissed her then, and I done so wholehearted, with my entire self. I seemed to melt like a snowflake on a cookstove from the hot sweetness of that kiss, and for a time there was no me at all nor her, but only us.

Then her hands were firm against my chest, and she broke away, her eyes wide and knowing. "Lordy," I said, in a deep, strangled voice I'd never heard before, "*Lordy*, Mary Alice."

"You're a sweet, good man, Merlin Fanshaw," she said, "and I *do* care for you. But so much has happened these last few days. I need time to sort out my feelings. Can you understand that?"

Well, I have to confess that right then I was more caught up in *my* feelings than in hers. I felt like I was a forest fire with the wind behind me, and she was a spruce grove; I was riding a runaway wagon and couldn't find the brake, nor did I want to. All I wanted was her, more of her, all of her, and her alone.

"Oh, Merlin," she said, "please understand. I've

never been *free* before, not even to love, or follow my own heart. I just need a little time, dear."

I found the brake, two feet from the cliff. A cold, drenching cloudburst broke just above the forest fire. My body was tremblin' like a locomotive on a greasy track, standing still with the throttle open and the drive wheel spinning, but I managed to give her a shaky smile and to say, in that strange, choked voice that wasn't my own, "Sure, darlin'—I understand."

And I *did* understand, or anyway *told* myself I did, not that it helped all that dang much. But Mary Alice had called me "dear" and I took my comfort where I could. She held my hand in both of hers and smiled her brightest smile. "I *knew* you would," she said, "thank you, sweet Merlin."

Right about then we pulled up in front of the hotel, and the driver drew rein. "Hotel Winslow, folks," he said.

The hotel was three floors high and well-lit by street lamps and by gas lights at each side of the wide front door. Windows flanked the doorway, and inside the lobby I could see potted palms and a plush divan underneath a fancy chandelier. I paid the driver and gave Mary Alice a hand down. We just stood there looking at each other as the hack drove off up the street.

"I'll be happy to stake you to a hotel room, Merlin," said Mary Alice, "you'll need a place to stay."

I was still wound tighter than a fiddle string, and wasn't sure I could trust my voice. "Much obliged, but I couldn't let you do that," I told her, trying to sound easy and casual, "there's a livery barn and wagon yard about two blocks south, and I believe I'll just bed down there, and see you in the morning."

"All right," she said, "if you're sure that's what you want."

Then she kissed me, and for a mercy it wasn't like our first kiss or I believe I would have ignited and set fire to the hotel gallery. Mary Alice picked up her bag, glided to the doorway, and, just before she went inside, turned and gave me a smile so sweet and bright it like to broke my heart.

Then she was gone, and I just stood there for a minute and looked at the doorway where she'd been. I picked up the bag that held my shaps, spurs, and trail clothes, and walked off lonesome into the darkness.

I had gone maybe three blocks when I came to a small but lively saloon called Kelly's Bar and stopped outside to listen. The smell of cigar smoke, stale beer, and wet sawdust drifted out through the open door, and somewhere inside I heard a piano, and a good tenor singing "Molly Dear, Good Night." The song was an old one, and I remembered my Pa singing it sometimes after he'd had a few. The sweet, sad words matched my mood to a fare-thee-well.

. . . Then Molly dear, good night.
Smile away the coming morrow
Till my sure return;
Why should fond hearts part in sorrow?
Grief too soon we learn.

The light from the windows and door cast bright squares out onto the boardwalk and street like yellow carpets on the blackness, and I stood there and listened as the tenor hit his stride.

Hours of bliss must come and go,
Constant pleasures none can know,
Joy must have its ebb and flow,
Then, Molly dear, good night.

I walked through the swinging doors and up to the bar, where I put my foot on the rail and set my carpetbag down beside it. The barkeep sized me up with a practiced glance, took the cigar from his mouth, and said, "So it's *whiskey* then, is it?"

"You bet," said I, "whiskey, and leave the bottle 'til it's time to open another. Are you Kelly?"

"Not me, lad," he said as he filled my glass, "Kelly is me father-in-law, may his black soul rot in hell. Tis himself owns this bloody tavern, but he's a man to share. He gets the *profits,* you see, and I do the bloody *work*."

I tossed back the whiskey and motioned for him to fill my glass again. "Life ain't fair," I said.

"Nor will it ever be," the barkeep said pleasantly.

I downed the second glassful, and leaned my elbows on the bar. "Life is *hell* when it's like this," I told him, "and it's like this *now*."

On thy form, with beauty laden,

All my thoughts will be;
Purer love ne'er blessed a maiden
Than I hold for thee.

I might as well have been drinking water for all the effect the whiskey seemed to have on me. The only thing I could think about was Mary Alice and the way her body had felt against mine. My longing for her was so strong it was like a pain. Even through the sour, rank smell of stale beer and old stogies I could recall clearly her lilac perfume and the clean, sunwashed scent of her hair. I heard again the breathy sound of her voice when she'd called me "dear" and "sweet Merlin" and my lips still burned from her kiss. It was like my body had its own memory, independent of my mind, and I didn't have no idea how to stop the torment.

I poured myself a third glass and drank it down, then turned and looked the room over. Down the bar from me an old man hunkered over his beer like a fortune teller reading a crystal ball. A hard-eyed gent with a broken nose stood at the far end drinking boilermakers, and three fellers in work clothes and derby hats sat at a table and listened to the music. The tenor was short and pigeon-chested, and he stood with one hand atop the piano and the other tucked inside his vest. His face looked the way an angel's might, and his eyes were closed as he sang the final strains.

While thine eyes in beauty glance,
While thy smile my soul entrance,

Still the fleeting hours advance,
Then, Molly dear, good night.

"Tell me, pardner," I said to the bartender, "who would you say is the toughest man *in* here?"

He looked thoughtful. "Well," he said, "present company *excepted,* of course, I suppose Dinny McBride, the dark-eyed lad there at the end of the bar."

I drank some more whiskey and tried to focus my gaze on the feller he spoke of. "Don't look so tough to *me,*" I said.

The bartender slowly shook his head from side to side, but he didn't lose his smile. "If you're about to do what I *think* you are, you'd best leave that *revolver* you're carryin' with me."

I had to reach for my Dragoon three times before I found it. I drew it from the leather and fumbled it onto the bar. "Don't—need—no gun—for likes of him," I said, and I moved out to make the gent's acquaintance. The room seemed to tilt, and I felt the way I did when I used to walk up and down the teeter-totter back at the Dry Creek schoolyard. I got my bearings after a false start or two and swaggered over to McBride with fire in my eye and mayhem on my mind.

"I can *whip* your sorry ass," I told him.

The last thing I recall was his smile. It was a spooky, gap-toothed grin, and it put me in mind of the way a wolf might look if charged by a feisty rabbit. "I think *not,*" said he, and danged if he wasn't right.

I was becoming used to waking up in strange places,

but when I first opened my eyes the next morning I had no idea where I was. I was sprawled on a narrow cot in a little room not much bigger than a closet, and it took some study to find places on my body that didn't hurt.

My left eye wouldn't open but a slit, and the flesh around it was puffy and tender to the touch. There was a lump on my jaw that throbbed like a heartbeat, and my back teeth felt loose. When I went to sit up my ribs said, "Oh, no you don't" and if I tried to take more than a shallow breath they said the same thing, only they hollered.

Finally, I managed to get my feet over the side and onto the floor, and I took to studying my surroundings. There were mops, brushes, and a push broom in one corner, along with some rags and a scrub bucket. A beat-up clock and a candle stub in a bottle set on an upended box beside the cot, and there were pictures of pretty women from *Leslie's* and *The Police Gazette* tacked to the wall. An old chair with its back broke off stood on wobbly legs nearby, and a raggedy shirt hung on a nail just above it. The little room was lit by a single dirty window and everything smelled musty and stale, while the cot itself stank of a body long overdue for a bath. I sure hoped it wasn't mine.

Then the door opened, and sunlight caused me to squinch my eyes against the brightness and hang on to the edge of the cot to keep from falling off the world. After a bit I opened my eyes a bit and the first thing I seen was the bartender from the night before, holding a cup of coffee in his hand.

" 'Tis mornin', lad, and time you were up and on your way," he said, "you get one cup of coffee on the house."

I took the cup and held it tight with both hands, and it seemed to help me get centered. "Much obliged," I told him, "was it you put me in here?"

"That I did. Tis a room me swamper sleeps in, but he's lately doin' thirty days for lewd and disorderly conduct. As you may or may not recall, you attacked young Dinny McBride last evenin', and Dinny sent you on a journey to the land of dreams."

"Yeah. Did I lay a hand on him at all?"

"Seldom, but you *tried,* lord love you. You were a wild, daft *juggernaut* of a man, if I may say so. You might have whipped him, too, had it not been for those first seven or eight lucky *punches* he landed. I don't know what came over you, lad, but if your goal is to become a bar fighter you might consider learnin' to *fight.*"

"Sorry. Reckon I was just carryin' a man-size huff and needed some help unloadin' it."

"Sure, and didn't I read the signs when you first walked in the door? Glad I am I could be of help. But now I need to open this grand saloon for business once again, and tis time for you to be goin'."

I stood up and moved out into the barroom. It was the hardest thing I would do all day. Sunlight streamed in through the open door, and I leaned for a moment against the bar and let the pain settle. The barkeep went around and fetched my Colt's Dragoon and carpetbag, then set them on top of the bar. He brought out my deer-skin poke and placed it beside them.

"Thanks for watching my goods," I told him, "what do I owe you?"

"Not a thing, lad," he said, "I took the price of the whiskey out, and there were no damages—except, of course, to yourself. You're more than welcome in Kelly's any time, but you might think about walkin' wide of Dinny McBride in the future."

I shook his hand and stepped out through the batwing doors. "Dinny who?" I asked, and I was even able to grin a little.

The day had dawned clear and fair, and from a corner signpost I learned I was on a street called Plata, which I later found out was what the old Romans called silver. By the time I commenced my careful walk up that noble thoroughfare, the local merchants had already opened their stores and were making ready for another day's commerce. I passed the Silver City Mercantile and a dry goods emporium, and I said my howdies to a storekeeper who'd come outside to wash his front window.

A family of sodbusters, long on hardship and short on hope, clattered past in a mud-spattered buckboard drawn by a sad-looking team, and a beer wagon rumbled up the street, maybe bound for Kelly's to replenish the stock.

A cowpuncher rode by on a well-muscled buckskin, and seeing the horse reminded me of Little Buck. I wondered where the little gelding had got to after he quit me back there in Shenanigan, and how he was making out. I didn't blame him none for leaving me, what with all the gunfire and ruckus, then running through the clothesline and all. I found myself missing the little horse, the way a man might miss a good friend. Which, of course, he was.

Mary Alice was still much on my mind, but somehow I didn't feel near as desperate and needful as I had the night before. There seems to be something about the coming of daylight that helps take away the fears and doubts of the night. It's not that a man's troubles are any different—or less—than they were in the evening, it's just that they don't loom as big or scary in the light of a new day.

My mind was more clear, and I was pleased to find that I even felt some better in my body. After the excesses I had visited upon my poor carcass at Kelly's, I reckoned I felt a good deal better than I had a right to. Somehow, just walking out into the morning air seemed to take away my various aches and pains, and even my ribs didn't hurt as bad as they had.

It was a curious fact, but that short train ride had in many ways put distance between me and my worries. Memories of Androcles Wilkes, Faunt Bodeen, and the bloody shootout at the Shenanigan Bank all seemed distant and faded somehow, as did my recollections of Original George, Shanty O'Kane, and the boys. I still remembered, of course, and I still wondered about things—like what had happened to *El Borrachon,* or

George and Shanty, Jigger St. Clare and Kiowa, for that matter—but I found I was no longer as spooked as I had been. I'd gone cat-eyed and wary for so long I had near forgot how to relax. It was a good feeling to know I still could.

The aroma of frying bacon and fresh-baked biscuits cut through my reverie like a shaft of sunlight through a cloud bank. I looked up out of my good eye to see I was directly in front of an eating house called the Early Bird Cafe, and the smell of vittles cooking caught me by the nose and pulled me right inside. I reckoned it a mark of Mary Alice's appeal that I hadn't thought to eat since we'd left Shenanigan together, but all of a sudden my appetite turned mean on me. I knew it wouldn't be put off no longer.

It was dark inside after the bright sunshine on the street, and it took me a minute to get used to the change and size the place up. The Early Bird seemed a cut above the hash houses and greasy spoons I was used to; there was white cloths and fresh flowers on the tables, and sturdy wooden chairs that matched. The place seemed nearly full of people at that hour, and the genteel whisper of eating tools on china plates fell mighty pleasant on the ear.

A waiter in a striped shirt and a waxed moustache looked at me like somebody had kicked over a rock. He finally asked, "Breakfast for one, sir?"

"You bet," said I, "Set me at one of them tables and bring on the vittles 'til I either fill up or founder."

He done his best to keep his poker face, but one eyebrow went higher than the other, and his lip sort of curled. "Yes, sir," he said, "right this way."

The cafe had potted plants—ferns and such—with polished wood and brass partitions that came up about chest high. I follered Stripes past three or four tables until he finally drawed rein and showed me the one he'd picked out for me. I drug out my chair and was about to set down when I glanced over at the table next to it, and froze.

Even with my one eye half shut, I would have known the old gent with the silver hair and the ice blue eyes anywhere. I could tell by the way them eyes narrowed and he jumped halfway out of his chair that he recognized me, too.

There was nothing to do but run a bluff, and I made it a good one. "Marshal Ridgeway!" I said, "Thank heavens I've found you!"

SIXTEEN

Bullsnakes and Robin's Eggs

U.S. Marshal Chance Ridgeway relaxed, but not much. He set back in his chair and studied me with them cold blue eyes of his. "So you've been looking for me, have you?" he asked, and I could tell he didn't believe it for a minute, "Set down and tell me *why,* Merlin Fanshaw."

"Yes, sir," I said, "but I had me a hard night, and I

216

haven't et in awhile. Be all right if we talk over breakfast? I'm buyin'."

"Appreciate the offer, son, but I had breakfast when it was breakfast time. *You* go ahead and eat; we'll talk after."

Well, sir, that was more than all right with me. Stripes, the waiter, handed me the bill of fare and I ordered most of what was wrote in it. "Bring me a double stack o' hotcakes," I told him, "some biscuits an' gravy, three or four eggs on the sunny side, a slab of ham, a side of sausage, a mess of fried taters, and a big pot of coffee. That orter get me started."

"Yes, I would think so," said Ridgeway, "if I et all that it would start *me* to a bellyache."

While I waited for the grub to arrive I sat there drinking water and trying to look as innocent as I could, which effort I have to admit was pretty much a total failure. There was a mirror across from the table, and I could see my eye had swole up still more and had gone purple as a plum. My jaw was lumpy and raw-looking, and there was a cut on my lip that hurt when I grinned, so I tended not to.

My battered old hat was sweat-stained, ragged, and dusty, and it still showed traces of the blue paint Ridgeway had put on it that day in the Brimstones. I wore it tipped back so as to go easy on my aching head, and I'd swung the stampede string around behind my ears so it wouldn't interfere with my grazing.

The banker's frock coat Mary Alice had provided me was a couple sizes too big around the middle, and held little specks of sawdust from the floor of Kelly's Bar. There were blood spots on my shirtfront, most of the buttons were missing from my fancy vest, and I had no idea where my silk cravat had gone. All the sleeves were short, my bony wrists hung well beyond my cuffs, and my knuckles were skinned and bloody from the evening's folly. That last struck me as curious, seeing as my fists had apparently come nowhere near my nocturnal opponent. The only conclusion I could draw was that I must have decided to help him out some and had beat up on *myself.* Considering my state of mind at the time, I figured that explanation was not only possible, but likely.

Add to all that my belted revolver, Romeo Flores' trail-weary Mexican pants, and my raggedy old riding boots and you can see that I cut quite a figure. Studying myself in the lookin' glass, I was forced to admit that I may have looked colorful, or comical, or quaint, or downright peculiar, but I did *not* look innocent, so I gave up trying and took to studying the tablecloth.

I could feel Ridgeway's eyes watching me, reading me the way I had read that pirate book of George's. He said nary a word; he just sat there a-studying me over the rim of his coffee cup, and I commenced to feel he understood things about me I didn't know myself. I decided then and there never to play poker with that old man, no matter what.

Directly, Stripes came through the double doors from the kitchen, carrying a tray full of vittles shoulder high, and I forgot all about Ridgeway's evil eye. The waiter set that steamin' chuck before me, and my mouth began to water like a pot-hound's at a barbecue.

"Will there be anything *else,* sir?" asked Stripes. Ridgeway took it on himself to answer, seeing as I was already a-forking it in. "I can't believe you have anything left in the *kitchen,* son," he said.

It hardly took any time at all to work my way through that grub pile. By the time I was done even the smell was gone, and there wasn't much left on the crockery but the glaze. I had ignored the pain in my jaw and had et myself into a happy stupor. All the while Ridgeway had patiently set there across from me and waited, his eyes savvy and alert.

He fished his watch out of his vest pocket, studied its face, and signaled across the room to the waiter. Ridgeway's chair skreeked like fingernails on a blackboard as he slid it back, and unfolded his lanky frame upward, all elbows and angles, like the sections of a carpenter's rule. I had nearly forgot how tall he was. From where I sat, his nickel-plated marshal's badge sort of glittered above me like the morning star, and my eyes were on a level with the ivory handles of his belted six-shooter.

"Watching you gorge yourself has been downright educational," he said, "put me in mind of one of them locust plagues from the Bible. But now it's time you paid the bill, and the *piper.* Let's go, son."

There was something in the old lawman's tone of voice that left no room for argument. I got to my feet, picked up my carpetbag, and gave Stripes enough coin to pay for my eats and then some. We'd hardly cleared the door of the Early Bird when Ridgeway lifted my Colt's Dragoon from its leather and stuck it in his coat pocket.

"No offense, son," he said, "I just figured we'd both be more comfortable if I lightened your load a bit. Rumor has it you've been a-studying the *pistolero* trade."

"Why, no such thing, marshal," says I, all innocence and virtue, "I wouldn't . . ."

"Of course not," he says, "and you wouldn't *run* on me, either. I trust you, son—that's why I didn't put irons on you. Besides, we both know if you *was* to make a break for it I'm too old to chase you. I'd just have to shoot you in the kneecap or somewhere, and that would be a bother for both of us."

Up to then my knees had been among the few parts of my body that didn't hurt, but as I imagined myself being brought down in full flight by a .44 slug *they* commenced to tingle some, *too.* "Oh, yeah," I told him, "I surely wouldn't want to cause no *bother.*"

He smoothed the silver hairs of his big handlebar moustache with his thumb and first finger, and just for a second there I thought I saw a twinkle in his eye. "My office is two blocks north of here," he said, "why don't we just mosey on up there and have us a friendly conversation?"

I felt trapped again, pushed into a corner, but I said, "Suits me right down to the ground. Let's go," and that's just what we did.

The U.S. Marshal's office in Silver City was on the second floor of the post office building. We got to it by way of a street level doorway and a steep flight of creaky stairs. Ridgeway unlocked the door at the top, and I stepped inside and looked around.

The building was made of thick, quarried stone, and the room was cool and businesslike. Navajo blankets served as rugs on the dark, oiled wood of the floor. Ridgeway's desk, cluttered with papers, circulars, and lawbooks, hunkered solid and four-square as a short-horn bull on the room's north side. File cabinets and bookshelves stood chest-high against the back wall, and a Regulator clock and a map of the district occupied the space above. A smaller desk and a couple of chairs stood out from the east wall, where a portrait of Honest Abe and a big American flag were displayed. At the room's center a rusty old potbelly stove offered the promise of heat during the winter months.

A gun rack holding a dozen rifles and shotguns stood between the windows on the south wall, the weapons secured by a long steel chain. Above that the dusty mounted head of a pronghorn buck seemed to watch the room through glassy, indifferent eyes. A hatrack stood nearby, and Ridgeway hung his pearl gray sombrero there on the way over to his desk. Thoughtfully, he placed my Dragoon atop the papers and sat down.

"Pull up a chair, son," he said, "and get comfortable. This here pow-wow could be a long one."

Once again, I did as I was told. I drug a chair over and

sat down. The marshal and me looked at each other across the scatter of paper that littered his desk. After a long pause, he said, "Now, then. You strike me as a decent, law-abiding young man. Would you say that's an accurate description of your character?"

"I always *aimed* to be decent and law-abidin', yes."

"That's good, son. You may recall that I place a high value on truthfulness. I make it a point to be truthful with people, and I expect the same from them. Are *you* a truthful young man?"

A blue-bottle fly buzzed busy but aimless at the window, caught like me between what he could see and what he could reach. For no reason I could put a name to I felt myself getting riled, and my jaw took on a stubborn set. "W-Well, yes, I am," I said, "I j-just wish others would be as truthful with m-me."

"You saying I deceived you?"

"I'm sayin' I don't know! Most everyone I've *met* these last few months has! I've got to where I don't know who I can trust and who I can't any more. I've been used, abused, rode hard and put away wet, by at least *two* cold-blooded scalawags, and *they're* just the ones I *know* about.

"You want the truth? Well, the *truth* is I don't know whether you're truthful or not. You *say* you are, but maybe you ain't telling the truth when you *say* it. I don't know whether you're an honest lawman or a badge-wearing hell-hound like Andy Wilkes. And I don't have no *idea* whether I can trust you or not—I don't know who the hell you are!"

222

With that I clammed up, crossed my arms, and sulled where I sat. I don't believe I'd ever made a speech that long before, and I was about half horrified by my outburst. I wasn't *raised* to get lippy with my elders, especially if they was federal marshals.

Ridgeway didn't seem at all ruffled by my tantrum. He just looked at me for a long moment. Then he said, "You've got sand, Merlin, and I appreciate your honesty. All right, let me *tell* you who I am.

"I grew up on a Kansas homestead with my folks in a soddy that was the highest point in ten square miles; everything else was prairie and sky.

"We were luckier than most, though, because we had us one genuine, bona fide tree in our yard. It was a young cottonwood my pa planted, and it had growed to where it was nearly eight foot tall.

"Lord, but we were proud of that tree. I was only nine, but one of my chores was to look after that little cottonwood. I carried water to it all summer and fall that first year.

"Well, sir, the little tree made it through the winter, and we were plumb tickled come spring when a pair of young robins flew in from somewhere and built their nest about four feet off the ground in its fork. We watched as the little mother robin laid her eggs and set on 'em, and I couldn't hardly wait 'til I could see the baby robins come out of their pretty blue shells.

"I was helpin' my pa dig a root cellar one day—or maybe I was just gettin' in his way—when I heard the most awful commotion coming from that tree. It was ma and pa robin, and they were chirpin' and chatterin', pitchin' theirselves a regular conniption fit.

"I came runnin' around the house to see what all the ruckus was about, and you won't believe what I saw. Them robins were flutterin' around in a dither, screechin' and screamin', and a big old bullsnake, thick as your wrist, had crawled up the trunk of that little tree and was eating their eggs!

"I don't know what came over me, but I felt so sorry for those birds and for their lost babies and so mad at that dern snake I could hardly breathe. I grabbed him by the tail with both hands and pulled, but he was wrapped tight around the trunk and I couldn't budge him.

"Everything was a red haze and I could hear my heart pounding like a trip hammer as I made for the house, got down my pa's shotgun, and rushed back to the tree. Them robin's eggs was that snake's last meal; the first shot blowed him out of the tree, and the second one killed him dead as a snake ever gets.

"Pa came a-runnin' when he heard the shootin', and so did Ma, but it was a few minutes before I came out of my rage enough to tell them what I'd done and why.

"Pa scolded me; he said bullsnakes were the farmer's friend, that the old snake was only doin' what came natural to him, but I didn't care, my heart was with them robins. Oh, they'd been foolish, of course, to build so close to the ground, but our little cottonwood was the only tree they could find for their homestead. I saw the whole thing as a clear-cut case of good and evil. That day set the course for my life, Merlin. Another kid might well have taken the snake's part, like my pa did, but my sympathies was otherwise.

"From that day to this I have made it my life's work to keep the snakes from doin' harm to the robins. I still see things in terms of good and evil, right and wrong, and while I may sometimes bend the law, I never cut evil any slack.

"And that, son, is who I am."

Ridgeway fell silent then, and the only sound in the room was the hollow ticking of the clock on the wall. I watched as a shaft of light struck the old lawman's silver hair like sunlight on fresh snow and flashed off the clock's swinging pendulum behind him. He pulled a tobacco pouch and a short-stemmed briar pipe from his coat, filled and tamped the bowl, and he took his own sweet time while he done it. Directly, he thumb-nailed a match with a snap and flare of fire and lit up, puffing slow and steady like he held title deed to Eternity.

There's something about the way pipe smokers look while they're a-smoking that makes them seem wise as all get-out. Sometimes a pipe smoker even takes on a smug, self-satisfied look like he reckoned he was a whole heap smarter than ordinary folk.

When I went to Sunday school back in Dry Creek the teacher told me King Solomon was about the wisest man who ever lived, but I believe if you was to teach even a boar hog to smoke a pipe he would take on a look of wisdom that would put old Sol in the shade. Far as I know, the good King never used tobacco much; his weakness seems to have been women.

Anyway, Ridgeway kept a-puffin' on his briar and studying me with them faded blue eyes, as the white smoke hung above his head like June clouds over a mountain peak. There was something about the way he studied me that gave me the feeling I was buck-naked in a courtroom. It seemed like he knowed everything I had ever done and mostly what I *would* do.

"And now," says he, "why don't you tell me what's been happenin' in *your* life since I seen you last?"

"I don't hardly know where to *begin,* marshal," I told him.

"Start anywhere, son. No need to run your thoughts through a cuttin' chute. Just get 'em corraled, swing open the gate, and let 'em out."

Well, to this day I can't explain why, but for some reason I done exactly what he asked. I told him about joining up with Original George at the mountain hideout, about renewing old acquaintance with *El Borrachon,* and about the murder of Mace Collyer. I told him of coming down the mountain and of the Dry Creek shootout (except, of course, the part where I cleverly put a bullet through my own leg), and I told him about the night ride to Rampage with Jigger and George.

Once I got started talking it seemed like I couldn't stop; it was like someone had blowed a hole in a dam and let the water pour out. I told Ridgeway about Slippery Mayfair and the layout of the outlaw town. I even told him about Bucktooth Betty, Jackrabbit Annie, and the Belgian Mare.

I recounted what I'd overheard George tell Shanty that day by the outhouse, and I told him about my ride to Shenanigan and my visit to Ollie Langford at the bank.

My capture by Wilkes and Faunt Bodeen, and the way they had done me back at the jail, was hard to relate but I told him that, too, and he puffed on his pipe and nodded his head like he understood and sympathized. I told him how I'd turned the tables on Bodeen and locked him in his own cell, and about my ride back to Rampage.

There was a point where I commenced to feel sort of guilty, like I was betraying George or something. Then I recalled how he had gave me them knockout drops and how he'd sent the gang on purpose into the bloody ambush at the bank, and the feeling passed.

I told Ridgeway how I'd tried to warn the boys, and I choked up for a minute and had to take hold of myself when I thought of the way Poddy Medford, Clete Potter, and Pike Fletcher had been cut down in that bullet blizzard out there on the street. I told him how Wilkes had gutshot the banker that day, and how I'd rescued Jigger St. Clare and Kiowa John. I even told him about Mary Alice, though I hadn't aimed to.

I have oftentimes been a mystery to myself, and I surely was that day. Wilkes and his deputy had put me through torture by water there at the jail and had throwed the fear of death into me, yet I had not told them what they wanted me to. But here a white-haired old lawman had set me in a chair, smiled at me like he was my grandpa or something, and I'd turned leaky-mouth and told him everything I ever knew or did.

Well, finally the water had all run out through the hole in the dam and nothing was left but the mud. I slumped back in my chair and said, "That's the whole of it, Marshal. Mary Alice is over at the hotel, George and Shanty O'Kane went their separate way and probably have dug up the payroll by now, I don't know where Kiowa John and Jigger have got to, and I haven't seen *El Borrachon* since we left the M Cross line camp."

For a time there, I just sat and listened to the ticking of Ridgeway's Regulator clock and the buzzing of the fly against the window. The old lawman's pipe had gone out, but he didn't appear to notice. For several seconds he just held the dead briar in his gnarled right hand and stared at me through narrowed eyes, like he was trying to make up his mind whether I had told him the truth or not. Finally, he struck another match and puffed until he got his pipe going again. It was several seconds more before he spoke.

"I appreciate your candor, Merlin, I really do," he said, "I believe you have told me the truth, leastways as you see it, and I believe you are a truthful young man.

"In more than thirty years behind the badge I have heard my share and then some of windies, falsehoods, and damnable lies, and I have knowed prevaricators and tale-tellers aplenty. I have got to where I can tell when a man is lying to me just by looking at him, and I can even tell when a *woman* is, most times, and that ain't near as easy.

"Anyway, I'm obliged to you for your honesty, and I'll try to return the favor. Emiliano Vasquez, or *El Borrachon,* as you call him, was shot dead and left beside the trail the day you boys left the mountain hideout. I thought Original George had done it himself, but you say him and Jigger St. Clare was with you at the time, so I reckon George must have ordered it done. I figure he found out the man was my deputy, and laid him off, permanent and final. That irritates me some. Emiliano was a good man, and a fair to middlin' deputy. He'll be hard to replace.

"Maybe *you'd* like to take up the law. What do you say, Merlin, do your sympathies lie with the robins or the snakes?"

"I don't know, marshal. The deputy business sounds near as dangersome as the outlaw trade."

"More so, I'd say."

"What about that feller I killed in Dry Creek?"

"Self defense, sounds like to me. Them four drifters made their play, and lost. There's hazards in the bounty huntin' trade, too."

"Well, then, what about the way I helped them bank robbers escape?"

"I have no interest in the Shenanigan Bank. My concern is with that stolen Army payroll. Besides, you were acting as my inside man with the gang at the time."

The office door opened, and I like to jumped out of

my chair. I had heard no footfall at all on them creaky wooden stairs, and the sudden sound of the latch after the stillness spooked me some. I turned toward the doorway just as Ridgeway's deputy, Luther Little Wolf, cat-footed through it in his moccasins. I could see he remembered me.

He gave me a slim smile as he passed my chair, walked over to the marshal, and handed him an envelope.

"Telegram, huh?" Ridgeway said, "much obliged, Luther."

He put his pipe aside, took a pair of gold-rimmed spectacles from his vest pocket, and put them on. He looked embarrassed. "I can see better'n some eagles when it comes to *far*," he said, "but I do sometimes have trouble with *near*."

Luther lounged beside the desk, a slight smile on his face and his black eyes heavy-lidded and unreadable. Ridgeway tore open the envelope and commenced to read the telegram, holding it carefully with both hands as he studied it. Finally, he laid the paper on his cluttered desk, carefully smoothed it with his fingers, and removed his spectacles. He sat back in his chair, and I seen a look of surprise and wonder on his face, as if he had just learned the earth is flat after all. "Well, I declare," he said.

"It's from Ernie Filmore, town marshal over at Dry Creek. According to him, Original George Starkweather and Shanty O'Kane were ambushed and *killed* there last night."

SEVENTEEN

Rain, Rain, Go Away

I've heard it said that sometimes when a feller is dying his whole life flashes in front of his eyes like a series of views in a stereoscope. Well, I have no idea whether that's true or not, but when Ridgeway told me what the telegram said a whole passel of pictures went stampeding through my mind, except they were all of Shanty O'Kane and Original George Stark-weather.

I saw Shanty at his dutch ovens by the flickering light of a cook fire, his laughing eyes the deep blue of summer sky, and his wispy red hair bright as flame. I saw him as I did the morning I woke up in Jackrabbit Annie's bed, with him grinning around the stem of his old clay pipe and bringing me coffee and vittles on a tray.

I saw Original George, too, the way I saw him the evening he rode across that high mountain meadow on his leggy thoroughbred and reined up before me. I saw in memory his grizzled beard, his strong, white teeth, and the ragged scar stabbing down across his cheek, and I looked into his yellow eyes and thought again of a proud, mad eagle.

I saw him as he was that day at the corral, his legs spread wide and his feet planted firm in the black mountain dirt. Again I saw him gun Mace Collyer, cold

231

and deliberate, like he was swatting a fly or slapping a skeeter.

I saw him again on that sun-scorched hilltop back of Rampage, reading a pirate book in the shade of a bawd's silk parasol, and then at last I saw him and Shanty in my mind's eye, lying side by side in death at the funeral parlor in Dry Creek.

For a long moment the only sounds in the room were the ticking of the wall clock and the nervous buzzing of the fly at the window. Then Ridgeway cleared his throat and said, "Well, there's nothing for it but to ride over to Dry Creek and look into this. I wouldn't take Ernie Filmore's word that the sun rises in the east."

Ridgeway came out from behind his desk and looked at his silent deputy. "Go on down to the livery and fetch our horses, Luther," he told him, "and pick out a good mount for young Merlin here, too. He'll be goin' with us."

Over the past few days my pride had been beat down like wheat in a hailstorm. I'd hid from the Progress County Sheriff in a pantry, Mary Alice Weems had kissed me and sent me away like I was her kid brother. I had discovered I couldn't hold my liquor in a peach basket, and I had been trounced by a total stranger in an Irish bar. Then, come morning I'd been swept out onto the street along with the old sawdust and cigar butts, and I had stumbled head on into the U.S. Marshal for the district and been took into custody. All that had been bad enough, but now Ridgeway was asking his smirkin' deputy to pick out a *horse* for me. The way I saw it, that was the straw that caved the camel in, and I wasn't a-going to stand for it.

"I d-druther p-pick out my *own* horse, if you don't mind," I said, "and anyway, I never *said* I was g-goin' with you."

"Sorry, son," Ridgeway said, "I would surely appreciate it if you'd ride along."

"Do I have a choice?"

"I would surely appreciate it if you'd ride along."

"Th-that's what I thought. What about my gun?"

"Go on with Luther and get you a horse. I believe I'll just hold your weapon a little longer."

Luther's black eyes had a shine to them like polished glass. He flashed his thin smile at me and nodded toward the door. For just a second there I gave thought to wiping the grin off his face, but I had lost considerable of my confidence, so I just took my shaps and spurs from my carpetbag, wrapped what was left of my dignity around me like a blanket, and we headed out for the livery.

The Blue Dog Livery Barn and Wagon Yard was the biggest and best of three such businesses in Silver City, and that's where Ridgeway and Luther kept their horses. The gift of speech had been wasted on Luther; he seldom used it, but somehow he did manage to let the young hostler know I was to pick out a mount from the loose stock, and the kid took me around back to the corrals.

Finding a decent saddle horse among that bunch took

some doing. The Blue Dog horses seemed to range from ordinary all the way down to sorry. At last I spied a deep-chested bay gelding that I judged to be the best of the bunch, and I threw a saddle on him and stepped aboard.

He commenced to skitter sideways like a crab, rolling his eyes and blowing his nose. I could see he'd been having his way with the town-folk and required someone to call his bluff. The mood I was in, nothing could have suited me better. I took a deep seat, spurred him sharp in the flanks, and the big gelding like to passed out from sheer surprise.

I had to laugh; it was clear he wasn't used to such treatment. He bellered like a bull calf and fell to bucking, but he'd lost the knack. He was plenty strong, just as I'd figured he'd be, but his pitching was awkward and ill-timed. I rode him easy and kept on a-spurring him until he quit.

The bay quivered like a wet dog while we made a circle of the corral, and I patted his neck and talked some calm into him. I was pleased; the gelding had proved to be both strong and halfway smart. It hadn't took him long until he'd seen he wasn't going to win no contest with me, and he'd cut his losses and gone to behaving himself.

By the time we came back around the second time, I saw Luther watching me as he sat his polouse pony just outside the corral. He had Ridgeway's Morgan behind him on a lead rope, and as I rode the bay out through the gate I saw a flicker of what just might have been admiration pass over his face. Of course, there's no way I could know for sure; I have seen granite boulders show more expression than did Luther Little Wolf.

The sky had took on a dark gray cast, and I noticed both Ridgeway's horse and the Appaloosa had rain slickers tied to their saddles. I stepped down from the bay, handed Luther my reins, and said, "I don't have no slicker, deputy. I'll ask the kid if he's got one he can spare."

I could feel Luther's hard eyes on my back as I ambled away toward the barn. The hostler had stayed behind to watch me ride the bay, and he stood now just outside the big doors, leaning on a manure fork and worrying a quid of chewing tobacco around in his jaws. He was short-built, curly-haired, and stocky—he put me in mind of a sleepy young bull a-chewing his cud in a pasture.

He carried a pencil stub in the front pocket of his dashboard overalls, and I took it off him and wrote a quick note to Mary Alice on the back of an old feed bill. "Two things," I told him, "I need to borrow a slicker if you have one you can spare, and I need you to take this message to a lady at the Winslow Hotel after I ride out. There's a dollar in it for you if you will."

For a minute there I was afraid I'd gave him more than his brain could digest. I had asked two things of him, but I had the clear impression one thought at a time was about his limit. He gave me his full attention, but stopped working his tobacco quid and just stood there slack-jawed and frowning while he tried to take it all in.

"I said there's a dollar in it for you if you'll do it," I told him, stuffing the note and the dollar into his pocket, "the note is for Miss Mary Alice Weems, at the Hotel Winslow. You savvy?"

I could have saddled a horse in the time it took him to answer, but I was relieved to see he understood. He grinned, and tobacco juice droozled out one corner of his mouth. "Mary Alice Weems," he said, "at the Winslow. You bet." Then he rummaged around inside the tack room and came back with a scabby old oilskin I believe must have belonged to Noah at the time of the flood. The kid held it out to me like it was some kind of family hairloom. I took it from him and turned away just as Luther rode up outside with the led horses.

The wind had turned colder now, and I could smell the coming rain in the quick gusts that tugged at my hat and peppered my face with grit from the street. Through half-shut eyes I watched as Luther kicked his tough little pony into a trot up the alley behind the post office. Ridgeway stood waiting, tall and thin as a crane on a sandbar. He caught up the reins to his Morgan and straddled him as the deputy and me came alongside. Then, with Luther in the lead and Ridgeway riding behind me, we left town at a high lope and lined out on the road that led to Dry Creek.

The skies turned darker as we traveled, and the light took on a greenish cast. Luther drew rein just this side of Brimstone Gap, took a look at the fast-moving clouds, and pulled on his slicker. Ridgeway and me followed suit. It was well that we did because right then a lightning bolt struck maybe two hundred yards distant, and the rain commenced to spatter down in drops the size of pullet eggs. The thunderclap that followed struck my ears like the crack of doom, and the bay horse shuddered, bug-eyed with fright, then surged ahead with a jerk like it was trying to outrun its fear.

It rained hard all the way to Dry Creek, and the thirsty earth sucked up moisture 'til it couldn't hold no more. Muddy water rushed and boiled in washouts that had been bone dry all summer, and the rain snuck in through my ancient slicker in so many places I wondered why I'd bothered to put the dang thing on in the first place. Rainwater crept inside the oil-skin and slithered down my spine in a chilly crawl that puddled where my crotch met the saddle before it moseyed on down my legs and into my boots. Having been born and raised in dry country, I'd come to appreciate rain, but right then I believe I'd have appreciated it more had I not been so *amongst* it.

The twenty-odd mile ride from Silver City to Dry Creek was cold and miserable. By the time we turned our steaming horses onto Dry Creek's mud-rutted thoroughfare it was coming dark. The rain had settled into a steady downpour which spattered the weathered board awnings of the buildings and drummed a soggy patter all along the puddled street. A few saddlehorses stood, eyes closed and heads down, at the hitchrack in front of the Oasis, and a mangy town dog shivered just outside the double doors, too wet and miserable even to bark. Now and then a thunderbolt lit the gloom with a blinding flash. For just a split second bright raindrops froze in mid-air and the world flickered stark black and white before the wet grayness covered everything over again. Lamplight burned a smoky orange in a few windows, but other than that the whole town looked drenched, glum, and deserted.

One of the places the lights were on was the Dry Creek Funeral Parlor, and it was there that Ridgeway reined up. He looked weary from the hard ride and stiff from the cold rain, but he had that dogged, resigned look that old men and critters sometimes wear, as he stepped down and loose-tied his Morgan to the hitchrail. Luther and me follered suit, and the three of us slogged around to the steps in front of the mortuary and went up the rain-slick planks into the relative dryness underneath the awning.

Right then the front door swung open, spilling a bucketful of yellow lamplight out onto the street, and I saw the unmistakable form of town marshal Ernie Fillmore bulk up the doorway. Even in shadow and lit from behind like he was now, there was no mistaking Ernie. He was built like a summer squash or a pear, narrow of shoulder and wide of hip like a woman; he carried a paunch he'd growed and nourished the way some men cultivate a moustache.

I hadn't been inside the funeral parlor since my Pa's passing, but near as I could tell it hadn't changed all that much. On the left side of the room was a space that served as a parlor for the kinfolk of the departed. The same big sofa and two armchairs I remembered stood huddled around a Sunshine stove, flanked by potted ferns. To the right stood a couple of fancy, polished coffins, one of which was propped open so as to show off its fancy white silk innards. On the wall, dusty black plush drapery framed a faded picture I supposed was meant to be a view of Heaven or the River Jordan, one or the other. It showed some peaceful hills, trees, and a crick, but there wasn't no deer, elk, nor horses in it so it didn't interest me all that much.

I had known old Ambrose, the undertaker, since my school days, when me and the other young hellions used to chunk snowballs at his high silk hat. Right then he came out through the curtain that separated the parlor from his living quarters, and when he saw me standing there with Ridgeway and Luther he gave me a look that was a perfect blend of surprise and curiosity. I knew he was remembering the day of the shooting affray at the Oasis when he'd seen me ride out of town with Original George and Jigger St. Clare. I figured he was wondering what the Sam Hill I was doing now in the company of the U.S. Marshal. He never let on, though; he'd been a bone merchant long enough to know how to keep a checkrein on his features, and when it came to poker faces I believe he could even have held his own with Luther Little Wolf.

"Evenin', marshal," he said to Ridgeway, "you boys made good time."

"We did at that, Ambrose," Ridgeway told him, "where are George and the Irishman?"

"*I'm* the one who *found* 'em," Ernie said, crowding in front of Ambrose, "inside the old Parker Hotel, they was." He looked puffed up and proud, like finding two dead outlaws was the high point of his career as a peace officer. Knowing Ernie, it probably was.

"They're downstairs, marshal," Ambrose said, "but they won't be goin' anywhere. Why don't you boys have a cup of coffee first?"

"Obliged, Ambrose, but I'll see them now," Ridgeway said, "coffee afterward."

Ambrose shrugged. "As you wish," he said, picking up the lamp from the table by the window, "follow me."

I druther have had my teeth pulled by a drunken blacksmith than follow Ambrose and Ridgeway down that dark, narrow stairway to the embalming room, but that's what I done. Worse than that, I acted like it didn't bother me a lick, like I done it all the time. I ran the worst bluff you ever saw. I even yawned, like I was bored stiff, but inside I was scared as a cottontail in a snake den. I reckon it's true, like the good book says, that pride can lead a feller to a fall, but I've found it can also turn him into a terrible hypocrite.

When we reached the foot of the stairs, old Ambrose ushered us through the door and smack into the center of his work room. The walls of the room were of rough-cut rock, and there were bottles and jars of different sizes and shapes on shelves all along the back. The whole place smelled of embalming fluid, the sick-sweet aroma of death and decay, and cigar smoke. As I looked the place over Ambrose set his lamp down and lit up another stogie from its flame. Under the shelves stood a long work table that held all manner of instruments, hoses, tubing, and what-not, The rear of the funeral parlor was cut below street level, and big double doors faced the alley side of the building. From Pa's funeral, I knew that through them doors Ambrose loaded the dear departeds into his rubber-tired hearse for their last earthly ride.

The fellers we had come to see lay side by side on two waist-high tables in the room's center. When Ambrose held his lamp high with one hand and drew back the sheets that covered them I like to passed out altogether. Shanty O'Kane lay still and waxy, his blue eyes filmed over, but wide open and staring. His mouth was open, too, and the face that had always been so rosy-cheeked and flushed was now a dreadful greenish gray. Only his wild red hair still seemed the same as it had been in life. He was dressed the way he was when I'd seen him last, but his faded flannel shirt and braces were soaked now with dry, blackened blood from a gaping chest wound.

My throat had gone tight, and I felt sad and sort of hollow, somehow. The feisty Irishman had fed me, joked with me, and showed me nothing but kindness during the brief time I'd known him, and I hoped that somehow he'd known how much I had appreciated him. I closed my eyes and swallered the memories; I

241

even tried to pray for him some, for whatever it might be worth.

Outside, a thunderclap cracked and rolled, loud as cannon fire, and I knew lightning had hit somewhere close. I sure didn't want to, but I lifted my eyes and looked at the other body then, and the sight stunned me like a blow to the face. The body wore Original George's black wool suit and fancy shirt, all right, and his hand-made boots and gloves, but where its face should have been there was only a mushy mess of torn flesh and splintered bone. "Took one square in the face from a shotgun," Ambrose was saying, "double-ought buck, from the pellets I found. Sawed off ten or twelve gauge, from the spread."

"But he'd been head-shot before that by a heavy caliber rifle or carbine," he continued, "probably the same weapon that took the Irisher in the chest. I'd say whoever erased his features with the scattergun prob'ly didn't *like* him much."

"I found 'em both where the old kitchen in the Parker Hotel used to be," Ernie said, "blood everywhere! I hightailed it over here and told Ambrose, and we fetched the bodies here. That's when I sent you the telegram."

"I'll want to see where it happened myself," Ridgeway said, "what happened to these boys' weapons?"

"Got 'em down at my office, along with of George's pocket watch and spurs," Ernie grinned. "He was packin' two revolvers, a derringer, and a Bowie knife, if you can believe it. Some bad man! He don't look so tough *now* though, does he?"

I heard a roaring in my ears. My heart commenced hammering, and I seemed to go half-blind, looking at the world through a blood-red haze. I spun and snatched Ernie halfway off his feet by his shirtfront.

"You whey-bellied, gutless, chicken-stealin' dog!" I hollered, "You bark pretty loud when the big dog's dead, but if that body even *twitched* right now, you'd hunt a hole so fast you'd be ten minutes ahead of your *shadow!*"

Ernie's face went white. His eyes bugged out, his lip trembled, and he stared at me like he figured I'd gone stark, staring loco, which I suppose I had. Ridgeway seemed amused. His ice-blue eyes seemed to twinkle as he reached out and gently but firmly pried my fingers off the pear-shaped lawman.

"You'll have to excuse young Merlin here," he drawled, "the boy had *feelin's* for the deceased, and I reckon your proud mouth offended him some. Offended *me* some, *too,* if the truth be told. Might be best if you just shut up awhile, Ernie."

Ernie glared at me and smoothed out his shirt where I'd took hold of him. "Hell, I'll do better than that," he huffed, "I'll just go on back to my office if I ain't wanted here. It ain't that I don't have *work* to do."

"Yes, why don't you do that?" Ridgeway said, "I'll be along to see you directly. And much obliged again, marshal, you've been most helpful and professional."

Ridgeway had thrown a bone to Ernie's injured

pride, and I saw it take effect. Dry Creek's fighting lawman squared his shoulders, throwed out his chest, and tried to pull his belly in. Then, with one last hard glance at me, he opened the door and I heard his boots go clomping up the stairs.

Luther leaned against the wall behind me, and I caught his eye. His gaze was steady, and his lips held a thin smile, but the deputy was not a book I knew how to read. I had no idea what he was thinking.

"I believe I'll go up and have a cup of that coffee you offered, Ambrose," Ridgeway said, "I've seen all I need to for the moment, and anyway, this place ain't exactly no rose garden."

Ambrose covered the bodies again and picked up his lamp. "It was never meant to be, marshal," said he, "this here is just a side-track depot on eternity's railroad."

We clumb the stairs to the rooms above and sat drinking coffee while Ridgeway and Ambrose spoke of the weather, cattle prices, and crime in the territory. I felt restless, fidgety. I finished my coffee and sat there as long as I could stand it. Then I stood up and told Ridgeway, "I need me some air, marshal. All right if I just step outside for a minute? That smell downstairs . . ."

The marshal's glance was sharp; he studied me for a moment, his wise old eyes wary. Then he grinned and raised his cup in a sort of salute. "Sure thing, son, go ahead," he said, "I don't reckon you'd run on me now, would you? There's no need."

"No," I told him, "there's no need."

Outside, in front of Ambrose's, I leaned against a building upright and looked out at the dark and muddy street. The rain continued as before, pattering on the board awning above with a drumming rhythm that somehow gave me a sad, lonesome feeling. Now and again a lightning flash would light up the street, and the shabby buildings across the way would stand out in stark light and shadow as the thunder rumbled overhead.

A cold breeze had started blowing, and it brought the scent of wet, rich earth and of sagebrush from the prairie beyond town. I turned my face into the wind and thought again of Shanty O'Kane and Original George, not the way they was now—cold, dead meat in the basement of a mortuary—but the way they *had* been, bold, reckless, and full of life.

And then—and I'm danged if I know why—my throat got tight, my eyes filled up, and I went to bawling like a dang baby there in the darkness.

EIGHTEEN
Dead, or Alive?

I slept that night, or anyway tried to, along with Luther Little Wolf up in the loft of Walt's Livery Stable. Mostly, I just laid there in the dark and listened to the rain a-pattering on the roof while I tried to quiet my busy mind and get me some shut-eye.

Collecting my scattered thoughts was like a man alone trying to move a herd; no sooner did I get my ruminations gathered and lined out than a stray thought would quit the bunch and bolt for thick timber. By the time I'd get that one turned back my other thoughts would have drifted off somewheres and I'd have to round them up again, too.

The loft was darker than the shady side of midnight, and I sensed rather than saw Luther a-slumbering nearby in the blackness. It came as no surprise to me that the deputy was as quiet asleep as he was awake; he neither tossed nor turned, and he never even snored or breathed heavy, far as I could tell. Being around Luther Little Wolf was downright restful, once a feller got used to the unnatural stillness.

Ridgeway had gone over to see Ernie Filmore at the jail, and I knew he'd smooth the town marshal's ruffled feathers some and learn what more he could about the killing of Shanty and George.

Every time I was about to drift off to sleep I'd recall the way the bodies had looked, lying cold and still there in Ambrose's basement, and I'd come wide awake again. I'd remember the way the room had *smelled,* too. I'd have to turn my mind away from the memory and center my thinking on the good smells around me there in the darkness—odors of cured hay and horseflesh, of leather and grain, and old wood.

Just about the time I gave up all hope of ever falling asleep, I fell asleep, of course, but my repose was any-thing but restful. Dreams came galloping through my mind—jumbled dreams and busy dreams, and silly dreams that I took serious while I was in the midst of them. Most of these fancies featured Original George, Shanty O'Kane, and the boys, but Andy Wilkes, Faunt Bodeen, and Mary Alice were in some of them, too. I could make no sense of my wild reveries at all.

Next thing I knew I was awake and back in the real world, where life is just as crazy as dreams but somewhat more solid. My mouth was dry, as though I'd been snoring or talking in my sleep, and I felt more tired than when I'd gone to bed. I judged the time to be just past dawn, because sunlight was already reaching in through the cracks in the wall and lighting up the dust motes that hung in the still morning air.

I pulled on my boots and dumb down the ladder to the barn below, to find that Luther had already grained the horses and was in the process of grooming Ridgeway's big Morgan with curry comb and brush. He wore his usual spare smile, and he nodded slightly when I came up to the stall where he was working.

"Sleep good?" he asked, and I nearly fell over from the shock. I'd never heard Luther talk before. "Tolerable," I told him, "I dreamed a lot. How about you?"

"You sleep *loud,*" he said, ignoring my question, "talk plenty."

"Well, that sure ain't one of *your* failings, awake *or* asleep. I'd about decided you *couldn't* talk."

I walked over to the barn door and looked out. The morning air was chilly and knife-edged, and I shivered as I surveyed Dry Creek's single street and the country

247

beyond. Pink light painted the rough wooden buildings and tinted the few tattered clouds that drifted above the mountains. The whole town looked fresh-washed, clean, and as good as ever Dry Creek could look.

The rutted street was a sea of mud that morning, with pools of water standing everywhere, and as I stood watching the town wake up I saw Ridgeway making his way across the street toward me. He was high-stepping through the muck like some long-legged marsh bird, and the way he kept studying the mire as he walked put me in mind of a big old blue heron looking for fish. As he neared the barn he looked up, saw me in the doorway, and smiled.

"The *good* news is old Ignacio has quit the sheep-herdin' business and opened his own cafe," he said, "word has it the man serves a fine breakfast when he's sober, and I'm told he's sober this morning. You boys interested?"

I've done some foolish things in my time, but I have never yet turned down an invitation to eat. "You bet," I told him. Luther, of course, said nary a word, but he favored Ridgeway with a quick, shy smile that I figured was equal to at least a thirty-minute speech. Luther put the marshal's gelding back in its stall, we washed our hands and faces in the cold water of the watering trough, and then the three of us slogged off through the gumbo to breakfast.

Ignacio hadn't changed a lick since I'd seen him the day of the gun battle at the Oasis. He gave me a gap-toothed smile when we came in, and I knew that, like Ambrose, he was no doubt wondering what I was doing in the company of the U.S. Marshal of the district. But Ignacio was almost as good at minding his own business as he was at cooking, and he never turned a hair nor said a word. At Ridgeway's request, he showed us to a private room in back, fetched us a pot of coffee, and took our orders from a dog-eared bill of fare. Then he sauntered off to the kitchen, and we were left alone.

"Ernie Filmore says he was out of town when George and the Irishman were killed, and that he found the bodies when he got back," Ridgeway said, "but I believe he was here in Dry Creek all the time.

"I think he heard gunfire over at the old Parker Hotel, but didn't act on it until after the shooters rode out of town. Ernie is—a *prudent* man."

"He's a yeller-bellied blowhard," I said pleasantly.

"Be that as it may, Merlin, your banty rooster outburst last evenin' put our good city marshal in a sod-pawin' mood. It took me a half quart of conversation fluid and a whole *mess* of soft answers to turn away his wrath.

"But it was worth it. Ernie did admit to hearing the killers ride out, and he says he talked to a cowpuncher who saw two riders leave town at a high lope a half hour after the shootin'. Said one of 'em was ridin' a thoroughbred of the kind Original George always favored."

Ridgeway took a long pull on his coffee, and set the cup down.

"What I believe happened is this. Original George

and Shanty O'Kane left Rampage on the day of the Shenanigan robbery and rode here to Dry Creek. I can't prove it, of course, but I suspect Ernie knew they were here, and looked the other way. George may even have paid him to do just that."

"More likely, George just threw a scare into him," I said, "Ernie seems to scare pretty easy."

"Could be. Anyway, I figure your tall tale to Wilkes about the boys having hid out at the Parker Hotel gave George an idea, so him and Shanty did just that.

"Now you told me Jigger St. Clare and Kiowa John were riding double on Kiowa's blue roan when they left you in Shenanigan. Ernie found a wind-broke, lathered blue roan wandering out south of town just after the shooters left, still packin' a saddle and pretty well used up. I figure the boys spotted George and Shanty's horses out back of the Parker and realized they'd caught up with the man who'd sent them into the ambush at Shenanigan. So they did a little ambushin' them-selves—took out both George and Shanty with a big-bore carbine, then gave their old boss a final touch with a shotgun blast to the face. Then they took George and Shanty's horses and lit out."

"Maybe," I said, "You been over to the hotel where it happened?"

"At first light this mornin'. But I'd like you and Luther to go over there with me after we've et. Might be you boys will find somethin' I missed."

Right then Ignacio came out of the kitchen with a prime load of steaming vittles on a tray, and I confess I lost my concentration on what Ridgeway was saying. I could smell them goldy-brown hotcakes, fried taters, and bacon strips before ever they reached our table, and the palaver came to a complete halt while we wolfed down the grub.

The old Parker Hotel was a ramshackle, two-story frame building at the south edge of town. When Ridgeway, Luther, and me approached it that morning I was surprised at how desolate and run-down the place had become. It stood there in the morning sun like a crippled old buffalo, its brown, weathered siding warped and water-stained and its second-story windows staring like sightless eyes out across the plains.

The Parker hadn't been a going concern even in the best of times, and its good times had been few. Then, five winters previous, a late evening fire had exploded through the place, sending the last few paying guests out into the sub-zero weather in their nightshirts and drawers. This event caused the innkeeper to give up at last, pack his bags, and catch the first stage east to what he hoped would be gentler climes and greener pastures. The Parker had stood gutshot, forlorn, and abandoned since that night.

And now it had become the place where Original George and Shanty O'Kane had died. If Ambrose was right about his mortuary being a side-track depot on the railroad to eternity, then this was the place where George and Shanty had bought their tickets. The cold breeze rippled the tall grass and moaned through the empty rooms and hallways of the Parker, and I felt as lost and dejected as the old place looked.

Luther and me followed Ridgeway up onto the rickety gallery and went inside. Pigeons flew up in a dusty commotion as we came in, and fluttered outdoors through the glassless front windows. Broken glass, old plaster, and pigeon poop littered the floors, and for some reason it felt colder inside than it had outside. I know that sounds strange, but if you've been around old buildings much you'll know what I mean.

The marshal led the way on back through what once was the hotel dining room into the kitchen, and it was there I saw where the killings had took place. Bloodstains, now a rusty brown, spattered the wall and colored the floor. Plaster, lath, and part of the door jamb had been torn away just below knee level by buckshot. Ridgeway held up a copper cartridge case and said, "Found this over yonder by the baseboard. Fifty-six caliber, from a Spencer carbine, I'd say, probably the Indian model. Would you know what weapon Kiowa John carried, Merlin?"

"Yessir. He shot a Spencer. Had it in a saddle scabbard the day of the Shenanigan ambush."

"Yes. What else do you see here, son?"

"Well . . . there's a pint whiskey bottle there by that pile of plaster, and what looks like beef jerky. And that broken clay pipe there is what Shanty called his *dudeen*. It's been filled, but neither lit nor smoked."

"What does that tell you?"

"Tells me George and Shanty were took by surprise,

which is about the only way a man *could* have got the better of George. They had et some jerky and drunk some whiskey, and Shanty was fixin' to light up his pipe when they were bushwhacked."

"That's about how I see it, too, son. One bullet took the Irishman in the chest, second caught George in the head. Neither man was able to get a shot off, but George *almost* did—he had a cocked revolver in his hand when Ernie found him. That bloody streak yonder is where George slid down, his head and shoulders still against the wall. Then one of the bushwhackers stood up close and personal and gave him a full charge of buckshot, right in the face. I have a feeling the killer was *annoyed* about something."

Luther had knelt down and was carefully examining the littered, blood-stained floor. "Well, deputy?" Ridgeway said, "What about it? Find anything that tells a different story?"

Luther paused, straightened, and stood up. His shrug told us that he had not.

When we got back to the livery, Ridgeway set himself down on a hay bale and lit up his pipe while Luther saddled the horses. "Well, son," the marshal said, "I reckon this trip puts a lid on the life and times of Original George Starkweather, and on the payroll robbery, as well. I figure only George knew where the loot is buried, and now that he's taken a one-way ride to the Happy Huntin' Grounds I don't reckon it ever *will* be located.

"Almost thought I'd found it once. When the gang split up after the robbery, George and a kid named Bobby Bowlegs wound up runnin' with the cash. But young Bobby had taken a bullet during the holdup, and he perished sometime before the sun went down.

"Reason I know that is Luther and me found his body next day in a shallow grave just west of the old windmill at Alkali Springs, but we found no trace of either the Army's cash or Original George. When first I saw that fresh-dug soil I was sure we'd found the money. No such luck, though; it was just young Bobby's burial place. Luther and me piled up some rocks to mark the spot and rode on. But the grave did surprise me somewhat. I thought, 'George Starkweather must not be *himself* these days.' Never would have thought he'd have took time to bury the kid."

Ridgeway looked thoughtful. His pipe had gone out, and he tapped it twice on the palm of his hand to knock the dottle out.

"As for Androcles Wilkes, and his part in all this," he said, "well, I know what I know—what we *both* know—I just can't *prove* it. But I'm a patient man, Merlin, and one of these days the high sheriff of Progress County will leave some scat he can't cover up. When that happens, I aim to *be* there, and I will pounce upon him like a cat upon a dickie bird."

The marshal stood up, all elbows, knees, and angles, and grinned. "What about you, Merlin?" he asked, "You ridin' back to Silver City with us? I can always use help keepin' the bullsnakes out of the birds' nests."

"Much obliged, marshal, but not right now," I told him, "I think I'll just stay around here a day or so, maybe see if I can hire on with one of the cow outfits along the river. All right if I keep the bay for a few days?"

"That'll be fine, son. Just bring him back when you get the chance."

I watched Ridgeway and Luther saddle up and get ready to ride out. The old lawman looked out along the road that led to Silver City, but it seemed to me his thoughts went a good deal farther. He sat a horse well, tall and straight-backed in the saddle. Before he touched spur to flank he reached back into his saddlebag and came up with my holstered Colt's Dragoon. "Almost forgot," he said as he handed it down to me, "I believe this hogleg belongs to you."

I thanked him and buckled the six-gun about my waist. Ridgeway crossed his hands on the saddlehorn and stood in the stirrups as he watched me. "I reckon advice that's free is just about worth the price, Merlin," he said, "but I'll give you some anyway. In my thirty-odd years behind a badge I have observed that them who follow the *pistolero* trade mostly have short life spans. I'd like to see *you* reach a ripe and mature old age."

I grinned, and we shook hands. "I'd like that, too, marshal," I said.

I stood and watched Ridgeway and Luther ride out on the road north until they disappeared from view over a low hill. From somewhere out in the sagebrush a meadowlark yodeled his bright music, and the breeze that sighed down from the Brimstones held a hint of ice, and coming winter. I smelled woodsmoke in the air and felt a chill through my shirt that made me wish I had thought to bring a coat instead of just a leaky, old, oil-skin slicker.

It had been my intention to say howdy to my former boss, old Walt, when he came down to the stable, but the old man never showed up. I figured he'd had the good sense to build up his fire and go back to bed. I paced around awhile, took comb and brush to the bay, and I even cleaned out his stall.

I was restless, nervous, for some reason. I couldn't seem to hold still, and that wasn't just because of the morning cold, neither. Something was worrying at the edges of my mind, a shadowy thought I couldn't quite put a name to, and I felt the need to get alone with myself and see if I could drag it out of its hole and into the light.

Usually, when those times come to me I get horse-back and ride the country until my thinking clears, but on that morning I felt the need for a quiet, warm place next to a stove, so I slogged across the muddy street and made my way uptown to the Oasis Saloon.

There was nobody in the place except the bartender at that hour; even the morning regulars hadn't showed up yet. I was glad to find it warm and dry inside, and the big, sheet-iron heating stove drawed me like a magnet to a table nearby. "Fetch me a pot of coffee and a cup, will you, pardner?" says I to the barkeep, "I need to spend a little time with myself and get warm, inside and out."

"*Coffee?*" he said, sort of snippy and sarcastic, "This ain't no restaurant, mister. We serve whiskey and beer here."

I brought my Colt's Dragoon out of the leather and placed it on the table. "I like my coffee hot and black," I told him, "and served without argument. When I *get* it that way I generally don't *kill* anyone."

It was like he hadn't really seen me at first. His eyes went wide and he swallered his sneer. I reckon he took a second look and saw where he might have misjudged me somewhat. "I'll have to make a fresh pot," he said, "it'll take a few minutes."

"That's all right, pardner," I told him, "I've *got* a few minutes."

The barroom looked the same as it had the day Jigger, George, and me shot it out with the drifters, or at least most of it did. The big oil lamps still hung above the tables, and sunlight slanted in through the front windows, just as before. Even an old spider web in the corner near the tin ceiling was as I remembered it. But there were some things that weren't the same, nor ever would be again.

There was Elmo, who had tended bar at the Oasis for so many years, killed in an "accident" by Androcles Wilkes and his mad-dog deputy. And there was Original George himself, gunned down in an ambush, cold and dead in an undertaker's cellar. And who

257

knew where Jigger St. Clare was?

I still had not let my eyes go to that part of the room where the shooting had taken place. The barkeep brought the coffee, and I drank most of a cup before I let myself look. Even then I sort of snuck up on the scene out of the corner of my eye.

The walls had been re-plastered and painted, the floor had been scrubbed and oiled, and the table scarred by the drifter's bullet now sported a new green felt cover.

The sounds, sights, and smells of that day came back to me with a rush, and I stood again with George and Jigger against the men who'd come to kill us. In my mind I smelled the bitter smoke, saw the stabbing tongues of fire belch from the revolvers, and heard once more the sharp, wicked roar of the guns. I recalled the sudden quiet when the shooting ended. I saw George tending my wounded thigh with whiskey, a bar towel, and humor. And then, suddenly, I found myself missing the old pirate and grieving his death.

Once, when I was just a little kid and living with my Pa on the home place, a pair of young foxes got into our hen house one night and killed every chicken. We must have had twenty hens, and those two bushy-tailed renegades just butchered them for sport. They didn't even eat what they'd killed.

I had taken care of those chickens, that had been my job. I'd fed the brainless, helpless things. I'd watered them, gathered their eggs, and helped Pa clean their coop, and I was about as outraged as a little kid can be. I thought those foxes had been as crazy mean as anything I'd yet heard of, and I told my Pa I *hated* them.

Pa's face went sober and sorrowful, and he was quiet for a spell. Finally, he said, "I know, Merlin, it *ain't* fair, and it don't make a lick of sense. But what's done is done, and you can't hate a fox for *bein'* a fox."

I've forgotten lots of things Pa told me, I guess, but I never forgot what he said that day at the chicken house. And I guess that's how I'd come to feel the way I did about Original George. I knew him for what he was; he'd been evil, treacherous, and completely ruthless, but I couldn't bring myself to hate him. I could, and did, hate what he had done, but I couldn't hate George for being George.

And then that nagging inside my head came a-nibbling at my memory again. I closed my eyes and tried my best to stir my recollection. What was it Ridgeway had said? Something about George burying Bobby Bowlegs near Alkali Springs, and about how that had surprised him. How had he put it? Oh, yes: "George must not be *himself* these days."

I poured myself another cup of coffee, and took a sip. "Well, *that's* a fact," I thought, "poor bastard is *not* himself these days. He's *dead.*"

Then another memory came into focus, sharp-edged and crystal clear. It was a picture of George, bare of foot and chest, that night in the house at Rampage. I saw again the scars from bullet and blade amid the thick matted hair of his upper body, and the blue death's head tattoo on his left arm. I remembered his cold yellow eyes, flat and unfeeling as a snake's, and I heard again

259

his deep, raspy voice as he said, "Sometimes a leader has to take *measures*."

And suddenly I knew, deep in my gut, what nobody else knew. George was still George, and he definitely *was* himself, as he had always been. Whatever else he was, I was certain sure there was one thing he was *not*.

Original George Starkweather almost certainly was not *dead*.

NINETEEN

Over the River and Through the Woods

Old Ambrose had a small bell mounted just inside the front doorway of his funeral parlor so he could hear when the Recently Bereaved came in to make arrangements for the Dearly Departed. As I closed the door behind me, he came a-hurrying upstairs wearing a claw hammer coat and his best sympathetic expression.

"Oh," says he, "it's only you. What do you want, Merlin?"

"I need to see them bodies again," I told him, "I need to see George's body."

"Sorry, son. I've already got them owlhoots boxed and ready to plant. Anyway, you seen them boys yesterday. They haven't changed all that much since then, except they've growed a little *riper,* maybe."

"It's important, Ambrose. I'll pay you for your trouble."

For a long moment the old undertaker studied my

face. Finally, he shook his head, kind of impatient-like, and turned toward the basement stairs. "Oh, hell," he said, "you don't need to pay me. Come on."

I followed Ambrose down the dark, musty staircase and through the narrow doorway at the bottom. The work room looked about the same as it had the day before, except the tables that had held the cadavers were empty. Two new pine coffins stood on sawhorses over by the big double doors.

"There's a hammer and a pry bar there on the work bench," Ambrose said, "if you want another look at George you can open the lid yourself. He's in the box on the left."

The smell of death was stronger now, thick, heavy, and pungent, and I gagged as I came near the coffin. I swallered, and kept a-swallerin', trying not to breathe. I saw my hands quiver as I wedged the flat blade of the bar betwixt the lid and the coffin. I remember thinking I druther be anywhere but where I was right then, but I had to know what I had to know.

Ambrose tapped me on the shoulder, and I dang near jumped through the roof. When I turned to face him he handed me a small open jar that held what looked to be some kind of grease. "Smell's gonna be even worse when you open that box, Merlin," he said, "better use some of this. It's a camphorated salve, and if you poke some up your nostrils it'll make the process a *little* less unpleasant, anyway."

Well, I was for anything that would do *that,* so I done as he suggested and it did cut the stink some, even if it didn't block it altogether. The pry bar dug in, the nails screeched as they were wrenched loose from the new pine boards, and all of a sudden I found myself looking once again at the faceless corpse that was supposed to be Original George.

Ambrose had folded the dead man's hands across his chest, and I gingerly took hold of the corpse's left arm and shoved the coat and shirtsleeve up as far as I could. The forearm was cold and clammy to the touch, and greenish-gray in color, but it had no skull-and-crossbones tattoo and there was no scar near the wrist. I unbuttoned the vest and shirt that had once been George's and saw that the barrel chest beneath was hairless and free of scars. There was no doubt about it; whoever the cadaver had been in life, he had *not* been Original George Starkweather.

My hands trembled as I buttoned up the clothes again and closed the coffin lid. The death smell was strong in the room, foul and putrid, and even with the salve poked up my nose it was all I could do to keep my breakfast down. The stench didn't seem to bother Ambrose none, though. He had lit up one of his cheap cigars, and was looking at me through the smoke with one eyebrow higher than the other, and with questions in his eyes.

"Well?" he said, "Find what you were lookin' for?"

"Yeah. Much obliged, Ambrose. I'll nail that lid down again in a minute, but right now I've got to get me some fresh air."

"Never mind. I'll do it. Ridgeway paid me to bury

these wrong-doers, but he didn't pay me much, so they ain't embalmed, perfumed, or fancied up none. But they do need to go underground soon, before the smell starts attractin' buzzards from as far away as Mexico."

He may have said some other things, too, but if he did I didn't hear him. I was already out the door and into the alley, gasping like a trout on a riverbank as I filled my lungs with cool, clean, air.

Ridgeway and Luther had been on the trail to Silver City just over an hour by then, but the bay horse they'd left me was a ripper and I figured I could catch up with them this side of noon if I put my mind to it. Ridgeway needed to know what I knew, that Original George was alive, that the case was far from closed, and that I even had a pretty strong hunch as to where the payroll money might be. I came around from the alley in back of the mortuary, quick-stepped across Dry Creek's muddy street, and made a bee-line for the Livery Barn.

There was still no sign of old Walt, and I pulled my borrowed saddle off the rack and carried it to the rear of the barn where the bay was stabled. The gelding nickered when he saw me, and I backed him out of his stall and eased the rigging up onto his back. I had tightened the cinch and had just turned to lead him outside when I heard the voice, high-pitched and giddy, and froze in my tracks. "Cock-a-doodle-do!" it said, "How the hell are *you?*"

My heart was hammering like a pile-driver, but I made myself stay loose, and I kept my voice calm and

263

steady. "Well, I'm just fine, Jigger," I said, "How the hell are *you?*"

Jigger St. Clare chuckled as he stepped out of the shadows and into the light. I turned to face him, and I was pleased, somehow, to see that he looked the same as I remembered—sandy hair, freckles, big ears, and all. So much seemed to have changed in my life right then that I was glad to find *something,* at least, had remained the same.

Jigger stood there, his feet wide-spread and his thumbs hooked behind his gunbelt. His eyes were sly and secret, as before, but his slack-jawed smile was open and friendly.

"Thought you was a *goner* back there in Shenanigan, Kid," he said, "thought you busted your *neck* when we hit that clothesline."

"Just lost my wind for a spell. Time I could breathe again, you'd already got up behind Kiowa and left the country."

The smile faded, and his eyes turned hard. "Kiowa's dead," he said, "Bastard went crazy an' I blowed him to hell. Som'bitch killed Shanty, an' shot George in the hip."

"Where is George?" I asked, trying to keep my voice calm.

Jigger froze. I saw he was watching a horsefly as it buzzed around his head, his eyes vacant and pulled back to some place deep inside him. Suddenly his hand flashed out, faster than a sidewinder's strike, and he caught the fly in mid-flight. He held his closed hand up to his ear, grinning as he listened to the trapped insect, then in one sharp move he tightened his fist, and the fly was no more. "George needs you, Kid," Jigger said.

For maybe three miles Jigger St. Clare and me rode northeastward in silence across the sagebrush flats that led to the blue fastness of the Brimstone mountains. At first I tried to make conversation, but Jigger had drifted off someplace inside himself again, and either didn't hear me or chose not to answer. Then, just when I quit making the effort, he suddenly came back from wherever he'd been and started talking again as if he'd never been away.

"Kiowa and me came all the way from Shenanigan to Dry Creek on his blue roan," he said, "Kiowa kept a-cussin' George and Shanty, sayin' they'd sold us out, that they knew about the ambush. Kiowa was talkin' wild, sayin' he'd get even, *kill* George, you know, crazy talk like that. I told him George wouldn't sell us out, and I said if he didn't shut the hell up his damn roan would only have to carry *one* of us and it wouldn't be *him*.

"He shut up all right, but I could tell by the way he spurred that horse and jerked on the reins he was still mad. Told him to go easy on the horse or we'd both be afoot, but the dumb bastard just kept on a-pushin' him.

"We came to Dry Creek, but the roan was wind-broke by then, hotter'n a stove, and drippin' lather like soap-suds. I figured the best we could do would be to steal fresh horses and keep on a-goin'. But then we came up to that old hotel and damned if we didn't see George and Shanty's horses hobbled in the shade out back!

"Kiowa stepped off the roan, pullin' his Spencer carbine as he done so, and commenced a-runnin' toward the hotel. 'The bastards are in *there!*' he hollered, and he ran up the front steps and went inside.

"Now I *knowed* he was loco, and I wasn't slow followin' him inside, but just as I cleared the front door I heard his carbine go off! By the time I got to the kitchen, Shanty was on the floor dyin' and the crazy fool was fixin' to shoot George, too.

"I kicked him hard in the back and drove him into the wall, but the Spencer went off and took George in the hip. Kiowa dropped the carbine when he hit the wall, and I snatched it up. He was just turnin' around when I put a ball between his eyes and watched him slide down that wall like a mush-rat down a crick bank.

"Shanty had brought a sawed-off ten-gauge with him when he'd come inside the buildin', and the gun was a-layin' there on the floor next to him. George grabbed it up and fired both barrels straight into Kiowa's face. Then he had me he'p him and I patched up his hip good as I could, after which he switched clothes with Kiowa. Said the law would figure Kiowa was him, and if them John Laws believed he was dead, that could maybe buy him some time."

"Time for what?" I asked.

"To heal up, I reckon. He never said. I helped him onto his horse, swung up on Shanty's, and he showed me the way to a hideout he knowed of where we could hole up for a spell. Then today I snuck back to town for some grub and whiskey, and was just fixin' to ride out again when I seen you come inside the livery."

"Did you ask George what he was doing in Dry Creek?" I asked. Jigger frowned. "No," he said slowly, "None of my business."

His frown deepened, "Don't reckon it's any of *your* business, *either.*" Jigger shifted in the saddle and turned so he could look me in the face. Then he said, "I ain't sure where *you* stand in all this, Kid. You saved my bacon back there in Shenanigan, and George seems to like you, so we'll go see what he has to say. If he tells me you're with us, then you're with us. If he says you ain't, then you ain't, and I'll most likely have to kill you."

A raw, cold wind was blowing down out of the Brimstones, and I could feel the chill right through my shirt. I don't know whether it was the weather or Jigger's words, but a sudden shiver took me, my mouth went dry, and my heart broke out of a trot and went into a fast gallop.

Jigger looked away from me, squinched up his eyes, and stared out at the country ahead of us. He was quiet for what seemed a long while, and then he said, "I don't reckon it'll be much comfort, Kid, but if I *do* have to kill you I don't expect it'll pleasure me none."

Jigger was right. It *wasn't* much comfort.

We came to the twisted silver ribbon that was Brimstone Creek just past noon, but instead of taking the trail that led to the old line camp Jigger cut off to the left, crossed the creek, and rode downhill through a stand of lodgepole pine that was thicker than hair on a dog. Studying the ground, he leaned forward in his saddle and picked his way slow and easy through the trees and deadfall on the dapple-gray horse that once had belonged to Shanty O'Kane.

I'd thought I knew that country pretty well, and it surprised me some to see the way we were heading. To the best of my knowledge there was nothing in the direction we were going but more lodgepole, thick brush, and scattered sliderock. Of course, there was no way a man could go quiet through that timber. It came to me that if we were headed for a hideout back there someplace that would have been one reason George had chose it. A man coming after him, afoot or horseback, would be heard long before he got within shooting distance, and the odds would be the way George liked them, with *him*.

The sky had turned the color of lead, and the cold wind through the treetops made a lonesome, breathy wail that sounded to me like the saddest ghost music there ever was. I jumped when I heard a loud pop-poppop sound close by, but after I'd looked around some I saw it was only a standing dead tree caught in the forks of a live one and a-rubbing in the wind.

From time to time Jigger would draw rein and study the way ahead, and at those times the woods would go quiet again. Now and then a squirrel would chitter, sharp, high-pitched, and nervous, or a pine cone would come skittering down and plop on the forest floor. Other than that the only sounds were the soft jingle of bit and spur and the sorrowful keening of the wind through the trees.

Then Jigger's horse raised his head high and whinnied. From somewhere just ahead a horse answered, and I knew we'd come to the hideout. We had broken out of the trees into a small clearing marked by down timber, blackened stumps, and fireweed, and I could just make out a small, low cabin set back in the shadowed woods. As the horse whinnied again I saw it was George's leggy thoroughbred, calling from a rough pole corral behind the cabin. Jigger stood tall in his stirrups and waved his hat back and forth in a big arc. "Cock-a-doodle-do!" he called, "It's me, and Merlin, too! Don't shoot us, Cap'n."

The rising wind came from behind us, carrying our sound toward the cabin, and if George called out an answer I didn't hear it. But I did catch a glimpse of movement just inside the cabin's open door, and Jigger seemed to believe we'd been given the go-ahead, so we rode out of the trees and across the clearing.

We slipped the saddles and bridles off our horses, hobbled them, and turned them out to graze on the thick, cured grass that grew among the aspens. Jigger untied the strings which held his blanket roll and cradled the bundle in his arms like a baby. "Got two bottles of Kentucky bourbon in here for the Cap'n," he grinned, "Be a hell of a note if I was to bring 'em all this way an' bust one now."

The cabin was old and low to the ground, and both Jigger and me had to duck our heads to go in through the door. Whoever built the place had not bothered with such frills as windows. It was darker than a prairie dog's pantry inside, and I hunkered down and waited for my eyes to get used to the gloom.

As I waited, I remembered a winter over on the east slope of the Brimstones, when I'd been stalking a big muley buck through thick timber and happened onto a gray loafer wolf with his foot in a trap. He was a big old lobo, lanky and rawboned, but I came near to passing by without seeing him at all. My gaze had been fixed on the tracks before me, and it gave me quite a start when I suddenly looked up and saw that old killer watching me. He had just sort of *appeared* out of the shadows, as he crouched there in the bloody snow, his jaws open in a toothy smile and his cold yellow eyes studying my every move.

Well, that's how it was that day. Original George seemed to just sort of come into focus out of the gloom. I suddenly found myself looking into his mad yellow eyes the same way I had that time with the wolf. The bandit chief lay propped against the far wall of the cabin, an old gray blanket around his shoulders and Kiowa's Spencer carbine in his hands. His canvas breeches were blood-soaked all along the right leg from waist to knee, and his scarred, bearded face looked feverish and strained. He squinted at me, and his strong white teeth flashed in a smile that I suppose was meant to be friendly, but which somehow just looked scary and tight on account of the pain behind it.

"Howdy there and welcome, Sir Merlin the Boda-cious," he said in his husky growl, "Set here by me, son, and I'll buy you a drink, soon as the Jigger uncorks that sippin' whiskey."

He gave me his hand, and gripped mine hard as I set down cross-legged on the cabin floor. "Much obliged, cap'n," I said, "but the *last* drink you bought me like to put me in a state of hibernation. I'm not sure I'm ready to snooze all winter."

His eyes glowed like there were lights behind them, and his chuckle started deep down in his chest and turned into a coughing spasm that racked his body and left him breathless and gasping. "Just—watching out for you, Kid," he said, "Young'uns—need their *rest.*"

Jigger had uncorked the bourbon, and he handed the bottle down and stood by, looking at George like a hunting dog looks at his master. There was something about the single-minded devotion Jigger seemed to have for the Cap'n that was almost spooky. I made a mental note never to do anything around Jigger St. Clare that he might figure was a threat to his leader.

George lifted the bottle in a kind of shaky salute, first to Jigger, then to me, and drank deeply. When at last he handed the bottle back to Jigger, he seemed to have gained strength, and some of the strain had left his face.

He slumped back against the logs and studied me in silence while Jigger and me each took a drink. Then he lifted the carbine and said, "Reckon Jigger told you what happened. This damn Spencer shot three men in as many seconds, and *one* of 'em was *me*."

"He told me. How are you makin' it, cap'n?"

"I've been better. But I reckon I ain't in too bad a shape, for the *shape* I'm in. You get that hundred I left you?"

"I did, and the note. Maybe you're right, maybe I'm *not* cut out to be a desperado."

George took another long pull on the bourbon bottle, swallered, and corked the quart. Then he pulled the blanket up, closed his eyes, and laid back. "Hell, Kid," he said, "maybe *none* of us are."

Jigger had killed a deer the evening before, and while I gathered wood and got a fire going, he sliced some steaks off a hindquarter and set them to cooking in an old black-iron skillet he'd found in the cabin. George had led him to the hideout and had told him it was an old trapper's roost he'd used once or twice before. He said he'd left the skillet, a coffee pot, and dishes cached there in case of future need. Jigger had brought coffee back with him from Dry Creek in his saddlebags, along with some taters, onions, a slab of bacon, coffee, salt, and a small sack of flour. While he fried up the steaks, onions, and taters, I got a pot of coffee going. When everything was ready, I woke the Cap'n up and the three of us made short work of the vittles.

When supper was over and we'd cleaned up the dishes, Jigger and me doctored George's hip, put on fresh bandages, and throwed the old ones in the fire. The wound was a bad one, raw and ugly looking, but it didn't seem to be infected. George had the stub of a cigar clenched in his teeth, and when Jigger rinsed his wound with whiskey he grunted and bit clean through it. As sweat broke out all across his forehead, I could see the pain in his eyes, but he never said a word. Afterward, when Jigger went out to take care of the horses, he lit up a fresh stogie and grinned at me through the haze. "Seems like no matter how many times a man gets shot, he never quite gets accustomed to it," he said.

He pushed himself up on his arms and rested his head back against the wall. "I'm glad to see you, young Merlin," he said, "but I ain't sure how you come to be here.

"The Jigger says you showed up in time to help him and Kiowa get away when the bank job went bad. How'd you get away?"

"Guess I just got lucky, Cap'n. A lot of the boys didn't."

"Every game has its winners and losers."

"The deck was stacked at Shenanigan."

George's head came off the wall. He stared at me, his eyes flashing. "Well, hell *yes* it was stacked, Kid. We're talkin' about the game of *life* here! The winners run the game, and they make the damn rules . . . that's what makes 'em *winners*.

"It was you, and your fool kid's notion of fair play, that put a wild card in the deck. I tried to keep you out of it, but you went a-chargin' in there like some storybook hero and upset the balance. If you hadn't helped that gut-eatin' Kiowa John get away, Shanty wouldn't be dead and I wouldn't be layin' here a-hurtin'."

His words stung, and I knew he was right about Kiowa, but right then a strange thing happened. I looked at George and I heard his words, and all at once I saw him in a different way than I had. Like Androcles Wilkes, Original George Starkweather was a man loyal only to himself. He would use other men. He would coax, charm, and persuade; he would bully, lie, and bluff. He would demand loyalty but never give it, he would sell out, betray, and kill anyone, do *anything,* in the service of his own ends, and he would never lose a minute's sleep because of it.

Long ago, I had wondered if George's conscience was the same as mine. There, in the cabin that night, looking into his crazy eyes, I knew it was not. More important, I finally knew I was on the side of the robins, not the bullsnakes.

TWENTY

In George We Trust

"Sorry, Kid," George said, "I ain't really blamin' you none. You done what you figured was right. But it did change the way the cards fell, and it has surely changed the way the game will play from here on out."

He put his head back against the logs and closed his eyes. The reddish light from the dying embers danced across his face in a flickering pattern. At first I thought he'd fallen asleep because for what seemed like a long time he was silent. Then he opened his eyes, looked at me, and said, "Why did you come out here with Jigger?"

"Jigger didn't give me much choice, Cap'n. He said you *needed* me."

"Well, he was right. I *do* need you, Kid. Nothin' against the Jigger, but I need a man at my side I can count on—somebody who can use his brain as well as his gun."

George closed his eyes again. For another long moment he was quiet. Then, his voice sounding tired and raspy, he said, "Shanty and me had planned to dig up the payroll money and move on to new range somewheres, maybe California, or Mexico. But old Shanty's dead now, and I've got a bullet in my hip. Them facts change the plan somewhat, and they mean that Lady Luck may have just gave you a big, sloppy kiss. How would you like to be *rich,* Merlin?"

"Well," I said, "I've been told money can't buy happiness, but I reckon I'd like the chance to find out for myself. What did you have in mind?"

"You get me to where that payroll is buried and help me dig it up, and I'll give you a thousand dollars, Kid. What do you say?"

"That's a heap of money, Cap'n."

"Yes, it is. It could set a man up for life if he handled it right. What's your answer?"

I wasn't fooled. I knew George was romancing me, but I also knew the lengths he'd gone to so as not to share that payroll money. He'd sent his men into the bloody ambush at Shenanigan, and he'd welshed on his deal with Wilkes. I knew he was capable of killing me, Jigger, or both of us if he seen advantage in doing so. I knew, too, there was no way he'd let me walk away now.

Still, I figured there was still a slim chance I could get free and slip away. If I did, I would do my best to get word to Marshal Ridgeway.

I concentrated on making my voice steady. "Like I said, that is a heap of money, Cap'n. But it seems to me your offer calls for a good deal of *trust* on *both* our parts."

George's eyes narrowed to slits. It seemed I could actually feel his eyes on me, like heat, or wind, as he studied my face. When he spoke, his voice was quiet, almost a whisper. "You saying you don't trust *me,* or that I can't trust *you,* son?"

I could feel sweat trickle down my backbone in an icy crawl. In the fireplace, a burning coal snapped like a tiny gunshot. Shadows danced across the walls, ceiling, and floor.

Before I could answer, George flexed his shoulders like a big cat and I saw the tension leave his face. "All right," he said, "I guess I *haven't* given you much reason to believe me. What can I do, Merlin?"

One thing remained. Over the past week or so, a notion had growed on me as to where the payroll was buried, but it was only a notion and not a fact. Only George could tell me if my guess was true; only George knew.

276

The Spencer carbine leaned against the wall beside him now, but he wore a belted Colt's revolver butt forward for a cross draw. His right hand rested across his belly just inches from it. I knew I was walking on mighty thin ice, but George had said he needed me, and I believed him. What I wasn't sure of was just how far his need would carry me, or how far I could push my luck. If he pulled on me now, could I beat his hand? And even if I did, what about Jigger? I swallered hard, and bet the farm.

"Talk is that after the robbery you and a kid named Bobby Bowlegs wound up with the payroll money somewhere near Alkali Springs. People say the law, and the Army, went over that country with a fine-tooth comb, but all they ever found was Bobby's grave."

"So?"

"So I think maybe *I* know where the money is."

George's words were so soft I could hardly hear them. "And where," he said, "*do* you think it is?"

"Underneath Bobby Bowlegs. Underneath his body, in the same hole you dug for his grave."

I have heard people tell of occasions when time seemed to stop and a moment seemed to stretch on forever. Well, until that instant I had never really understood what they meant. I crouched there on my bootheels, facing Original George as he slumped back against the wall, his eyes nearly shut and his hand an inch from the gun at his waist.

Then the moment ended, time came unstuck, and life began again. George's laugh boomed as it broke the stillness, and his left hand slapped his good leg with a loud smack. "Well, I will be damned, and *double* damned," he said, "How in the blue-eyed hell did you figure *that* out?"

Tension drained out of me like water from a broken dam. I could breathe again. Sweat ran past my ear and on down inside my collar. My mouth was dry, and tasted like copper pennies. I chuckled, reached for the whiskey bottle between us, and handed it to George.

"*You* told me," I said, "when you loaned me your big book on pirates. The book said that's what them old-time buccaneers like Kidd and Morgan used to do when they'd go to hide their loot on some lonesome desert island. Them old boys would bury the treasure deep in the sand, then butcher one of their henchmen with a cutlass or something and plant the poor devil on *top* of it. Anybody who dug there later would find a carcass and figure it was just a grave, and nothing more."

Original George chuckled, and took a swig from the bottle. "That's pretty good, Merlin, pretty *damn* good. Now there's *two* people in this world who know where that Army payroll is. We'll talk more about it come mornin', but right now I'm gonna get me some shut-eye. Might be a good idea if you did, too."

After a bit Jigger came in, rolled himself a smoke, and sat watching the red and black embers in the fire-place until he finished smoking. Then he yawned, took off his boots, hat, and gunbelt, and turned in. I spread my blankets on the other side the room and lay there staring at the ceiling while I listened to the bandit chief and his faithful gunslinger snore.

It was good that at least *two* of us could sleep.

I came awake with a sense of surprise. I had lain long awake the night before, thinking about the twists and turns my trail had taken and the way it had led me back to Original George. It was hard for me to believe at first that I'd slept at all. The cabin was cold and damp inside as I stirred up the coals and kindled a blaze in the fireplace to take the chill off. George still lay huddled in his blankets, but Jigger had already rolled his bed and gone outside. I pulled on my boots and did the same.

Morning broke clear and sunny, with nary a cloud anywhere in sight. A heavy dew had turned to frost during the night, and I shivered as I watched the welcome sun come a-crawling over the peaks. There was a spring out back among the trees, and I washed up there in water so cold it was like ice that had forgot to freeze. Already, the aspen leaves had commenced to yellow and drift, and a rising breeze scattered a double handful across the grove like new-minted coins.

Which brought my thoughts back to the Army payroll, of course, and the offer George had made me. I had often heard men talk on the subject of honor among thieves, loyalty to the gang, and what not, but I had seen precious few of them virtues in actual practice. My experience with Androcles Wilkes, Original George, Kiowa John, and the boys had all been to the contrary. It seemed to me outlaws were men who had *forsaken* honor, and who were loyal only to themselves and to their greed.

Wilkes may have been the high sheriff of Progress County, and George Starkweather a black-hearted killer, but I couldn't see a nickel's worth of difference between them. They had both proved there was nothing they wouldn't do, from lying to torture to betrayal to murder, in order to get their hands on that stolen money. I knew neither of them would hesitate to take my life, no more than they would to step on a bug. All of which is to say that I had come to trust Original George about as far as I could throw a hot locomotive.

Right then Jigger came back from looking after the horses and cooked up some more venison and taters for breakfast, while I boiled coffee and George said good morning to the bourbon. George seemed to be feeling a bit more perky than he had the previous evening, maybe in part because of the painkilling properties of that sippin' whiskey. He asked Jigger and me to help him outdoors, and we done so. Jigger had carved him a crutch out of mountain ash wood, and George used it to give us what help he could as we got him through the door and over to a grassy patch in the sun. He leaned back on one hand, laid the crutch across his legs, and lit up a cigar.

"Well, boys," says he, "I still ain't quite ready to take on a bronc-bustin' job, but I do believe I'm on the mend. It is a sad, but true fact that takin' a fifty-six caliber slug in the hip at close range can put a real crimp in a man's horseback enterprises. I don't expect I'll be able to set my stud horse for a while yet, but I can gimp around pretty well with this here crutch.

"I figure it's time to go get that payroll money and leave this country behind us. With folks believin' I'm dead and buried in the Dry Creek bone orchard, nobody will expect us to be treasure huntin' 'til we're long gone and livin' in tall cotton."

George fixed his gaze upon me and breathed out a cloud of cigar smoke. He took a deerskin pouch from his vest and tossed it to me. "There's a hundred dollars in coin there, Merlin," he said, "I want you to ride on in to Dry Creek and rent a buckboard and team from old Walt. Pick us up some grub, supplies, and a shovel and come on back. Make sure you ain't followed, and if anyone in town asks what you're up to, tell 'em to mind their own damn business, or say you've took up a homestead or some such."

Jigger stood in his loose-jointed, lazy stance, listening slack-jawed and intent. George swung toward him and pointed at him with his stogie. "Jigger," he says, "I want you to fetch the axe and rig me up one of them Injun *travois* from some of them limber lodgepole pines. We'll hitch the outfit to my horse, and you can take me out of here in high style."

George got the crutch under him and struggled to his feet. It could have been my imagination, but it seemed he studied my face even more carefully than usual before he spoke again. "Jigger and me will meet you where the trail crosses Brimstone Creek some time this

281

evenin'. I'm countin' on you, son. You have my full and total trust."

Yes, you trust me because you think the promise of a thousand dollars has bought me, I thought. *Once, I would have followed you through hell just out of loyalty, George Starkweather, but no more. Maybe you trust me, but I damn sure don't trust you.*

The bay gelding took it on himself to come undone when I went to get astraddle of him, so for a couple of jumps there he pitched a regular fit. Maybe it was the chill morning, or hanging out with all us wicked outlaws, but whatever it was, the old fool blowed up there among the aspens like a true bronco and took to crow-hopping and warping his backbone until my rein arm and spurs convinced him it was folly.

To tell the truth, I was *glad* the gelding had throwed his tantrum. Dealing with the sometime rebellion of horses was a thing I savvied, and the doing of it settled my nerves and eased my mind. When the bay turned reasonable once again, I lined him out across the clearing and wove him through the thick, standing lodgepole while George tipped his hat and Jigger stuck his thumbs in his armpits and hollered "Cock-a-doodle-do!"

By the time I was clear of the trees and had splashed across Brimstone Creek the big gelding had settled down somewhat. We covered the ten miles from there to Dry Creek without further disagreement.

Twice I topped a ridge and checked my back trail, just

in case George had coppered his bet and sent Jigger to follow me, but each time I saw no sign of horse or rider in all that big land. Just before noon, I reined the big horse onto Dry Creek's crooked main street and pulled up at Walt's Livery.

I found Walt himself out front, setting on a bench and mending harness in the shade. Now you would think at his age he'd be past embarrassment at being caught wearing his spectacles, but he took them off when he seen me, out of vanity's old habit, I suppose.

I had always liked Walt, and I believe he felt the same about me. The old man had hired me when my Pa got himself killed, and he'd always seemed more like a grandpa to me than a boss. Somehow, Walt made me feel *approved* of. He never acted like he thought my notions and opinions were idiotic, even when I knew they were myself.

"Well, good day to you, Merlin," he said, "Where you been a-keepin' yourself?"

Lying to old Walt made me feel bad, so I kept my falsehoods as close to the truth as I could. "Here and there, Walt. Been ridin' for a horse outfit over across the river."

He squinted up at me from where he sat. "*Heard* you've been around town," he said, "What can I do for you?"

"Feller I work for sent me in for supplies. I need to rent a buckboard and team for a few days."

Walt laid the harness down and rubbed his chin. "Take your pick, son," he said, "They's two of 'em out back. You can take the good Morgan team, too."

"I'm not sure how long I'll need the outfit, but you can trust me—I'll have it back soon as I can."

Walt snorted. "Hell, kid, I know that," he said, "Gimme four dollars, hitch up, and go. I'll see you when I see you."

I figured there had been speculation aplenty around town about my riding with Original George and the boys, and about my coming back to Dry Creek in the custody of the U.S. Marshal, but if Walt had heard the talk he never let on. That is, he didn't until I turned to go. As I started to walk around to the corral, I heard him say, almost as if he was talking to himself, "Be *careful*, son." I turned around quick and looked at him, but his head was down and he'd picked up the harness again. He busied himself with needle and awl at his mending, this time *without* his glasses. I figure he put them on again as soon as I was out of sight.

I bought a shovel, groceries, and a camp outfit at Bender's Store, along with some ammunition and sundries, a roll of barbwire, and a pound of staples. Bender was born nosey. I told him I had a job building fence for a nester over on Careless Creek. It was a poor lie. We both knew it would be a rare sodbuster in those parts who could afford to hire *anyone,* but Bender never cared if a man's answers made sense; he just liked to feel he was in the know.

At the Oasis, I bought two quarts of bourbon and had myself a beer while the barkeep told me everything he knowed about women. It didn't take long.

From there I drove up the street with the buckboard loaded and the bay gelding following, and stopped at the telegraph office.

For a minute I just stood there on the boardwalk outside and thought about what I was fixing to do. I planned to send two telegrams. I knew that once I did, the cards would all be dealt and the final hand would commence to be played out. There would be no turning back. I took a long, deep breath, let it out, and went inside.

Percy Purcell, the telegraph agent, looked up at me with some curiosity when I ambled up to his counter, but he saw I wasn't there for conversation and just pushed a pencil and pad of paper over to me. I nodded my thanks, picked up the pencil, and wrote. Then I slid both telegrams across the counter to him.

"First one goes to Sheriff Wilkes, over at Shenanigan," I said, "George Brown, the feller I'm workin' for, asked me to send it for him. Don't know what it's all about, but he said it's important, so I need you to read it back to me."

"To Androcles Wilkes, Progress County Sheriff, Shenanigan," Percy read, "MEET ME ALKALI SPRINGS. COME ALONE. WILL GIVE YOU WHAT YOU GOT COMING. GEORGE."

"That's just fine, Perc. Second one's from me. It goes to U.S. Marshal Chance Ridgeway, at Silver City. Read it back, too, will you?"

Percy studied the paper for a moment, and read:

"THE WOLF IS ALIVE AND DIGGING UP A GOLDEN BONE AT BOBBY BOWLEGS'S PLACE. MEET ME THERE SOONEST. MERLIN."

"I'll wait while you send 'em," I told him, "I need to know they got through."

Percy opened his key, looked at the paper, and the telegraph stuttered its code. When he finished sending, Percy stopped, waiting. A minute later, the key clattered briefly and was still. "They went through," Percy said, "operators at Shenanigan and Silver City both acknowledge receipt."

"Much obliged, Perc," I said, paying him for the telegrams, "I don't guess I need to ask this, but those messages are strictly *private,* ain't they?"

Percy frowned. "You know damn well they are, Merlin. Contents of telegraph messages and identity of their senders is confidential by law. I'm a telegraph agent, swore to secrecy—just like a lawyer, or a priest."

"No offense, Perc," I said, "I just needed to hear you say so."

Back out on the street, I took the reins, stepped up onto the buckboard, and started the team. I figured Percy Purcell was as good as his word regarding the confidential nature of the telegrams, but only up to a point. One of the first things Marshal Ridgeway had told me was that the telegraph agent at Dry Creek showed him copies of all incoming and out-going messages. My hope was that Ridgeway was Percy's *only* exception.

Old Walt had named his Morgan team Lewis and

Clark, and the horses seemed almost eager as I set out that afternoon. Ahead, to the east, the moody bulk of the Brimstone mountains loomed tall and aloof. As I thought of their shadowed canyons, tall timber, and clear water, I wished I was headed there instead of to a face-off at a gravesite.

Two miles down the road I passed a homesteader couple in a wagon. A rawboned farmer was driving, and a red-faced woman in a gingham dress and matching sunbonnet set beside him on the spring seat. I grinned and tipped my hat as I drove by. The farmer gave me a curt nod, but didn't smile. The woman did, though— just a quick, shy flash of a smile—but it raised my spirits like birdsong after a rain.

Maybe it was seeing the woman that brought Mary Alice to mind again. I recalled the way she had felt in my arms that warm summer's night in Silver City. I remembered the clean, sunshine scent of her honey-hued hair, the tender fire of her kiss, and the sweet promise she seemed to carry deep in her soft, brown eyes.

I thought again of my mother, gone these many years, faded now in memory's mist like an old tintype. I thought of Pa and the good times we'd shared as we hunted the wild, free mustangs. I thought of the crazy black stud who had carried Pa to his death at the bottom of a rimrock. I remembered the numb, hollow hurt I'd felt at his funeral. I believe I would have gave everything I ever had or hoped to have right then for a chance to talk to him once more, but I knew from trying that I could not. No, there was no one I could turn to for advice or help, no one to back my play or see me through what lay ahead at Alkali Springs but myself.

When I was a shirt-tail young'un I would sometimes climb to the top of some big old cottonwood tree and get paralyzed with panic by the height. I'd be scared to climb down or even move, and I'd hug that tree and holler for Pa until at last he heard me and came to where I was. He'd look up 'til he spotted me high among the branches, and then he'd grunt and say, "You got yourself up there, Merlin Fanshaw, and you can get yourself down." Having no choice, I discovered that I sure enough could.

I had growed up since then and had become a man, but I reckon the same principle applied. I had got up this particular tree, so it was up to me now to get myself down. I had drawed cards in a man's game, so I would play my hand as a man. I was through being rode rough-shod over by anybody.

Still, being a man is a lonesome business, sometimes.

TWENTY-ONE
Openers and Hole Cards

By the time I reached Brimstone Creek the sun had already gone to bed beyond the mountains and had set fire to the clouds as it went. The night air had took on a chill with the sun's passing. A lonesome breeze that was second cousin to a winter wind sighed down through the pines, and I figured it would be a cold night. There was no sign of George or Jigger at the crossing, so I watered the horses and just sat there a-listening to the stream chuckle across its rocky bed while the colors in the sky bled out and went to gray.

The tall trees along the creek loomed black and still against the sky as the world fell silent all around except for the good sound of the horses grazing and the wild, free scream of a nighthawk somewhere up the canyon.

I never have liked to tarry. Just setting still and waiting leaves a man too much time for worry and imagining. I find it all too easy to make mountains out of molehills and fear out of nothing at all.

As I stepped down from the buckboard, I stomped my feet so as to warm them some. I had tied an old sheepskin coat behind my saddle, and I was just about to loose the strings and slip into it when the bay lifted his head and nickered, low and nervous.

"Cock-a-doodle-do! Good evenin' to you!" said Jigger St. Clare, somewhere close behind me. If I didn't spook so's you could see it on the *outside* I must have jumped plum over the *moon* on the *inside*. I turned around slow and easy, as if being slipped up on by a grinning gunslinger with jug-handle ears was the most normal thing in the world. "Evenin', Jigger," I said, hoping I *sounded* calm, "Where's George?"

Jigger's slack-jawed grin faded like smoke, and there was just a hint of pain behind his cold, sly eyes. "George ain't doin' so good, Kid," he said, "I rigged a travois to his stud horse, like he wanted, and we set out to meet you. But his hip got to hurtin' bad, and I never even got him out of the trees. Built a fire and left him a-settin' back yonder in a clear place."

I put the sheepskin on and stuck a quart of whiskey in each pocket. "Tie up the team and show me where you left him," I said, "I'll have a look at that hip."

It took us maybe thirty minutes to ride back through the lodgepole to where Jigger had left George. The first thing I thought when I saw him was how much he resembled that foot-trapped wolf I'd seen some years before. Jigger had propped the travois against a tree at the edge of a small clearing, so George could lean back on it in front of a warming fire, wrapped in his gray blanket and with his pistol in his hand. His face was haggard and shiny with sweat. His deepset yellow eyes had took on a funny kind of glow, like there was light behind them. He grinned when he saw me and put up his revolver, but there was no strength in his smile. I could see that his pain had grown worse.

"Sorry I didn't meet you at the crossin', Merlin," he rasped, "but my damn hip is hurtin' me a good deal more than somewhat. Figured I'd just rest here for a spell. You get everything?"

I hunkered down on my heels beside him, took a quart of whiskey out of my coat, and gave it to him. His hands trembled some as he took it, and he grinned that old wolfish smile as he pulled the cork. "Everything," I told him, "grub, tools, supplies and cartridges. All in Walt's best buckboard, pulled by his good Morgan team. Fetched you that bourbon, and some cigars, too."

George tipped the bottle back, and I watched his Adam's apple bob as he swallered down a healthy portion of its contents. When he came up for air the gratitude in his eyes gave me a sad feeling. I was surprised to find my fear of him was mostly gone. It's hard to be scared of a man you pity.

George shut his eyes and sagged back against the travois. When he spoke, his voice had lost some of its tightness and seemed to come from a place far away and deep inside him. "You done good, Sir Merlin, "he said, "You're a man to ride the river with."

"Damn! I'm more pathetic than George," I thought, *"All he has to do is hand me a little soft soap and I forget everything I know about him and puff up like a carcass in the sun."*

"Let me take a look at your hip," I said, trying to sound gruff.

George gave me a sad, reproachful look as I splashed some of his sippin' whiskey onto my hands, but he rolled sideways and pulled his breeches down without comment. When I removed the old bandage I could see, even in the flickering light from the campfire, that the wound had changed since the previous day, and not for the better. The flesh around the hole in his hip where the rifle ball had entered was swollen and bright, flaming scarlet in color, with little red lines streaking out from it like trails on a map.

"Well?" said George, "How does it look?"

I straightened up and looked him straight in the eye. "It don't look good," I said, "I think blood poisoning may be settin' in. I'm gonna have to cut you, George."

For a long moment he was silent. Then, his voice calm and steady as if I'd asked him to pass the sugar, he shrugged and said, "Do what you have to, Kid."

I could feel Jigger's eyes on me as I opened my clasp knife and ran its sharpest blade through the flames. I turned and met his gaze, silently holding the knife out away from me. Jigger's thumbs were stuck in his gun-belt. He frowned as he watched me, but I just raised an eyebrow and kept looking at him until at length he nodded and took a step back. Then I said, "Here she comes," and cut a deep cross with two strokes right across the bullethole. I felt George stiffen and heard him grunt, but he never cried out, not even when I squeezed the poison out and rinsed his wound with whiskey.

"If—you're—about done—pourin' that good bourbon on my hind-quarters," he panted, "I believe I *will* have me another drink."

I grinned, and lifted the bottle up in mock salute. "First, one for the doctor," I told him, and swallered amber fire.

Afterward, we had us a cold supper of venison and fried taters left over from the morning. When we were through George lit up one of the stogies I'd brought from Bender's and squinted at me through the smoke. "I figure Alkali Springs to be maybe twenty mile from here, by way of the West Fork road," he said, "Now I

292

still can't set a horse, but I reckon I can ride the buck-board all right, so come sunup Jigger and me will head out in Walt's rig.

"I want *you* to ride over ahead of us, Merlin, and make sure there ain't anybody around when we get there. If you leave around three I figure you can be at the springs by first light."

George studied the ash on his cigar, then looked up at me, his gaze intense and steady. I had that same strange impression there were lights on behind those mad, yellow eyes. It was all I could do to meet his stare.

"There's an old, abandoned homestead maybe a mile north of the springs," George said, "and a big log barn back along a dry wash. Scout the place well, Merlin, and if everything looks all right just wait for us. But if things *don't* look right, ride on back up the road and meet us."

"Sure, George. You expectin' trouble?" I asked.

"Always," George replied.

After George had settled back, I took my blankets from my saddle and bedded down near the fire in the hope of catching a little shut-eye. That's just what I caught, a *little* shut-eye, and *dang* little at that. First off, the night was cold as a gambler's heart, and as the fire died down it turned colder yet. Even wearing my sheep-skin coat didn't help much, and the chittering of my teeth put me in mind of Spanish castanets. Besides that, my mind decided *it* wasn't tired, even if the rest of me was, and kept going over things I knew, and worrying about things I didn't, like a fool dog chasing its tail.

If all *that* wasn't enough, Jigger St. Clare took to snoring with a din like the day shift at a sawmill 'til I wanted to jump up and stuff a sock in his pie-hole. I reckon there's squirrels in those woods that are deaf as a post yet, just from that one evening.

Anyway, I kept a-stewing and a-fretting, and somehow I must have fell asleep in spite of it all. When next I opened my eyes I could see that the Dipper had rolled around the North Star to the two o'clock position, and I figured I might as well be miserable standing up as laying down.

I had hobbled the bay gelding just outside the clearing, and I found him not thirty feet from where I'd left him the night before. I rubbed the big horse down with a handful of grass before I saddled up in the dark thinking about Alkali Springs and wondering what the day would bring.

George had accused me of putting a wild card in play when I dealt myself into the Shenanigan raid, and I surely had. Now, what could be the last hand in the game was about to be dealt, and I had done a double shuffle and a cathouse cut on the deck George had so carefully stacked. I swung up onto the bay, picked up some jerked beef and a can of peaches at the buckboard, and set out on the road to Alkali Springs.

First light found me on a low butte above the Springs, hunkered down among scrub cedar and yucca while I waited for the sunshine to take the chill off the land, and me. Over east, the sun dumb above the far ridge like a hot red balloon. Pink light flowed down the long hills as if the Almighty had upset his paint can. I had brought my old brass telescope along, so I used it to look for signs of life in the valley, but saw none.

Just below me I could clearly make out the abandoned cabin, weed-grown and fallen in on itself, and the big log barn George had mentioned. A hundred yards or so below stood an old windmill amid a big patch of greasewood, some of it as tall as a man. Just east of the windmill I saw the rockpile that marked the final resting place of young Bobby Bowlegs, and the temporary resting place of the stolen Army payroll.

I had hobbled the bay gelding again, and he stood head down as he tried to make a meal from the short, sparse grass of the slope. I folded up the telescope and made my way down to him through the cedars. The big horse looked up when he saw me as if to say he thought the range I'd set him on was pretty damn poor. I took the scant provisions I'd brought out of the saddlebags and told him I knew the grazing was thin but that it was for me, too. "Fact is," I said, "I believe I'd trade *you* right now for a steamin' stack of hotcakes and a pot of coffee."

The jerky and peaches didn't really break the fast but they bent it some. Meanwhile my belly growled "is that all there is?"

I had made good time. It wasn't likely either Wilkes or Ridgeway could have got there ahead of me, but I held cards in a high stakes game. I had to be sure. I clumb to the top of the mesa and once again scanned the whole country, slow and careful, through the long glass. Nothing stirred, neither on the road nor anywhere else in all that broad land, except a pair of ravens out a-hunting *their* breakfast. I laid up there another twenty minutes or so until I was satisfied there was no one down below, then I made my way back to the bay gelding and took his hobbles off. I snugged up his cinch, swung into the saddle, and pointed the horse downhill toward the homestead.

The descent was steep. It dropped off through red dirt and loose shale, so I gave the big horse plenty of rein and leaned well back in the saddle to help him. The gelding stepped slow and careful, his nose nearly on the ground at times. I watched his ears work as he concentrated on finding and keeping his footing amid the sliding, rolling rock.

There have been occasions in my life when I figured I was too dumb to live, and that day turned out to be one of them. I had looked the valley over through Walt's telescope and declared it empty, even though I could not be certain that it was. Then I had steered my horse downhill in a sliding, skittering avalanche of loose rock, red dirt, and enough noise and clatter to wake the dead. Worst of all, I was too sure of myself; it did not seem possible anyone could be down below watching me.

That is, until I saw the bright flash of sunlight on metal just inside the dark doorway of the old barn.

The last sound the bay gelding ever made was a short,

shrill scream that spoke of pain, fear, and surprise. His big frame jerked as though it had struck a wall, and in that instant he actually seemed to back *up* the hill against gravity through the red dust and shale. The loud, deep bark of the rifle came just after the shock of the bullet, and then the horse was down, tumbling and flailing the last forty feet to the bottom. My right leg was beneath him as he rolled, the sharp-edged rock tearing through my shaps and breeches as I fought to free myself. Then the bay turned a somersault and fell heavy and dying amid the rattling dirt and rock.

I had been thrown clear, and my hip and shoulder struck the ground first before I bounced briefly onto my feet, then fell hard on my face and belly and slid to a stop. Through the dust and the shock I saw a man in a black hat and canvas duster come walking toward me from the barn. At first I couldn't make out who he was, but I could see he held a long-barreled rifle. I scrabbled like a crab across the loose shale and reached for my holstered Colt's Dragoon while I tried to get my feet under me. Then the man spoke, as I looked up to see that he stood, his legs wide apart and the rifle aimed directly at my brisket. I knew I'd lost my chance.

"Don't even *think* about it, Kid," he said, "You try to pull that six-gun and you're wolf meat!"

Well, I knew that voice. I knew the man behind it, too. I looked up into the muzzle of the Sharps buffalo gun and beyond it to the broad, flat face, the close-set eyes, the broken nose, and the gap-toothed grin that made up the features of Faunt Bodeen. I had the definite feeling my day was off to a bad start. My clothes were torn, my elbow was bleeding, and a big, plug-ugly deputy had the drop on me. But spunk is available to all, and a rabbit can sass a rattlesnake, though he may do it only once. "I ain't all that impressed by your marksmanship," I said, "It don't take much skill to shoot a horse."

Faunt's eyes lit up and he smiled his demon's grin as he came toward me. Quick as thought, he stepped close and caught me just under my rib cage with the rifle butt. I lost my breath, fell on my back, and nearly passed out from the pain. Spunk may come easy, but it don't always come cheap.

I wasn't quite ready to stand up again, but Faunt took my revolver off me, stuck it in his waistband, and jerked me up by my hair. It was then I tried to spit in his eye but hit his cheek instead. He said something about my birth that either insulted my mother or slandered the canine species, and knocked me down again.

"That will do, Faunt," said Androcles Wilkes, coming out of the barn behind the deputy, "Fetch young Merlin inside, will you? I'd like to ask the boy a few questions."

Faunt drug me inside, pulled a length of rope from the pocket of his duster, and tied my hands tight behind me. Then he shoved me backward and I came down hard in the dust and dry manure of a long abandoned stall. The barn was dark and cold after the sunlight outside. The chinking had long since gone from the square-hewn logs that made up its walls, letting some sunshine slant in through the cracks on the east side that turned the dust motes into bars of light. Toward the back, in the gloom, I could make out three saddled horses, corraled in an oversize stall behind a stretched lariat. I had seen neither horses nor men before; it was clear to me now they had been concealed from my view inside the barn. I called myself six kinds of fool for being so sure nobody could have got to Alkali Springs before me. I hoped my mistake wouldn't cost me my life, but had to admit it would be my own dang fault if it did. It was early of the morning, but late in the day for hindsight.

Wilkes had found an old barrel somewhere among the trash and debris, and he pulled it up before me and eased his big rump down onto it. For a long moment he just studied me without speaking, like he was trying to see if he'd missed something. Finally, he blowed out a long sigh and said, "Well now, Merlin. I don't hardly know what to say to you, son. You have crossed me and *double* crossed me over these past few months. You have sorely tried my patience. On several occasions, you have interfered in matters that were not your concern. You betrayed my trust, you took sides with my enemies against me, you lied to me, and you've rejected my friendship. In short, you have been a major disappointment to me.

"Now I need some straight answers from you, Merlin. You need to know that you have overdrawn your account in the bank of my good will. Should you lie to me, or refuse to answer my questions, I will let Faunt here have his way with you. Do you understand the gravity of your situation?"

I glanced over at the deputy and saw that he had fixed his gun-barrel eyes upon me and was grinning his snaggle-toothed, demon grin. I remembered how he'd helped Wilkes give me drowning lessons at the jail. I knew *he* remembered the way I'd tricked him and locked him in his own cell the day I busted out and hightailed it back to Rampage. I met his cold stare and gave him a little wink, just for the hell of it.

"All right," I said, turning back to Wilkes, "What do you want to know?"

The sheriff took a folded piece of paper from his coat, opened it, and held it in front of my eyes. "First of all, this message you sent me from Dry Creek," he said, " '*Meet me Alkali Springs. Come Alone. Will give you what you got coming. George.*' Now I know it was you who sent it, because Percy Purcell, the telegraph agent, *told* me it was. Oh, he *refused* to tell at first, but he got more helpful after I had Faunt break the man's *arm*. What I *don't* know is whether you sent that telegram on your own hook or if somebody *told* you to.

"Now I could almost believe George Starkweather had you send it, except that George and his mick pardner got themselves killed and planted in the Dry Creek bone yard last week. Or, maybe they *didn't*. What about it, son?"

Well, by that time several things were going through my mind. I hadn't expected Wilkes to find out it was me who'd sent the telegram, but it didn't change anything. I had wanted him to come to Alkali Springs and he was here, even if he had come earlier than I'd planned. I

300

wondered when George and Jigger might show up, and what they'd do if I wasn't on hand to meet them, and I also gave some thought to U.S. Marshal Chance Ridgeway and the message I'd sent him. Had Percy told the sheriff about that one, too?

Something else was working at the edges of my mind. I had seen *three* horses under saddle in the gloom at the back of the barn—three horses for two men? Did Wilkes figure to pack one saddle horse with the payroll money? Or was there a third man, someone out watching the road even now?

"What *about* it, son?" Wilkes said again. His voice had a hard edge to it, and his face looked flushed as he stared at me.

"Well," I stalled, "it could be George didn't *stay* dead. Or maybe his *ghost* had me send that telegram."

I didn't expect what happened next. Wilkes's eyes bugged out, his jowls commenced to tremble, and his face turned beet red. Suddenly, he jumped up off his barrel and flung himself at me, clubbing, kicking, and bellering in a fury as wild as it was unexpected. The sheriff was so caught up in his rage that his blows and kicks didn't do the damage I reckon he intended. I pulled in my head like a terrapin and weathered the storm as best I could until, at length, it passed.

Wilkes stood over me, the cords in his fat neck standing out like cables and his chest heaving as he gasped for air. "You—damn—snot-nose-whelp!" he choked, "I've—had—a bellyful—of your smart mouth! I'm—gonna—let Faunt take a knife to you—see how

many pieces he can cut off you without killin' you altogether!"

I was getting mad myself. "G-Go ahead, you lard-ass
t-tub o' guts!" I yelled, "D-Do your worst! I *druther* be
dead than tell you yellow bastards a damn thing!"

Wilkes had sunk back onto his barrel, and his hand
shook as he wiped his face with a bandanna. His shirt-
tail was out, his chest and belly still heaved, and the
color had begun to drain from his beefy face. Faunt
Bodeen had started towards me, but Wilkes lifted a
hand and stopped him.

"I—thought—you might—prove stubborn," Wilkes
said. He nodded at his hulking deputy. "Go ahead,
Faunt," he said, "show smart-mouth here our *hole*
card."

Bodeen gave me a cold grin as he walked past me to
the dark stalls at the back of the barn. I saw him bend,
straighten, and turn back toward me. Then I saw
what—I saw *who*—he held, and all my bull-headed,
brass-bound bluff vanished like a raindrop in a forest
fire.

Bound hand and foot and gagged, her pale green trav-
elling dress torn and stained with dirt, Mary Alice
Weems looked straight at me with soft brown eyes that
were wide with fear.

TWENTY-TWO

Reunion at Alkali Springs

The first elk I ever shot was a four-year-old dry cow. I had jumped her out of her bed in a spruce grove one fall in the last good light before dusk. She had waited until I was nearly on her before she lost her nerve and broke out ahead of me with a racket that I believe spooked me even more than I'd spooked her.

My shot was mostly reflex, and it was pure luck that I hit her at all. She went down, then sprang to her feet and ran straight up the mountainside and into a narrow draw, while I stumbled and crashed through the brush and deadfall after her with my heart a-pounding louder than my footfall.

By the time I found her the light was nearly gone, and so was she. The cow lay sprawled in a blood-spattered thicket of elk brush, lung-shot and dying, and she struggled to get up when she saw me but couldn't. "Rest," I told her, "it's over now." Then I saw her eyes. They were warm, brown, and deep, and filled with unspeakable dread and anguish, a kind of resigned acceptance of the fate that had fell upon her and taken her life.

I never forgot that first elk, or the mysteries I saw in her eyes. There, in that old, abandoned barn above Alkali Springs, I looked into the wide and staring eyes of Mary Alice Weems and remembered an elk brush thicket, red blood, and twilight.

Faunt Bodeen's smile was an ugly thing. His long-barreled rifle stood propped against the stall as he held Mary Alice close against him from behind, his left arm about her slender waist and his right hand holding a knife to her throat. Her hands, like mine, were tied behind her, and the gag that stopped her mouth made her eyes seem bigger, somehow, and magnified the fear I saw there.

There was a purple bruise on her left cheek, and the shoulder of her dress had torn away to show the white, smooth skin beneath. Her hair was tangled and mussed, and her bosom rose and fell with the ragged rhythm of her breath. But it was her eyes that held me, eyes full of fear and pleading. All at once I didn't feel near as bold and reckless as I had before.

"All right, Wilkes," I said, "I'll tell you what you want to know. There's no call to hurt the girl."

"Well, now, that's fine, son," Wilkes said, "I *hoped* you might be reasonable. But first I need to tell you a few things."

Wilkes glanced over at Bodeen and Mary Alice, and nodded. "You see, Miss Weems admitted that she told you about my little business arrangement with her late friend, Ollie Langford. Banker Langford offered to pay me a small monthly fee if I'd help keep his little secret from *missiz* Langford and the community. I have a sentimental nature, and I was plum' tickled to help the cause of true love, so I agreed. But then I learned Ollie had commenced dippin' into the bank's funds and divertin' them to his own *personal* use.

"Well, sir, as the duly elected sheriff of Progress County I could not turn a blind eye to such dishonesty. Ollie had become an embezzler as *well* as a philanderer, and I was duty bound to take action.

"However, like yourself, son, I am inclined to be reasonable. Rather than arrest the poor devil, I levied a fine against his ill-gotten gains in the amount of fifty per cent of the take.

"Of course, my ownership of such illicit funds—if discovered—could harm my reputation, compromise my political career, and could even result in criminal charges. I allowed Ollie to hold the money. Between his share and mine, this fund eventually amounted to almost ten thousand dollars. The money was kept in a safe at the little love nest he shared with the charmin' Miss Weems.

"Well, sir, that same little house somehow caught fire and burned to the ground the night after Ollie was killed—the very evenin' you and Miss Weems left town on the train to Silver City.

"Naturally, I opened the safe as soon as it could be retrieved from the fire, only to discover that the money had disappeared. Now, since only Ollie and me knew the combination to the safe, I was forced to conclude that he'd somehow confided it to his paramour, Miss Weems.

"So I caught a ride next morning on the early freight to Silver City and found the young lady gettin' ready to leave for San Francisco. I took her into custody and searched diligently for the missing money, but without success. I was not able to find you, *either,* son, so I brought Miss Weems back to Shenanigan, where my deputy and I questioned her at some length. She finally told me she doesn't *know* where the money is, and that *you* now have it, Merlin Fanshaw!

"About that time, I received your telegram from Dry Creek which told me to come here and 'George' would give me 'what I got coming.' Well, I figured that could be either my share of the Army payroll, or something more *personal.* When the telegraph agent admitted it was you who sent the message, I rode here in all haste with Mr. Bodeen and Miss Weems. As you can imagine, son, I've had a real *longing* to see you again."

Wilkes hunched forward, his hands braced on his fat thighs, and stared at me. But he seemed nervous and uncertain, and a tiny muscle near his right eye had commenced to twitch.

"Now I need some straight answers from you, son, and I strongly urge you to come up with 'em. Miss Weems is a handsome woman, and the manner in which you respond to my questions will surely determine whether she *remains* that way. The next time you stall, or lie, or use your smart mouth to irritate me, my deputy Mr. Bodeen there will cut her pretty face with his sharp knife. Scars oft-times give a *man's* face character, but they don't do a helluva lot for a woman. You *follow* me, son?"

I glanced over at Bodeen and Mary Alice. The big deputy grinned a lewd smile, pulled her face close to his own, and, with his black eyes fixed on mine, put his tongue in her ear. Then I saw the blade in his right hand catch light as he brought it up and laid it against her cheek. Mary Alice closed her eyes, as I heard a mewing sound from beneath her gag like a kitten in a sack.

"Yes, sir. I follow you," I said.

"That's good. Now, about the money Miss Weems says you have. Do you have my ten thousand, and if you do, where is it?"

I didn't dare glance at Mary Alice, or make any other move that might cause Wilkes to doubt me. I figured she'd put the money in her valise just before she fired the house and we caught the train, and that she must have hidden it somewhere in Silver City. But she had told Wilkes I had it, and I knew I'd better tell him the same. "Yes, sir, I do," I said, "Mary Alice gave it to me for safe-keeping. I had a bartender friend in Silver City lock it up for me."

"I see," Wilkes said, "And who would this bartender friend *be,* son?"

"Kelly's son-in-law, at Kelly's Bar on Plata Street," I lied. The fact is, I surprised myself. I had told my bare-faced lie so skillfully and well, my eyes meeting Wilkes's and without stammering or hesitation, that I really began to believe I had a flair for falsehood. For a minute there, I even thought about going into politics.

Wilkes looked thoughtful. "You're doing fine," he said, "Now let's go back to the *big* question. Keeping Miss Weems's welfare in mind, tell me—is Original George Starkweather dead, or alive?"

I had wondered whether Percy had told Wilkes about

the second telegram, the one I sent to Marshal Ridgeway. Wilkes's question convinced me he had not.

"He's alive, and on his way. He had me send you that telegram."

"He's comin' to dig up the payroll money?"

"All I know is what the telegram said."

"Do *you* know where the payroll money is buried?"

"No, sir. I don't reckon George would tell *anybody* that."

Slowly, the sheriff got to his feet, walked over to the doorway, and looked out. "No," he said thoughtfully, "I don't suppose he would."

"All right," he said, looking at Bodeen, "here's how we'll play it. Tie young Merlin's feet, put a gag in his smart mouth, and let's you and me go see how the land lays. This barn is a good place to hide in, but a bad place to be trapped."

Bodeen carefully drew a strand of Mary Alice's honey-colored hair taut, and cut it free with a quick stroke of his knife. Roughly, he shoved her away and watched as she toppled to the barn's dirt floor. "Don't see why we don't just kill 'em now," he said, "don't need 'em no more."

"I'm still not sure how young Merlin fits in all this," Wilkes said. "He may yet have some value if it comes down to a showdown with George. As for Miss Weems, she's still useful for keepin' the kid in a helpful frame of mind. Now do what I told you."

Faunt Bodeen wadded up a rag and shoved it in my mouth. Then he jammed a bandanna between my teeth, knotted it at the back of my head, tied my feet, and dumped me on my face.

The answers I gave to Wilkes's questions seemed to have brought back some of his old arrogance. He came strutting back from the horses with his Henry rifle crooked in his right arm, and just before him and Bodeen walked outside, he turned and said, "Faunt and me will be back directly. You young folks *behave* yourselves now, y'hear?"

I rolled onto my side and lifted my face out of the dirt. Through the doorway, I could see Wilkes and Bodeen walk to the foot of the mesa where the bay gelding lay sprawled and lifeless amid the loose rock. Ravens and magpies, who were already working on the big horse, flew up as the two men drew near. I noticed they didn't fly far, but lit just a few yards away, waiting patiently for their chance to go back to the carcass.

I saw Wilkes speak earnestly to his big deputy, his hands talking, too. I watched him point toward the top of the mesa, then downhill toward the windmill. Bodeen carried his long-barreled Sharps rifle, and I saw him nod, turn, and start to climb. Wilkes watched him for a moment, glanced quickly back toward the barn, and moved on down the slope.

I turned back onto my belly, straining and flexing my wrists and ankles against the cords that bound them, but there was no give to the rope. All I got for my trouble was sore wrists and a dirty face. I had to admit that whatever skills he may have lacked, Faunt Bodeen surely did know how to tie a knot.

Dirt had got in my eye and I wanted to rub it, but couldn't, of course. There was grit in my mouth, too, but with the gag Bodeen had gave me I couldn't spit, neither. I felt baffled and irritated as a bob-tailed bull in fly time, and was commencing to lose my sunny disposition. Then I rolled over again, and came face to face with Mary Alice, just five feet away from me. She lay on her side, her soft brown eyes fixed on mine, and I saw the white tracks her tears had made through the dark dirt on her face. I saw something else, too, or thought I did. The fear that had been in her eyes was gone, replaced by a kind of hopeless despair. As I watched, her tears began again.

I lay close to the edge of an old stall, where weathered, dusty planks were fixed to a rough-hewn upright with rusty spikes. One big nail had not been driven all the way in, but had buckled under the hammer and lay against the wood, bent at an angle an inch from its head. I wiggled like a sidewinder til I could get my face up against it, hooked the bandanna of my gag onto it, and pulled. It took several tries and a scratch or two, but finally I gave a hard yank, heard the cloth tear, and pulled free. It took a bit more time before I was able to spit out the wad Bodeen had stuffed into my mouth, but when I finally did I felt like I'd hung the moon.

My mouth was dry and my cheek stung where I'd gouged it on the nail, but the cool air tasted sweet and I rolled back toward Mary Alice and grinned. "Don't you quit on me now, darlin'," I whispered, "we're not whipped yet." Deep in her eyes I saw a flicker of hope, a kind of glow, like a campfire ember in a rising breeze.

"Listen to me now," I said, "Wilkes and Faunt can come back any minute. I've got a clasp knife in the front, left-hand pocket of my pants that I can't reach, but you can. I want you to turn on your side, with your back to me. I'm gonna roll over close behind you so you can reach beneath my shaps and into my pants pocket. Get me that knife, Mary Alice, and I'll cut us loose."

"One good turn deserves another" was an old saw I'd learned as a kid. When I used to camp out with my Pa and share his bedroll, he'd sometimes grin at me and say, "One good turn gets most of the blankets," and the truth is it oft-times did. Well, there in that drafty barn at Alkali Springs one good turn, more or less, put Mary Alice in range of my pocket knife. After that it wasn't long before I'd cut us both free and took off her gag.

Now I'm not sure you'll understand what I'm about to tell you, and the truth is I don't quite understand it myself. I looked at Mary Alice Weems kneeling there in the dirt, and I marveled. Her dress was torn and stained, her eyes and nose were red from weeping, her honey-colored hair had gone dull and mousey, and her dirty face was bruised and muddy from her tears. I looked at the soft lips I remembered so well, now all swole up and puffy, and my throat got tight. It seemed I had never before in my life beheld such beauty. I felt like bawling, but instead I pulled her close to me and held her until I could again trust my voice. Then I drew back, grinned, and said, "Lordamighty, Mary Alice, if you ain't a sight!"

Some of her spunk had come back, anyway. "You don't much resemble the answer to a maiden's prayer *yourself,* Merlin Fanshaw," she said. Then she kissed me, quick and shy, and added, "but you *are* one."

I left her sitting inside the stall, her back against the boards as she rubbed her wrists to get the blood flowing again. With a glance outside through the barn door, I made my way to the horses in back. I went rummaging through the saddlebags in the hope I'd find a spare weapon or some such, but all I came up with was a little jerked beef and a canteen of water. "We may have to make a break for it," I said, "Can you ride, Mary Alice?"

"As well as you, I imagine," she said, shaking the dust from her skirts, "Remember? I told you my daddy was a horse rancher."

"I remember a *lot* of things you told me, and some things you didn't," I said, "like the ten thousand dollars you told Wilkes you gave me. I understand now why you wouldn't let that valise out of your sight when we took our trip to Silver City."

She bent over, and I caught a glimpse of her trim ankle as she tore a strip from her petticoat. She splashed water from the canteen on the cloth and washed her face and hands. "That money is my future," she said, "and I don't intend to lose it to Androcles Wilkes or anyone else."

312

"Yes. Especially since you had to *work* so dang hard for it."

"Don't you judge me, Merlin Fanshaw," she snapped, and her eyes flashed fire, "When a woman takes up with a man for money she earns every penny ten times over!"

"I'll take your word for that, I reckon."

I walked to the barn door and took a careful look outside. There was no sign of Bodeen, and I figured he'd made his way to the top of the mesa and was keeping an eye on the road. Wilkes was hunkered down in a patch of greasewood near the old windmill and seemed to be bent over relieving himself. He was not twenty yards from Bobby Bowlegs's grave, and I had to smile. If the sheriff had known he was sixty feet away from the buried payroll he would surely have postponed his call of nature and would be digging up the earth like a hound after a gopher.

I felt bad about the *way* I'd spoke to Mary Alice. Like I said before, I never yet wore no halo, and last time I looked there weren't no wings a-sprouting from my shoulder blades. It wasn't my place to judge her, nor anyone else. I don't reckon I'd have been so spiteful if it wasn't for the green-eyed critter that lived in my gut and woke up whenever I thought of her and Ollie Langford together. Anyway, I felt sheepish and plum' ashamed of myself, but not quite bad enough to tell *her* that.

The horses were our best chance. If we could mount up and ride out pronto we could be into the tangled breaks behind the barn and well away before Wilkes and Bodeen could stop us. The trouble was, there was only a narrow door in the back of the barn, too scant to take a horse through, and going out the front would put us in range of Wilkes's Henry repeater for two hundred and fifty yards, and Bodeen's buffalo gun for four hundred and better.

I didn't like the odds. I had seen Faunt Bodeen shoot, and despite my taunting him, the carcass of the bay gelding bore witness to his accuracy. But I knew if Mary Alice and me could reach the breaks there'd be no stopping us. One thing was sure: Wilkes and Bodeen wouldn't be able to follow us; we'd be a-straddle of their *horses*.

I turned back to tell Mary Alice to get mounted, and it was then I saw her eyes staring wide and fearful past my shoulder toward the doorway, and I knew we were too late.

I turned, and saw the thing I feared. Faunt Bodeen stood backlit at the door of the barn, his big frame bulky and dark against the brightness outside, and the long-barreled Sharps held waist-high and pointed directly at us. "I *figured* it might be a good idea to slip back down and check on you two," he said, "you're gettin' to be more damn trouble than you're worth."

The only thing I had left was surprise, and I used it. I took a deep breath, ducked my head, and charged the big deputy like a runaway train. His eyes went wide, he took a step backward, and the Sharps exploded somewhere near my left ear with a roar like a cannon. My shoulder struck him high and hard in the chest, and I heard him grunt and felt him lose his footing. I saw the rifle slip from his hands and fall away. Then I was hammering at his face, belly, and groin with everything I had and trying to come up with more.

At first, the pure momentum of my headlong rush carried the day. Bodeen fell back and went down like a felled tree, with me a-pummeling, pounding, and whupping on him like a man insane, which I sort of was. He still carried my six-gun in the waistband of his breeches, and my hand found its familiar plow-handle grips and jerked the weapon free. But by that time Bodeen had rallied from my wild attack, and his big paw closed on my wrist like a vise while his other hand clubbed me hard upside my head.

I cocked the revolver and was trying to bring it to bear when Bodeen clubbed me a second time, and my eyes lost their focus. Then he was on top of me as I squirmed in the loose dirt of the barn's floor and tried to hit him with my left hand. He captured my hand with his right, and, holding me spread-eagled and pinned, drove his big, ugly head hard into my face. He let go of my left hand, but it was only to hit me again. I felt the shock of his blows, once, twice, and a third time, before I lost my hold on the Colt's Dragoon and felt it fall away.

It seemed I was falling away myself, into some great dark whirlpool. I heard a loud, buzzing sound inside my head while the barn and the whole dang world seemed to slowly tilt and roll over on itself.

My eyes had commenced to water and everything had

gone blurry, but all at once my vision cleared and I could see Bodeen's face above me, his big yeller teeth bared like a loco wolf, and his eyes hot with hate. He had the heavy Sharps rifle in his big hands again and I waited for the shot that would end my life.

All of a sudden, Mary Alice jumped him from behind like a mama wildcat, her small fists hammering at his head, her fingers clawing at his eyes, and her teeth sunk into his neck. He reared up and roared like a grizzly in a trap, with her still hanging onto his back. Bodeen flung her away and onto the ground like a child's doll. She rolled, found her feet, and came at him again, but the deputy stepped aside and met her rush with a hard, backhand blow that felled her. This time she didn't move.

I wanted to get up and fight some more, and my mind sent the rest of me a message to that effect, but it seemed I had a mutiny on my hands. My body told my mind to go to hell, that it was all through with combat for the moment, and maybe forever. And then I looked at Faunt Bodeen and knew that it *would* be forever, because he had the rifle aimed point-blank at my head.

I laid there and watched my death come, like a spectator at a stage play. I looked up into the terrible dark of the rifle's bore and absolutely knew that it was my time to die. Bodeen's face was flushed deep red, almost purple, with rage, and his crazy eyes left no doubt of his intention.

My life didn't pass before me like a lantern show, as folks say it does at such times. I just held my breath, closed my eyes, and waited for the bullet that would punch my ticket.

The gunshot was loud inside the barn, and it racketed off the walls like the echo of falling rock in a canyon, but it hadn't come from Bodeen's rifle. I looked up to see him thrown back and bloodied, shock and surprise stamped on his face like a brand. Bodeen slumped hard against the doorway of the barn, staggered, and nearly fell. Turning, he slowly brought his rifle to bear again, pointing it not at me but beyond and behind me.

The second shot hit the big deputy like a wrecking ball, and the impact slammed him into the wall. For a moment, he seemed to just hang there, his eyes wide, his white canvas duster torn and blood-spattered. Then the heavy rifle fell to the dirt floor as Faunt Bodeen slid slowly down the wall and lay lifeless and still in the dirt.

Gunsmoke drifted toward the open door in a white, acrid haze. I turned onto my side and struggled to find its source, and the source of my deliverance.

And there he stood, his tattered gray blanket across his shoulders like a cape as he shucked the empties from Shanty's shotgun and loaded it again. He looked haggard and worn as he leaned heavy and hurting on his homemade crutch, but his mad eagle eyes glowed like before and his strong white teeth flashed in the same old grin.

"Sorry to *intrude,* Merlin, but it appeared to me you needed a little *help,*" said Original George.

TWENTY-THREE
Day of Reckoning

Even during the most desperate and trying times, I never lose my quick wit or my glib tongue. "Uh— where—uh—where did, um, *you* come from, Cap'n?" I inquired.

"Let myself in the *back* way," George said, easing himself down onto the barrel. "When a smart mouse is in cat country," he added, with a nod toward the narrow door at the rear of the barn, "he don't *use* the *front* door."

"Took a bit of doin'," he went on, "but I *was* able to get myself up onto my horse this mornin.' Rode around through the badlands and slipped inside the barn while you was fussin' with the deputy. Noticed you'd already lost your fight and your dignity, and was fixin' to lose your *life,* so I drawed cards in the game. Didn't mean to butt in, son."

I hauled myself to a sitting position. "Glad you did, Cap'n," I said, "but Wilkes will . . ."

"Wilkes will be along directly," George said. He pulled out a stogie and bit the end off. "I sent Jigger down yonder to invite the old som'bitch to join us."

My concern was for Mary Alice. I looked away from George to where she lay, pale and still, on the barn's floor. When I moved to her side it seemed like everything on me hurt but my hair. George fished a match out of his vest and popped it to flame with his thumbnail. He leaned back on the barrel, the shotgun across his thighs, and gave her a one-eyed appraisal. "Kind of hard on horses and women, ain't you, son? That one yours?"

"Not exactly," I said. I wet a cloth with water from the canteen and dampened her face some, and she began to come around. Her cheekbone was red and swollen where the late Faunt Bodeen had struck her. I glanced over at the deputy's crumpled corpse and felt glad he was dead.

"Not *exactly?*" said George, "She either is or she *ain't,* son. And if she ain't, you'd best let her be and go get yourself *another'n.*"

Through the doorway I could see Wilkes trudging up the hill to the barn, herded by Jigger St. Clare. The sheriff held his hands shoulder high, and the scowl he wore on his craggy face made him look like a constipated owl. Every now and then Jigger would goose him with the rifle. Wilkes would do a quick little shuffle and go back to his regular pace, at which time Jigger would grin and goose him again. It didn't take much to entertain Jigger.

When Wilkes came inside the barn, he barely glanced at Bodeen's body, but set his jaw and glared at George. "You're settin' on my barrel," he said, "and you owe me *money.*"

George took a deep drag on his cigar and grunted. "Got squatter's rights to the barrel. As for money, how much do you figure?"

"Fifteen thousand is what we agreed on."

"That's what *you* agreed on. My offer was *ten*."

"Make it twelve, and we'll call it square."

George snorted. "You've got more gall than a buffalo's liver, Androcles," he said, "I *could* just *shoot* you."

"You could, but you won't. Whatever else you may be, you're a man who pays his debts."

"Maybe I'll pay you and *then* shoot you," said George.

Jigger had been drawn to Bodeen's body like a fly to a cow pie. He was going through the dead man's pockets, happy as a pig in hot mud while he sang "Mary had a little lamb" off-key to himself.

I shook my head and marveled. A crooked sheriff and a ruthless killer were dickering over a stolen Army payroll like a pair of horse traders at a county fair. Meantime, a harebrained desperado with jug-handle ears sang nursery rhymes and prospected a corpse while a poor, semi-honest young cowboy knelt in old dirt and pigeon poop, playing nursemaid to the former mistress of a gutshot banker. We were, I believe, a sight to behold.

George studied Wilkes for a spell with his cold, one-eyed squint, puffing slow and thoughtful on his cigar. Wilkes glared back like a wet rooster, but neither man seemed inclined to further talk for the moment. Finally George took the stogie from his mouth, fixed the sheriff with his cold, mad eagle stare, and said, "All right. I'll give you twelve, but you do the diggin.' That is, if you can still remember which end of a shovel goes in the ground."

I saw greed sweep over Wilkes's face like a prairie fire in dry grass. He opened his mouth and for a moment there I thought he was going to try to bargain some more, but he must have seen something in George's yellow eyes that changed his mind. He nodded his head, just a short choppy jerk, and squatted on his boot heels in the dirt facing George.

Mary Alice had come awake, but she seemed confused about where she was, and who I was. Her fingers clutched my arm and her eyes went rubbering around the room like a drunk seeing phantoms. "It's all right, honey," I told her, "it's me, Merlin. Everything's gonna be all right."

"Merlin? *Help* me, Merlin," she said, "Take—me—away. Need to sleep . . ."

"Put her yonder, by the horses," George said, still watching Wilkes, "and get your ass back over here. I want you where I can *see* you, son."

She clung to my neck like a frightened child when I picked her up. I carried her gentle and careful to the rear of the barn and laid her down in the softest spot I could find. I took off my sheepskin coat, covered her with it, and told her again how all right everything was going to be. As I turned to leave, her small hands gripped my sleeve again. I had to pry her fingers loose before I could go back to where George and Wilkes sat staring at one another.

I could see George was in pain, but the old fire inside

him had flared bright again now that he was about to dig up the loot. Jigger was still singing about Mary being in the sheep business while he went through the dear departed deputy's duds. George reared back and hollered, "Jigger! Let that deputy alone, you damn ghoul! Go fetch the buckboard up here; I ain't a-fixin' to *walk* down yonder."

Jigger stepped away from Bodeen's body, grinned his foolish, slack-jawed grin, and scurried out the door like a dog chasing a stick.

"Down yonder *where?*" Wilkes asked, sudden interest in his voice.

"Down yonder where you *was,* Androcles," said George.

It didn't seem any time at all before Jigger came driving Walt's buckboard up the hill toward us, with Lewis and Clark, the matched Morgans, stepping high and pulling easy like they was in a parade. I doubt it was much more than two hundred yards down to the windmill and the rocks that marked Bobby Bowlegs's grave, but it was evidently farther than George figured to walk. He looked weary and spent as he leaned on me to climb up beside Jigger on the spring seat.

"You and Androcles walk on ahead of us," George said, "that way I can shoot you boys in the back, should I take the notion." Of course, I knew that was just George's way of talking, but Wilkes looked fidgety and wall-eyed, like he wasn't all that sure.

As our procession started downhill from the barn a

gust of wind swept across the valley and peppered us with blown dust and grit. The sky had been clear at sunup, but gray clouds had swept in since then, and the rising wind had a cold bite to it. Beside me, Wilkes marched along with his eyes straight ahead, and I knew his mind was on the money and what it could buy him.

It seemed to me then—and I've had no reason to change my mind since—that a man comes to be ruled by whatever he gives his hankerings to. Some men crave whiskey like a locoed horse craves the weed, and they will do anything to get it. Some look for meaning in the arms of women, and some in their own strength, or their quickness with a gun. There are men who lust for power over others, and that hunger comes to ride them like a man rides a horse. And there are those, like Wilkes, who corrupt their office and twist their authority in the service of a golden god called Greed. I had been surprised the day before to find I felt sorry for Original George. I was downright astonished right then to discover I also felt a little sorry for Androcles Wilkes.

Jigger drawed rein and brought the buckboard to a stop just this side of the old windmill. George sat hunched on the seat beside him. I could tell by the set of his shoulders that the wound in his hip was giving him grief aplenty.

Wilkes turned, his hand gripping his big hat against the wind, and looked up at George with a question in his eyes.

"That's right, Androcles," George said, tossing the

shovel down to him, "just move them rocks off Bobby's grave and go to diggin'. First, you'll come to Bobby, and below him you'll find the Army gold."

I figured maybe George wanted me to help, and I began to move the rocks that marked the gravesite, but he soon made it clear that was not his desire. "Just step on back a piece and set down, Merlin," he said, "I want the high sheriff of Progress County to do this job all by his lonesome."

Wilkes was more than eager to do just that. He flung himself into the work like a man possessed, which I guess he was. Seeing the feverish look on his face made me feel like a Peeping Tom peering through a window. I felt like I was like looking at the man's naked soul.

Minutes later, the mortal remains of Bobby Bowlegs saw the light of day once again. Gasping for air and dripping sweat, Wilkes bent over the body. The sheriff's face was the dull red color of an overheated stove as he dropped the shovel and dragged the corpse up and out of the grave.

I had no real wish to look at the moldering carcass, and in fact tried not to, but my eyes had a mind of their own. They went ahead and gave the outlaw the once-over before I could stop them. The skin had drawed tight over the bone and looked like old yeller parchment. Young Bobby's cadaver stared out at the world through its hollow eyesockets and grinned from ear to ear, maybe at the folly of it all.

George slumped in the buckboard seat, holding his ragged blanket tight about his shoulders, the sawed-off shotgun laying loose across his knees. Jigger sat beside his captain and gaped and snickered at the sight of a sheriff doing hard manual labor to uncover a desperado's treasure. Wilkes had long since shed his coat and sweated through his shirt, but he continued his fevered excavation and even seemed to increase his efforts.

When the shovel hit paydirt with a scrape and a chunk, all time and motion seemed to stop. Wilkes's blistered hands gripped the spade's handle, his hefty body frozen in mid-stroke, even his labored breathing stilled. In the buckboard, George lifted his head to look at the grave with a dreamy smile, his pain forgotten. Jigger St. Clare leaned forward over the dashboard and stared at the spot where the shovel's blade had come to rest, and I held my breath and did the same.

The moment ended. Wilkes dropped to his knees and brushed loose dirt aside with his hands, revealing several bulging canvas bags. As he lifted one up, the fabric gave way and let fall a shimmer of glittering, golden coins all down across his paunch onto the ground. Wilkes's wordless beller told of his joy as Jigger shrieked a hoot and a holler that startled the Morgan team and caused them to shuffle nervous in their traces.

Then I heard a voice I knew, a voice that spoke beyond its words and told of right and wrong, of law and lawbreakers, and declared a day of reckoning to be at hand. And, I guess, it spoke of bullsnakes and robins' eggs, as well.

U.S. Marshal Chance Ridgeway stood up from the

greasewood thicket not fifty yards away, tall as a pine and thin as a rail. Luther Little Wolf and five other hard-eyed gents stood up with him, their rifles at the ready and pointed at us.

"Raise your hands, boys, high and empty," Ridgeway said, "The dance is over and the fiddler needs paid!"

Then time, which had already played its trick on me, pulled another joker from the deck. Everything seemed to slow down, like a phonograph in need of winding as I watched events unfold at half speed or slower, in sharp and clear detail.

Again the voice came, clear and strong: "Chance Ridgeway, United States Marshal. I said raise them hands, boys, *you're under arrest!*"

I saw George turn his head toward the sound of Ridgeway's command, his hands still holding the gray blanket closed at his throat, the oiled wood and dull metal of the double-barreled gun still resting across his thighs. Sheriff Androcles Wilkes stood, hip-deep in the grave, clutching the now empty canvas sack. His face had a sort of stupified look, like he could neither under-stand nor accept what was happening. His hands dropped the money bag and began to tremble.

My own hands were the only ones that obeyed the marshal's order. They rose hat-high like they had a will of their own, and I stood stock-still and staring.

Jigger St. Clare rose up off the wagon seat, turning toward the lawmen as he put himself between their guns and George. Even at half speed the quickness of his draw was hard to follow. I saw his guns come clear of the leather, saw the barrels glint in the cold, gray light and the white smoke blossom at the muzzles even before I heard the shot.

At the same time I heard Wilkes cry out in a strangled voice, one word, a scream, "No!" He bounded out of the grave, covered the distance to the buckboard in three long strides, snatched the shotgun from George's lap, and raised it toward the men in the greasewood patch. His thumb found the hammers and eared them back as he brought the weapon to his shoulder.

It was then that time's sprocket wheel suddenly slipped its cogs back into the gear teeth. The region around the grave of Bobby Bowlegs turned into hell with the hide off. Ridgeway took aim with his revolver, cool and deliberate as a marksman at a shooting match, and sent three slugs into the chest of Androcles Wilkes. The big man staggered and jerked as each bullet struck him, the shotgun fired into empty air, and the sheriff of Progress County fell to his knees and toppled dying into the dirt.

It was a rifleman, or more than one, who killed Jigger St. Clare. The jug-eared *pistolero* stepped off the buckboard and into a hailstorm of lead. I saw him go down with his fast guns still blazing. Even then, he tried to raise up and fire one last shot, but could not. While I watched, Jigger grinned his foolish, reckless grin, then fell on his face, to rise no more. The silence that followed seemed louder than the gunfire.

TWENTY-FOUR

Profit and Loss

George stood stiffly, the blanket falling as his hands went up. I could tell he was hurting worse than ever, but he tried not to let it show. He grinned his go-to-hell grin at Ridgeway and said, "You're mighty damn polite, for a bureaucrat. I s'pose you want my weapons now, too."

"If you would be so kind."

Under the marshal's watchful eye, George shucked his gunbelt and pistols, including a .44 Derringer he carried as a hideout.

"There's a knife in my right-hand boot," George said, "but I'd appreciate it if one of you law-dogs would take it off me. I've got a fifty-six caliber hole in my hip, and it is a mite hard for me to bend these days."

"I appreciate your candor," said Ridgeway, "but it always *was* hard for you to bend, as I recall."

Original George Starkweather was many things—outlaw, killer, and thief, to name a few—but one thing he was not. He was no fool, and he was smart enough to know when the odds were too long. He sat on the wagon seat as before, his hands still holding the tattered blanket tightly about his shoulders. He didn't watch Ridgeway or his deputies as they came toward us out of the greasewood thicket, but thoughtfully fixed his yellow eyes upon me. For a moment I was able to meet his gaze, but only for a moment. My eyes dropped before his hard, cold stare, then met his again. I believe it was a measure of my conscience that allowed them to do so.

"You dealt this hand, didn't you, Merlin?" he asked softly, "You stacked the deck and dealt the cards."

"I invited the players," I told him, "that's all. *You* boys played out the hand."

One of Ridgeway's men turned Jigger onto his back and dragged his body out away from the buckboard by his arms. Two others did the same with Androcles Wilkes. Ridgeway sauntered up to George and pointed his long-barreled Colt's at the bandit chief. "George Starkweather," the marshal said, "you are under arrest for stealing the Army gold that lays yonder in that hole, and for the murders you committed in the process. Stand up and raise your hands, sir, if you please."

I told Ridgeway about Mary Alice being up at the barn, and he allowed I could go fetch her. I went up the hill at a run, but when I got there she was nowhere to be seen. Neither was George's thoroughbred stud. I found her tiny tracks in the dirt along with the horse's hoof-prints where she'd turned him around and sprung up into the saddle. I saw where she'd jumped him out at a gallop into the badlands beyond. While we boys had played our game of showdown she had rode out on business of her own. I wondered if I would ever see her again.

I never did. Later on, Leonard Peabody, the night clerk at the Winslow Hotel in Silver City, told me he'd locked up a valise for her in the hotel safe. Said she'd paid him fifty dollars not to tell anyone about it, especially Sheriff Wilkes. Well, Leonard liked money and pretty girls a *lot* more than he liked Sheriff Wilkes, and he liked whiskey even more than that. He told me he *would* have lied had it been required, but it never came to that as he was still out drinking up the fifty on the morning Wilkes came a-hunting Mary Alice and the money.

The ticket agent at the train depot didn't recall seeing her, or said he didn't, but that didn't mean much as she could have sent someone to buy a ticket for her. Leonard, the hotel clerk I mentioned, did say he'd seen her once or twice that week in the company of a good-looking high roller with a waxed moustache and a gold-headed cane. I told him I didn't want to hear such gossip. I *didn't* want to, not because I was so dang high-principled but because it hurt me so to hear it.

I reckon Mary Alice made it to San Francisco all right, and I hope she found the life she was looking for. I never told Ridgeway about the ten thousand, maybe I should have. I had turned against Original George and had chose the side of honesty over crime, but I had done exactly the *opposite* when it came to Mary Alice. I could see that letting my conscience be my guide didn't necessarily guarantee I would do right, and that thought has troubled me more than once over the years.

I still think of Mary Alice from time to time, especially on warm September evenings in Silver City when dusty moths frolic in the soft light of the streetlamps, and in the springtime when the sweet smell of lilacs comes a-drifting on the breeze after a rain.

But I really don't think about her much any more. Well, some, maybe.

I was called as a witness when George went to trial, but I didn't have to say much because the lawyers didn't ask me much. I had no real first-hand knowledge of the payroll robbery, anyway. The jury found George guilty of robbery, and complicity in the murder of the paymaster and troopers, and the judge sentenced him to life without parole.

I visited George in the Silver City jail just before they took him up to State Prison. Luther Little Wolf sat guard at the doorway across from his cell with a Winchester across his knees, and he looked up, his black eyes alert, and gave a slight nod when I came in. I pulled up a chair next to the bars and asked the old bandit how he was doing. George said he was looking forward to some quiet time and regular meals. Said there was a doctor he knew up at the prison who could fix his hip good as new, and that he didn't know how long he'd be staying there after that. The way he said it was like he was checking into a health resort and could leave whenever he had a mind to. Knowing George, maybe he could.

Our palaver was mostly small talk. We spoke of the weather some, we laughed a little at memories of our time over in Rampage, but I think we both knew we didn't have much to say to each other any more. I was about to take my leave when George got quiet and looked at me with his old one-eyed squint.

"Why'd you turn on me, son?" he asked.

"Why, I guess because I came to believe you were *wrong,* Cap'n," I told him, "and because I knew you'd turn on *me.* Seems like you turn on *everyone,* sooner or later."

"Seems that way, don't it?"

He was quiet for a long moment, and his eyes took on a far away look. When he spoke again, his voice was so soft I could hardly hear him.

"Just you and me left now, of the old Starkweather gang," he said. "Yes, just you and me."

I took the package from my coat. It was wrapped in brown paper, and tied up with store string by the clerk at the Mercantile, and I held it up so Luther could see it. He nodded, and I passed it through the bars. "This is for you, Cap'n," I told him, "Ridgeway said I could give it to you."

George looked pleased, like a kid at a birthday party. "For me, huh? Now how'd you get the Belgian Mare in this teeny little package?"

When he'd unwrapped the book, he touched its covers with a kind of reverence, and opened it to the title page. "*Two Years Before the Mast,*" he read, "*by Richard Henry Dana, Jr.* Why, this is mighty fine of you, Merlin. Is it a pirate book?"

"I don't believe so, but from what the storekeeper said, there's a sea captain in it who sometimes has to take *measures.*"

"Well," I said, feeling awkward, "I guess I'll be goin.' So long, Cap'n."

"So long, Bodacious."

I was almost to the door beside Luther when I heard George say, "Tell me true, Kid. You didn't sell me out for *money,* did you?"

I turned and looked back at him. George stood, his hands on the bars between us. Once again I was reminded of the trapped wolf I'd stumbled on that time up in the Brimstones. "No, Cap'n," I said, "I surely did not."

His yellow eyes went hard and flat. "Then you're a damn fool, Kid," he said.

What I told George was true. I not only didn't sell him out for money, I didn't accept the reward Ridgeway offered, either. He said there was five hundred offered for Jigger St. Clare and a thousand for George, and while I surely could have used the cash it felt too much like blood money. My better half said "no" while my worser half hollered, "Are you out of your *mind,* Merlin Fanshaw?"

Marshal Ridgeway shook his head as if he, for one, thought I was crazy to turn the money down; but I caught a gleam in his ice-blue eyes that made me think maybe the old lawman admired me some for my decision. I did ask him if maybe he could help me get Little Buck and my saddle back. Two days later they both came in on the morning train from Shenanigan.

Ridgeway offered me employment as a part-time

deputy, but I declined. I'd had a great plenty of danger, high adventure, and delicate moral insights, at least for awhile. I elected to take the team and buckboard back to Dry Creek and go to work again for old Walt at the Livery. Figured I'd look for a riding job come spring, maybe sign on with some cow outfit for the roundup.

There were times during the next month or so when I cussed my pride, principles, or whatever it was that had made me turn down the reward money. I had my little buckskin horse and gainful employment, but as far as money was concerned I'd have had to borrow some even to qualify as a pauper.

At least, that's how it was until the 18th of December when an envelope came for me marked simply, "Merlin Fanshaw, General Delivery, Dry Creek." Now I don't get much mail; fact is, that envelope was the first one I'd ever received, so I was some curious as to what it might contain.

Well, in my wildest dreams I never would have guessed. There was no letter inside, nor word as to who had sent it, but there was something else: *fifteen one hundred dollar bills.*

At first I thought maybe Marshal Ridgeway had sent me the bounty money in spite of my prideful refusal, but it was not so.

Anyway, the money lifted my spirits considerable, coming right before Christmas like it did. I treated Old Walt and myself to a Yuletide dinner and all the trimmin's over at Ignacio's.

Later that evening, after I'd stuffed my paunch with

enough goose, ham, taters, gravy, mince pie, and plum puddin' to stagger a packhorse and after Walt had gone to bed, I stood out under the cold glory of the starry sky and said my thank yous to the Almighty. Then I wished myself a Merry Christmas and a Happy New Year and slipped into my blankets, happy as a sleeping cat by a hot stove.

I didn't keep the money. Late one night the following week I slipped it under the front door of the Shenanigan Bank, along with a note that read, "I believe this is yours." But I did keep the envelope, and I have it yet, for it smelled faintly of lilac and its postmark reads "San Francisco."